Whispers in the Attic
A Magical Papillon Mystery

Sabine Frisch

Thinking Dog Publishing

Thanks for reading

I'd be extremely grateful if you'd leave a review...Amazon, Goodreads, Bookbub, or whatever site you use. Independent authors live and die by reader reviews.

Sabine

Reviews for Other Books by Sabine

Writing as Sabine Frisch:

<u>The Cannabis Preacher Series</u>

GoodReads Review: "The subject matter and title intrigued me having been around some of these sorts of dealings. From the beginning of this book had my attention; I picked it up to "just have a look" and suddenly found myself eight chapters into it. As the main characters were introduced, I started to feel that I had met all of these people before.Read on as Connor, the main protagonist, battles his demons up and down the shady side of Wall Street. There are just so many moving parts for any one control freak to manage. The greatest deal of all time starts to get out of control but every time he seems about to fall, he finds a way to land on his feet.We keep guessing:• Is he our hero or his own worst enemy?• Is this a runaway train or a slow-motion train wreck?• Will he end up in Financial Heaven, Regulatory Hell, or just a Fool's Paradise?Read to the end of this fun little tale and wait for the movie to come out."

❧

Writing as Sabine Keevil

The SoundMaster Romance Series

<u>**Guitars & Cadillacs**</u> (Semi-finalist in the BookLife Fiction Prize Contest, 2023)

Editorial Reviews:

"Sabine Keevil has constructed the perfect fantasy romance in her novel Guitars & Cadillacs, the latest in the Soundmaster Romance Series... At the same time, she appeals to that part of us that longs to see the behind-the-scenes footage of celebrity lives."-Rachel Jagt, Rambles.net

"Ms. Keevil is a good storyteller, I'll say that right out. She has a good grasp of storyline, she's succinct and to the point, her characters are engaging, and she knows where she's taking them."-Laurie Joulie, Takecountryback.com

"Guitars & Cadillacs is the entertaining story of the fire and fury stirred up by the relationship between Reanne (Parker) and fictional country superstar Colton Wright...Offering surprise twists, intrigue and mystery...Keep turning the pages to see what happens next in the well-paced plot."- Pat Mandia, Country Weekly, the world's #1 Selling Country Music Magazine

Foolish Pride
Editorial Reviews:

"Keevil spins an engaging romantic tale and does a credible job of taking us backstage into the minds, lives and hearts of her characters."
-Pat Mandia, Country Weekly Magazine
"Canadian author Sabine Keevil (Guitars & Cadillacs) has done it again -- she revisits the world of SoundMaster with originality, humour and a large share of romantic spirit.
One of Keevil's strengths as a writer is her ability to create realistic characters, even in the midst of a story about the world of big money show business. She is unpretentious and honest and her characters are likeable from the beginning...Even in two nights, the characters became

beloved -- a sure sign of a good story." -Rachel Jagt, Rambles - a cultural arts review magazine

Contents

Chapter 1

"This is the house you want us to move into? Seriously?" Cory's voice dripped with skepticism as he peered out of the car window. "Was it on sale or what?"

"Cory, language," Sarah snapped and tilted her rear-view mirror to glare at her son. *Sixteen going on thirty,* her mother would have said and ruffled his unruly dark hair, but just then Sarah had to battle her irritation with his attitude – hard.

"The least you could do is give it a chance."

"The flowers are so pretty," little Emma whispered, her voice filled with wonder as she craned her neck at the stately Victorian house before them. Like a grand lady in her garden, the old home looked stately, a riot of colorful blooming flowerbeds extended to the left and right, and a rolling green lawn that reached to the road. Their new home.

"So pretty," Cory mocked his sister when he didn't think his mother was looking, then wisely kept his mouth shut. *Not the time,* Sarah thought, *not the time.*

The last few months had been tough on all of them, ever since Michael, the kids' dad, and her husband of twenty years, had one day put down his fork and knife during dinner and told them he was leaving. "It's not you — it's me." Did anybody even use that sentence

— ever, Sarah had thought at the time, before it became all too real. Michael telling them he'd fallen in love with one of the partners at the ad agency they owned together, packing a few things, and leaving. No anger, no tears — unless you counted those shed in silence when Sarah closed the door so the kids wouldn't see.

To his credit, Michael had been exceedingly generous. He had bought out her share of the ad agency and provided her with a substantial settlement and ongoing support – ample to ensure she wouldn't have to worry about finances for a long time, if ever.

He had been accommodating with custody arrangements and remained composed when she informed him about her plans to move for a fresh start.

"If the kids stay with me a couple of weeks at the end of summer and maybe Christmas – that'll be just fine," he had said. Sarah knew he was already planning a new family without looking back, and she understood that mending a broken heart at her age would take time.

This, she thought as she parked the car in the generous driveway, this house would be the place where she could do that. She'd spotted the pretty old blue and white Victorian on a trip she'd taken years ago with Michael and admired the wide wrap-around front porch, the white porch swing that invited you to linger, and the gingerbread trim on all of the eaves. It looked – enchanted and magical to her eyes. Sarah had inquired about the house back then, drawn to its charm and history. Fate had intervened when she received a call from the estate agent just as her life seemed to crumble around her, 'did she still remember the house in Rosewood Hollow she'd been interested in a few years ago?'

Emma's eyes widened in wonder as she took in the enchanting porch swing and the delicate flowers in all the window boxes. Sarah knew deep down that Emma would be fine in this new place, but her heart ached for Cory. Her sweet little boy had become withdrawn and sullen since his father left. He would need time. They all would need time.

"Go on in," Sarah said, trying her best to sound cheerful despite the lump in her throat. "You can choose your own rooms upstairs."

"It doesn't matter," Cory mumbled as he awkwardly climbed out of the car, all gangly limbs and jerky motions. He thrust his hands into the pockets of his Punk sweater and glared at the house as if it were a personal adversary.

"Cory..." Sarah sighed, unable to finish her sentence. They needed time.

Someone had lovingly cleared the front porch, adorning it with cheerful pillows on the swing and oiling the grand white entrance door. The intricate lock alone was almost the size of Emma's hand. With a silent sigh, the door swung open, inviting them into their new home.

A grand entrance hall unfolded before them, boasting a magnificent double staircase with banisters intricately carved like mythical creatures. "Are those dragons?" Cory asked, showing an interest for the first time.

"Griffins," Sarah said, putting a hand on the polished mahogany. "The original builder probably had a thing about mythology."

Emma gingerly touched the beak of the griffin. "There's an L carved below," she said, running her finger over the letter.

"Really? Maybe it was..."

"Mom, what's the wireless password?" Cory waved his tablet impatiently.

"I think they're only coming tomorrow to hook it up, Cory."

Even paying extra, she hadn't been able to get an earlier time slot.

"Tomorrow, that's not fair, you said—"

"I'm sure one day without Facebook or WhatsApp won't hurt, okay?"

That came out more harshly than she'd meant, and Cory's face darkened. He retreated further into his sweater, shutting himself off from the world again, and Sarah cursed silently.

"I'm taking this room," Emma called from somewhere above. It was probably the one on the corner, with the wallpaper of angels and roses. Sarah had always felt that room suited Emma perfectly.

Her daughter appeared on the landing again, all bright eyes and smiles, and Sarah sighed. Time, she told herself again, more time.

∽

As Cory took a few steps upstairs and Sarah casually placed her bag on the massive, intricately carved mahogany hall table, a knock on the front door startled them all. The sound reverberated through the entire house, making her shiver for an unknown reason.

"Yoo-hoo, Anderson family! Is everything alright?" A familiar voice sang from beyond the door. The front door creaked open slightly, revealing a head of curly white hair.

"It's me-e..." their new neighbor, Mrs. Jenkins, greeted them. Sarah had met the kindly old lady when she purchased the house and made a few arrangements.

"Mrs. Jenkins, thank you so much for tidying up before we arrived. Your kindness made all the difference," Sarah said softly.

"Nonsense, dear. What are neighbors for?" The elderly lady stepped inside, setting down the white plastic airline carrier she had brought along.

"Welcome to Rosewood Hollow," she beamed, her face crinkling with a warm smile. "I hope your trip was uneventful."

"Yes, thank you. The moving truck should be here any minute now," Sarah replied, her curiosity piqued by the carrier at their feet. "Is that...?"

Mrs. Jenkins nodded and could barely contain the huge grin on her face.

"Kids," Sarah called out, "why don't you come down and say hi to our new neighbor? She has brought us a lovely welcome gift."

"Do we have to?" Cory's voice floated from somewhere on the second floor. Sarah closed her eyes for a moment, taking a deep breath before counting to ten.

Emma, on the other hand, came down the staircase like the lady of the manor, touched the griffin at the bottom, and stood before Mrs. Jenkins.

"I'm Emma, and I live here now. Are you our new neighbor?"

"Why yes I am, Emma. I'm Mrs. Jenkins, and I happen to bake the most scrumptious chocolate chip cookies you've ever tasted. If you ever find yourself hungry..."

Emma's face lit up with delight, and even Cory couldn't resist joining in. "Cory," he muttered, his gaze fixed on the floor. "Do you have wireless next door?"

"Cory," Sarah's voice held a hint of caution but Mrs. Jenkins only chuckled warmly.

"Oh, my dear boy, I wouldn't even know what that is. But I've brought something far more exciting for you."

They all stared at the crate now, and Sarah nudged her oldest.

"Go on, Cory, might as well..."

With the kind of sigh only a bored sixteen-year-old could produce, Cory knelt and fumbled with the flap of the crate.

"Is that... whoa!" Cory exclaimed in astonishment.

As his fingers loosened the door of the crate, it burst open, and even Mrs. Jenkins couldn't contain a fit of giggles. Quite suddenly, something red and white exploded from within and landed straight in Cory's arms. A bundle of pure, unadulterated energy in the form of a little white dog with pretty reddish markings on her face and sides. The pup's large, expressive ears perked up, and a glimmer of excitement sparkled in its dark, intelligent eyes. With a sudden burst of energy, she bounced out of Corey's arms into the room, tiny paws barely touching the ground as she practically floated in the air for a split second, resembling a fluffy cloud of happiness.

The dog's silky coat gleamed in the soft sunlight that streamed through the open window, casting a halo-like glow around its petite frame. Its feathery tail wagged in ecstatic delight, a metronome of pure joy.

The pup spun around like a tiny whirlwind, darting between legs and leaving a trail of smiles and giggles in its wake.

With a graceful leap, the dog bounded onto the nearest couch, seemingly weightless, and then hopped onto the armrest before standing tall on its hind legs, a little circus performer showing off its endearing charm. All of a sudden the room seemed brighter, and the mood lighter as the dog's antics continued, weaving its way into the hearts of everyone present.

Emma reached out, and the little dog responded eagerly, gently nudging her hand with its tiny, wet nose. Emma giggled in delight, and in that simple gesture, a bond was formed that would last a lifetime.

"Whoa," Cory repeated, his eyes wide with amazement. The tiny dog bounced from Emma's lap to his, planting her paws on his knees, and then leaped onto Sarah before returning to Cory again.

"This is Pixie," Sarah explained, her laughter bubbling over. "Pixie is a Papillon dog, and I adopted her before we moved here so you'd have a new friend right away."

Cory lifted the small red and white fluff ball, holding her up to his face. The long fringe on her ears danced, and her fluffy tail twitched with excitement. Pixie shook her head, pointy, fluffy ears flying, and lovingly licked his nose.

"It's a girl's dog," Cory declared, gently setting Pixie back down. Pixie sat and glanced between him and Emma, seemingly trying to gauge their response.

"I wouldn't be so sure, dear," Mrs. Jenkins chimed in. "This little one has enough attitude and energy for three. I bet you two could have a fantastic time playing ball together."

Cory rolled his eyes, and Sarah hurriedly thanked Mrs. Jenkins before she had the chance to call him dear again. Deep down, she felt they had just got off to a fantastic start. She hoped that this little dog would be a significant step towards healing their hearts.

Outside, Sarah caught sight of the Ryder truck and heard a honk, signaling that it was time to unload their belongings.

"Alright, kids, let's thank Mrs. Jenkins properly," she said, taking charge. "Emma, please make sure Pixie stays safe while the front door is open. Cory, could you lend a hand in directing the movers? Let's go, Anderson children." She re-tied her long blonde French braid, wiped her hands on her old jeans, and went outside to wave in the movers.

❧

It's been a huge day, Sarah thought later that night, as she tucked the blankets first around Emma, then Cory. Emma, as always, looked like a little angel, on her back with her little hands folded, while Cory curled into a tight ball with his back to her.

Sarah sat on the edge of his bed and gently touched his hair. "It will be fine, Cory," she whispered so as not to wake him. "Everything is going to be just fine, I promise." It wasn't a promise she could keep, but she made it anyway. The moon peeked through the old half-circle window, and Sarah pulled the curtains a little closer.

"Everything is going to be fine," somebody said behind her and, for a moment, she was startled, but it was only Pixie sitting in the doorway to Cory's room, her head cocked, her beautiful feathery tail draped elegantly over her back. Just her imagination. The pretty little dog seemed to smile at Sarah, and in the moonlight, the white of her fur all but glowed.

"You startled me," Sarah whispered and put a finger over her mouth.

"Mom," Cory turned around now and lifted his head off the pillow so the moonlight drew dark shadows on his face.

"Everything is fine, just go to sleep now, Cory."

"Mom, how come Pixie came to be adopted? Did somebody abandon her?" The unspoken end of that sentence broke Sarah's heart all over again, *Just like me.* Sarah made a fist and dug her nails into her palm until she could trust herself to speak normally again.

"No, honey, Pixie was well-loved. Her owner had an accident and passed away," she whispered. "Mrs. Jenkins saw her at the humane society and thought she would be a fabulous companion for you and Emma."

"She's home now," Cory said and snuggled deeper into his blankets.

Sarah turned around, but Pixie had already disappeared down the hall again, probably into Emma's room. Emma didn't think her mom knew, but she encouraged Pixie to crawl into bed with her and snuggle under the blankets, a habit the fluffy little dog would hopefully tire of as the summer grew hotter.

Chapter 2

The old kitchen featured the original wooden cabinetry and a deep sash window where she could grow herbs once they had settled, Sarah decided the next morning. With the sun streaming in through windows on two sides, the kitchen was a cheerful space that hinted at noisy family meals and joyful banter. Right over there, on that big wooden trestle table, the kids could do their homework and— A screech from the garden summoned Sarah from her daydreams, and she wiped her hands and sprinted onto the back porch. What she found made her laugh out loud.

Emma had slipped away from the cozy confines of her room, like the playful sprite she was, enticed by her curiosity about their new home. The yard with its riot of colorful flowers beckoned, as did the old-fashioned swing she had discovered the night before. Now she was swinging ever higher on that old chestnut tree, while down in the grass, Pixie ran back and forth, along with the rhythm of the swing, playfully nipping at Emma's toes and the hem of her pink flowered dress.

Sarah tried her best to be stern and reprimanding – she had told Emma they would need to have that swing checked first — but the innocent game of swing and catch between the girl and her new dog was irresistible. Sarah stood on the porch, her hands on the white railing, and watched her daughter squealing with delight.

"Emma, didn't we say—"

"Mom," the moment she spotted her, Emma dragged her feet to stop the swing. "I know, you wanted the swing checked," she said, looking down at her bare feet. "But Pixie said it was fine."

"Pixie did?"

"Yes. She said the ropes were old but very solid, and it would be just fine."

"Aha. Did Pixie also remind you that we agreed not to play on or with anything in this old house until somebody said it was safe?"

"No." Emma raised her eyes just a little and gave her mother the saddest look from bright blue eyes. The one that always worked on her mother, because it was the same one her father used. Had used. Whatever. A tear formed, and Sarah opened her arms.

"It's okay, Emma, nothing happened. Just remember to ask an adult to check things first. There's an old well on the property somewhere, and I don't want anybody to get hurt."

"The well is back there on the far end by the fence," Emma mumbled and vaguely pointed over her shoulder. The fact that she already knew sent a shiver down Sarah's back. "But Pixie said it was very dangerous, and I should never go near it."

Sarah took a breath and blew it out again. The well needed to be capped ASAP, and the fact that her daughter had found it already... The thought of what might have happened made her knees shake.

"You make sure to listen to what Pixie said," she warned, trying to keep her voice firm, and ignoring for the moment that Emma tried to blame her curiosity on the little dog. As long as she stayed away from the well.

Her children needed friends – human friends – as fast as she could make that happen. Pixie was meant to be a sprinkle of joy and enchantment in their new life here, not a sole confidante.

Sarah stepped off the porch to take her daughter's hand and ruffled Pixie's ginger head with the other.

"Come on, you two ladies, enough adventure for one morning. Time for some breakfast."

As the pair of delightful little ones ascended the porch steps, innocent laughter and excited yipping filling the air, a flicker of anticipation danced within her heart. Just for a brief moment, a mischievous twinkle adorned the tip of Pixie's enchanting tail, casting a magical glow. Yet, in the blink of an eye, it vanished, leaving behind a sense of wonder. Today promised to be a radiant day made of sunshine, adventure, and anticipation.

∽

Cory had found his way into the kitchen and remained strangely silent while Emma couldn't stop chattering about her early morning adventures in the garden.

"What do you want to do today, Cory?" Sarah asked and was met with a silent shrug.

"You can help me unpack and put your things into your room, perhaps? Later on, we could drive into Rosewood Hollow if you like. They must have a community center, perhaps there is a basketball court or a soccer field... You think that might be fun?"

Please let them have a basketball court, Sarah prayed silently. Basketball had become Cory's passion, a game he could play on end with his dad and, if she understood correctly, he was quite good at it.

But Cory only shrugged.

"Maybe," he said when it became clear his mother wouldn't let up.

"Can we go to the library?" Emma asked, proud of her budding career as a young reader. "Pixie said they have the most delightful section on—"

Cory slammed his hand with the napkin in it on the table hard enough to make the dishes rattle.

"Why don't you just go to the library then, if it's what you want so much? And your dog…. You do know that dogs can't talk, silly."

In a huff, he abruptly rose from his seat and stormed towards the back door, seeking solace on the porch, just as his mother had done moments earlier. His hands gripped the railing tightly, mirroring her stance from not long ago.

"Cory," Sarah's voice called out, trying her best to hide her frustration, but he remained silent, consumed by his own anger.

"Cory! You know the rules, in this house, we try to remain civil with one another, and we don't run from the table. Now come back. Please."

Their eyes met through the open back door. The boy's stare was hard, his jaw set with defiance. Sarah opened her mouth to say something, something she knew would probably come out wrong and likely seem disciplinarian, when Pixie quite suddenly disentangled herself from Emma's arms, gracefully hopped to the ground, and approached Cory. In her mouth she carried a little tennis ball she must have found under the table. Eagerly, she dropped it at Cory's feet, her body lowered on her front paws, tail wagging with a universal invitation to play.

Cory's eyes shifted between Pixie, Sarah, and Pixie once again. Still that tail wagged, and suddenly, joyous laughter escaped his lips. He scooped up the ball and threw it as far as he could into the expanse of the yard. In a blur of white and sable, Pixie darted after it, and Sarah hid a huge grin behind her napkin. How that little creature possessed the remarkable power to mend her wounded son's spirit, even if just for a moment.

Mere moments later, Pixie returned, dropping her ball at Cory's feet, and the boy picked it up again. Try as he might, he couldn't hang on to his sullen expression. His young face lit up as he threw the ball time and again, trying each time to propel it further and further into the yard, and without fail Pixie would return it within moments.

As Emma joined in after a few attempts, the joyful laughter of the children echoed throughout the house and yard. Sarah, savoring the sweetness of the moment, folded her hands and smiled. How long had she waited for such a lighthearted moment from her children?

"All right," she finally said. "All right. Help me clear the table, then you take half an hour to play with Pixie in the yard. We still have to unpack a lot of boxes, though, and I will need your help."

Never had the dishes been cleared faster or without any bickering between the siblings. Pixie nestled into a cozy pink dog bed on the front porch, seemingly content – a gift from Mrs. Jenkins, perhaps? For one fleeting moment, it seemed as if the little dog winked at her, a mischievous glint in its eye.

Blinking in disbelief, Sarah looked again, only to find Pixie peacefully snoozing. Perhaps it was her imagination playing tricks on her, but a small part of Sarah couldn't help but wonder if there was more to Pixie than met the eye. With a faint smile, she shook off the notion and turned her attention back to the tasks that awaited her.

She had not been kidding, they did have a lot of boxes to go through, even though much of their old life had been left behind in the city. But no matter what lay ahead, they were moving forward and making new memories out of sweet moments with her children and their enigmatic canine companion.

"Hello, Anderson family…"

The screen door opened, and Mrs. Jenkins stuck in her curly head. "I'm here to offer help, and I will not take no for an answer."

In her hands, she carried a plate of cookies Sarah knew the children would devour.

"Then I will not say no, there's still a lot to do."

"I see the little sprite found her place in your family right quick."

"Yes, they made fast friends…" Sarah looked down at the sleeping Pixie. "This might be a silly question, but did you make a little – dog bed for Pixie when you brought her over?"

Mrs. Jenkins blinked and cocked her head, looking down at Pixie and back at Sarah.

"If I had thought of it, I would have, Sarah. The little one is just too precious, but it looks like you have the perfect little bed for her anyway. How sweet. Now let's get started – the upstairs hallway has a large, vented linen closet you are going to love. Why don't you point me to your boxes of linens, and I can organize and refold everything just so?"

The woman might be old, but apparently, she had an inexhaustible supply of energy, Sarah thought and did as she had been asked. It was just easier.

Around lunch, they all found themselves in the kitchen again, and as she had expected, the children devoured the cookies.

"I probably should make them eat something a little more healthy," Sarah said guiltily, sneaking a cookie herself. "But they've been so good the last few days."

"Nonsense, they have all the time in the world to eat healthy," Mrs. Jenkins said. "Let them have this treat. How was your first night in the new house anyway?"

"How was it?" Sarah asked a little confused. "Fine, I think? Any particular reason you ask? I know I have to find someone to cap the well in the yard, but everything else was – fine."

"Nothing strange happened?"

"Should it have?" Sarah asked with a frisson of concern. "Is there something I don't know?"

"Of course not, dear," Mrs. Jenkins patted her hand. "You know – whatever you dream on your first night in a new house will come true, that's all."

"That's disappointing. I didn't dream anything. I rarely ever do."

Sarah took another cookie and smiled. "Now – we have made fantastic progress this morning, I think I want to take the children into town this afternoon. Emma's a voracious reader. Is there a library or a bookstore she might enjoy? And a community center or sports center where Cory might make some friends? I thought we would do some exploring."

Chapter 3

Armed with the address of a bookstore, the community sports complex, and the local historical society, Sarah set out a few hours later with two freshly showered children and a little white and sable princess on a leash to explore Rosewood Hollow. Nothing bad ever happened in these parts of the country, Mrs. Jenkins had assured her, and the kids could quite easily ride their bikes into town. Just for now, Sarah wanted to be there.

The bookstore they sought was nestled in a weathered, clapboard building situated on the outskirts of town. Sarah knew Emma would lose herself amidst the shelves for hours, so she decided to grant Cory the freedom to explore the nearby sports field. He was old enough to venture on his own.

"Stay out of trouble," she called out to him with a mischievous grin, and Cory responded with a sly wink, gesturing towards Pixie.

"Don't worry, she's keeping an eye on me," he reassured Sarah, his voice lighthearted and happy once again.

Emma needed no further encouragement to explore the bookshelves, and Sarah stood browsing by a table at the front. "Local Authors," a sign proclaimed, and Sarah found herself with a lot of mysteries and ghost stories.

"Anything in particular you are looking for, an author I could help you find?"

Sarah looked up into the kind green eyes of a smiling woman her own age. Her auburn hair fell in a riot of curls just below her shoulders, barely contained by a multi-color scarf around her forehead.

"I'm Lily Morrison," she said with a broad smile. "I own this amazing bookstore, and if that little one you came in with is your daughter, then you raised her right. I see she has her eyes on some fabulous new releases."

"Sarah Anderson," Sarah said and stuck out her hand. She instantly felt self-conscious in her old jeans and t-shirt, compared to Lily's chic flowing dress of pink and purple and orange and... "We just moved to the area," she added.

"Oh, then you're the family who bought the old Thompson place. I heard about that. What's it like inside?"

"It's – quite beautiful," Sarah said with a smile. "I bet the house has a long history. Maybe that's where I should start," Sarah looked over the offerings on the table before her. "A history of the area?"

"If you're interested in the history, then you need to see Matthew over at the historical society about that," Lily said. "He can totally get you the lowdown on everything. The old Thompson place has been empty for years now, I'm so excited someone is finally living there again! And welcome to Rosewood Hollow! Anytime you need to know something, just stop by here. Glad to help."

"Wow, thank you." Sarah looked to find Emma still engrossed in books. "To tell you the truth, we are all – starting over. I probably will have questions. Mrs. Jenkins said—"

"You be careful with Mrs. Jenkins, now, Sarah."

Sarah felt that odd shiver creep down her back again. "Why do you say that, she's a lovely old lady, isn't she?"

"A lovely old lady with nothing to do all day," Lily warned and spread her arms in a move that made dozens of little gold hoops on her wrists tinkle and chime. "You tell Mrs. J anything, and the next day the entire town will be aware, I can promise you that."

"Oh. I guess I know what that's about," Sarah said, relieved. "Now, would you happen to know of any sports clubs?"

Cory ambled along the edge of the soccer field and sat on a bench, Pixie at his feet.

"Guess we forgot your ball, huh?" he murmured apologetically to the little canine companion gazing up at him, her expressive eyes seeking understanding. "I'm sorry, I don't have anything to play with."

Pixie tilted her head inquisitively and gave a short, little yip as if to console him. Cory's hand instinctively reached down to caress her velvety head, finding comfort in the warmth of their connection.

At the distant end of the field, a quartet of young boys congregated, their presence drawing Cory's attention. One of them clutched a basketball tightly against his side, and his gaze fixed on Cory. Sensing their curiosity, Cory averted his eyes, torn between a burning desire to join them and an invisible force that kept him tethered to that narrow, metal bench.

With an easy gait, the tallest boy sauntered over, idly kicking at a speck of dirt and casting an appraising glance at Pixie.

"Isn't that a little girl's dog?" he challenged, immediately stoking irritation within Cory.

"Pixie is the fastest dog I know," he swiftly defended, his voice carrying a hint of defiance, which only served to ignite the other boy's laughter.

"Pixie? That's the dumbest, girly name for a dog I've ever heard," the boy taunted, relishing in his attempt to undermine Cory's companion. "Here, Pixie dummy."

"Pixie is smart," Cory defended her again. "And she is fast, faster than any dog."

"Oh yeah," the boy reached out for Pixie, his intentions clear, but with a graceful twist that required minimal effort, she eluded his grasp. Undeterred, the boy made another attempt, trying to seize her by the neck or trample on her leash, yet Pixie effortlessly evaded him with each maneuver. Cory thought he detected a flicker of delight in her eyes. It was as if she silently declared, *I can do this all day, can you?* Eventually, the boy conceded defeat.

"Stupid dog," he muttered and kicked the dirt for good measure. "What good is it anyway with all that long hair?"

"Hey Damian," one of the other boys called over. "You want to play basketball or chase that dog all day long, huh?"

Basketball. Cory's gaze wistfully drifted towards the hoop at the far end of the field, and Damian didn't miss the longing in his eyes.

"So, can you play basketball, or are you just here to walk stupid little dogs?" Damian taunted, his tone dripping with skepticism.

"I can play ball," Cory responded with a mischievous grin. This was one area where he excelled. "I'm Cory."

"Damian. And make sure that dumb dog doesn't get in the way," Damian cautioned, the tinge of competitiveness lingering in his voice.

෭ඬ

"Emma, we've been here for an hour and a half," Sarah suddenly said and looked around for her daughter in a panic. It was just so easy to chat with Lily and the lovely young ladies who dropped into the bookstore.

"You've all been so welcoming," Sarah said, fear mounting in her stomach. Lily only pointed and winked. The bookstore, once an ancient home, had undergone numerous expansions over the years, resulting in a series of interconnected rooms with steps leading up or down.

Lo and behold, tucked away in a cozy corner one level up, Emma sat nestled in a deep armchair with an open book resting on her lap, completely engrossed and unaware of the bustling world around her.

"She'd be delighted if I left her here to spend the rest of the afternoon," Sarah said with a sigh. "But Cory, my son, is out at the community center – somewhere. I'm afraid he may not be too pleased with us."

Lily dismissed her concerns with a wave of her hand.

"Oh, don't worry about your boy. There's always some pickup game going on. He's probably already made some friends."

"Cory's a bit shy," Sarah explained while searching for her wallet. "Let me just pay for our purchases here, and then we'll go find him."

Emma reluctantly handed over her beloved books.

"He's got Pixie with him," she said making a face. "Pixie will watch out for him."

"Thank you, Lily. This afternoon has been wonderful, and we truly needed this break."

"It's my pleasure, please feel free to visit anytime," the young woman said, winking once more. "I'd love to have a conversation with you about your beautiful house. Oh, and I must introduce you to Matthew."

Suddenly, mischievous sparks danced in her eyes, and her golden bangles jingled and danced with excitement as she continued in a low voice.

"Matthew Turner is a history professor and works at our local Historical Society. He knows absolutely everything about Rosewood Hollow. Everything, mark my words. I'll arrange for you to meet him, maybe right here, it'll be fun."

"Matthew Turner, the historian," Sarah repeated, handing over her credit card. "I'll try to remember," she finished lamely. An ancient history professor was the last person she wanted to meet just then.

"He's truly the best person if you want to learn about the history of Rosewood Hollow," Lily replied with enthusiasm. Leaning in, she lowered her voice again, "And trust me, he's quite easy on the eyes if you catch my drift."

Sarah chuckled a little and touched her hair. *Do I look that old?* she thought but Lily seemed to read her mind.

"Trust me, you'll enjoy meeting him. Now, go find your son, but I can guarantee he won't have even had time to miss you – I promise!"

With a thankful smile, Sarah gathered her belongings in a large hold-all and set off to find Cory, looking forward to both the meeting with Matthew and the intriguing history of Rosewood Hollow.

❧

"That lady was really nice," Emma said, skipping excitedly toward their old station wagon. "I'll have to come back here. They have a whole section of authors I've never heard of!"

Sarah smiled and bent down to give her youngest a quick hug. "You're more than welcome to come back as often as you like," she whispered. "But let's make sure Cory gets to do something equally fun and exciting, okay?"

"He got to have Pixie with him," Emma grumbled, but she obediently settled into the backseat of the car.

Maybe it was time to have some sort of locate function on their phones, she wondered as she looked for a parking spot at the community center. Yes, it was kind of invasive, and people did keep mentioning nothing ever happened in Rosewood Hollow, but still...

However, her worries about finding Cory were quickly put to rest as she arrived at the soccer field. The boisterous sounds of screeching laughter and jeers filled the air, signaling an energetic game in progress. Shielding her eyes from the sun, Sarah spotted the basketball court on the other side of the field and Cory, showing off his remarkable skills with a basketball. His face drawn tight, he set up for an impossible shot – and sank it flawlessly.

"Nothing but net," Sarah whispered to herself, clenching her fist in pride. "Go Cory."

In the cool shade of a nearby tree, Pixie sat calmly on top of Cory's jacket, enthusiastically commenting on the game with loud barks. Two of Cory's new friends exchanged high fives with him, while a third one, his face dark with thunderclouds, set up a similar shot. Unfortunately, he missed, and in response, Pixie jumped up and barked even louder than before, adding her unique touch of enthusiasm to the game.

Pixie spotted Sarah and Emma and bounded toward them, putting excited paws on their knees and dancing in circles. Sarah waved at Cory. You can stay for a while, she wanted to say, but her son exchanged high fives with the other boys again, slung his jacket over his shoulder, and bounded across the field to them in easy, loping strides.

"See you later, Cory," one of the boys called after him. "Great game."

Cory waved over his shoulder without turning. How like his father, Sarah thought with a pang and shoved her hands deep into her pockets so she wouldn't reach out and ruffle his hair.

"Good time?"

"All right," Cory slipped into his jacket now and picked up Pixie's leash again. "Damian thought Pixie was a dumb girl's dog." He rolled his eyes. "Shows you what he knows."

"Pixie is not dumb," Emma said, glowering back at the boys as if she were ready to go over there and give them a piece of her mind.

"Easy, Emma," Sarah put a hand on her shoulder. "Looks like you had a good game anyway."

"You bet." Cory automatically sat in the passenger seat, stretched his legs, and folded his hands behind his head. "Tough luck for Damian though. After he called Pixie – a name – he couldn't sink one single shot. Not even an easy one, and he's supposed to be some sort of a star or something. Said it was because she looked at him and her tail glowed," Cory rolled his eyes dramatically. "Excuses – nothing but excuses. But I sank every single shot I set up for – every single one. It was cool."

Her son was happy, that was what counted, except Sarah tilted the rear-view mirror and looked at Pixie, snuggled tightly against Emma, snoozing once again. Her feathery tail fanned out across the seat, shining pure white. Not a glow anywhere. And yet...

Chapter 4

That night Sarah sat on the porch swing, letting it sway gently, enjoying a book she had purchased that afternoon and a glass of wine. She felt that she had made the right decision moving to Rosewood Hollow with its friendly people and small-town charm. They'd be happy here, she believed.

"Storm coming in," Mrs. Jenkins waved at her from the next yard. "Better get all of those patio cushions inside and batten down the windows."

Sarah waved back and finished her wine. She could live with nosy neighbors, that was fine. A gust of cool wind breezing through the porch reminded her that Mrs. Jenkins was likely right after all. She sent the kids to bed and told them there'd be a thunderstorm overnight. Cory, of course, rolled his eyes.

"No biggie, Mom, I'm not five."

Emma clung to Pixie. "Can Pixie sleep in my bed?"

"Sure," Sarah sighed. The whole, 'this dog will sleep in her crate at night,' thing had gone out the window the first night anyway.

Pixie gave a little yip and put her paws on the window sash to look outside. The enjoyable evening on the porch had turned into a dark, almost sinister moment in a hurry, and Sarah shivered involuntarily.

"Wash up and then to bed, kids. You can read for another half-hour if you like, Cory – no more iPad, please."

"Yes, Mom," they chorused and disappeared upstairs.

Sarah pulled her cardigan a little tighter and checked both doors and all the windows. Something in the air felt electric and tense all of a sudden. She jumped when she heard a metallic rattle, but it was only Pixie rubbing up against her legs, her tags clinking softly.

"Hey there, little girl," Sarah whispered and caressed the silky head. "Something's got you spooked too? I don't blame you."

Pixie cocked her head and spun around once in front of her, then she headed toward the stairs as if she meant for Sarah to follow.

"Go on then, check on the kids."

Pixie stood still at the bottom of the stairs, her dark eyes on Sarah's, one paw lifted.

"Go on, Emma is probably looking for you."

Why did it look like that little dog understood every word she said, and, moreover, wanted her to go and check on something?

"You're not Lassie," Sarah said a little louder than she had meant to. "And those kids are old enough to call out if they need something."

Just then a bolt of lightning lit up the dark, and the massive roar of thunder followed almost immediately.

In a flash of white, Pixie disappeared upstairs. The lights flickered briefly, and Sarah shivered.

Maybe I'd better check, she thought and set her book aside again. No point pretending to read now.

Sarah almost jumped out of her skin when she turned and literally bumped into Cory, dressed in a t-shirt and shorts.

"Weren't you headed for bed half an hour ago?"

"I am," her son pointed down at himself, a mischievous twinkle in his eye, "See. I just wanted to get some water. And the streetlights flickered."

"I know," Sarah said, smiling warmly as she put her arms around his shoulders. "Where's Pixie? She tore upstairs like a flash."

"Emma's room. Probably hiding under the blankets."

Another flash of lightning and a thunderous boom confirmed his suspicions, and Sarah shivered again involuntarily. The eerie shadows cast by the lightning danced on his young face, giving him an almost ghostly appearance. Sarah went to the kitchen to fetch a bottle of water, handing it to her son.

"Here you go, want to sit with me for a little while?"

Bedtime was usually a sacred ritual in their family, but it was summer, not a school night, and he looked as if he might finally open up to her with all the emotions he'd bottled up inside since his father left.

Cory nodded and dropped into a deep upholstered chair.

"That was weird," he finally said.

"What, the flickering lights? That's just—"

"Not the lights," Cory shook his head and chewed his lower lip for a while. "Mom, what kind of dog is Pixie?"

"Pixie," Sarah cocked her head. "She's a Papillon dog. The long fringes on her ears and that fluffy curly tail? That's how you recognize them."

"I know the breed," Cory said, spreading his hands with the frustration of searching for words. "What I mean is – you know how there are specially trained dogs for people who are blind or in a wheelchair? They help them?"

"Service dogs?"

"Yes – is that what Pixie was?"

"I don't think so… Her owner taught her a few tricks. I can tell that – but, why do you ask?"

"Because she – it's like she knows when I'm feeling crappy. She comes around and puts her paws on me. I just thought…"

"Oh honey," Sarah knelt beside the armchair and put her arms around his skinny frame. "That's just what dogs are. They can sense when you're not well and they comfort you."

"That's what Emma said," he mumbled and looked down at his hands. "I guess she has a book on it." Cory rolled his eyes. "But this afternoon, when Damian called her dumb, she just sat and stared at him. And he really didn't make one more shot after that. Isn't that weird?"

"It's weird if you're Damian," Sarah chuckled and leaned against her son. "I got Pixie so you and Emma wouldn't feel alone and without somebody to talk to. I'm happy she's doing that. You do like her, don't you?"

"She's pretty cool," Cory said, a faint smile breaking through, probably as much of a compliment as any sixteen-year-old could manage. "And she does know a few really neat tricks."

At that moment, a chilling scream pierced the air, shattering the serenity of the moment. Sarah sprang from her seat so abruptly that she nearly knocked over Cory's chair. The urgency in the cry propelled her into motion, racing up the stairs, taking two steps at a time, her heart pounding like a drum.

"Emma?" she tore into Emma's room. "What's the matter?"

Her daughter sat upright in her snow-white bed with the pink linens and had pulled the blankets all the way up to her face.

"What's wrong, Emma?" Sarah sat on the edge of the bed and awkwardly tried to put her arms around her daughter. Emma struggled to find her words, her entire body trembling with fear.

"Hush, baby, it's all right, everything is all right," Sarah said softly. "I'm here..."

"I heard – I heard something." Emma's bottom lip quaked, and a big tear fell.

"The thunderclap, is that what scared you? It startled all of us, I'm sorry."

"No, there was a voice... A scary woman's voice."

Could it be a nightmare? An intruder? Did she hear people arguing outside? Sarah checked, but the tall half-moon windows in Emma's room were tightly closed.

"Maybe someone outside? Somebody walking by, perhaps?" Sarah offered tentatively, hoping for a simple and mundane explanation.

But Emma's response shattered any hope of such reassurance. "No, Mom, it was inside the house," she said softly, her voice trembling.

Inside the house. Those words sent shivers down Sarah's spine, and her maternal instincts kicked into overdrive. Clasping her daughter tightly to her chest, she tried to quell the pounding in her own heart. The eerie thought that an intruder might be in their own home sent her mind racing.

"Hush, it's over now, maybe it was a nightmare."

"It was not, Mom. Pixie tried to protect me."

Pixie! Where was the little dog in all of this? Sarah looked between the mounds of blankets on Emma's bed just as Cory wandered into the room.

"I brought you a cookie," he said matter-of-factly and handed Emma one of the precious chocolate chip cookies on a white napkin. "And what is Pixie doing over there?"

In her worry about her daughter, Sarah had never looked at anything but Emma in her bed. Now she saw it too. At the far wall of the room, Pixie scratched with all of her five-pound might against a section of the wall. A few inches of floral wallpaper just at the bottom of the wall had already been torn off the backing.

"Pixie, stop! What are you doing, stop?" Sarah pleaded with the little canine, desperately trying to understand the significance of her actions.

Pixie momentarily paused, her eyes darting between Sarah and the wall, before resuming her frenzied effort to expose whatever lay concealed beneath the wallpaper.

Now lying on her side, Pixie fervently dug away at the wall, pouring all her strength into the task. A section of wallpaper finally yielded, presenting an opportunity that Pixie couldn't resist. Swiftly, she clamped her tiny jaws around the edge of the wallpaper and leaped backward, exerting all her strength as she pulled with vigor.

"Pixie, for God's sake, stop right now," Sarah exclaimed, perhaps a touch concerned about what insects or rodents her curious pet might uncover.

Cory merely stared at Pixie and her relentless scratching, his own cookie uneaten in his hand. Suddenly he dropped it carelessly and pointed at the wall.

"Mom, look, Pixie found a door!"

What lay hidden beneath the tattered pink floral wallpaper was far from the anticipated whitewashed wall. Where Pixie had ripped the paper away, the outline of a simple wooden door was now appearing.

Satisfied with her work, Pixie sat back and shook, panting hard. Emma called out to her again, and gracefully Pixie jumped up on the bed and snuggled up to the girl.

"Naughty girl," Emma giggled, her earlier fright all but forgotten, but the appearance of a hidden door chilled Sarah all the way to her core.

Sarah couldn't help but wonder if there was a connection between the hidden door and the faint voice Emma claimed to have heard earlier. The thought of something unknown lurking just beyond their threshold filled her with a mix of curiosity, fear, and trepidation.

"Cory, be careful," she snapped as her adventure-loving son had already crossed the room and was feeling along the edges of the exposed door panel.

"No door handle," he said quizzically. "That's kind of weird. If Pixie hadn't started digging like crazy, you'd never even know there was a door there."

Sarah felt an icy grip around her heart. All of the reasons why someone would hide a door flooded her mind, and none of them were any good.

"I don't know what it could be," she said tonelessly.

Cory reached out to touch the door, but Sarah stopped him.

"Don't touch it," she snapped. "It's probably just a storage closet, but I'm not about to take any chances."

Cory frowned. "But it looks so interesting," he said. "I bet there's something cool inside."

Sarah sighed. "Maybe," she conceded. "But we'll find out tomorrow. Right now, it's too late to be poking around in old storage rooms." Her voice sounded almost panicked to her own ears. Emma stopped patting

Pixie and stared at her mother, and Cory raised both hands and took a step back.

"Geez, I'm not a little kid, you don't need to worry about everything, you know."

"I'm not worried about you, Cory."

Another thunderclap roared as if it were right above the house, and a bright flash of lightning bathed the entire room in a flash of blinding white.

Was that…? Did she hear something?

Sarah strained her ears, but all she could hear was the pouring rain against Emma's window.

"This is an old house," she finally said, forcing a measure of calm into her voice, calm she did not feel. "It's been renovated a lot, so who knows why they covered it up, or what shape whatever's behind it is in. I'm not about to find out tonight."

"Yes, Mom."

"And if it wasn't renovated, the floor there could be beyond rotten. Maybe that's why it was capped. I don't need you crashing through a weak ceiling tonight, okay?"

"Yes, Mom." Cory pushed his hands into the pockets of his sweater, but his eyes never left the section of torn wallpaper and the edge of a door beneath it. She knew he wanted to grab some tools and get to work on it right now. With a sigh, she pushed the thought away and listened for a moment. No voices, that was a relief.

"Tomorrow," she said. "Tomorrow, we'll get a handyman to check out what's up with that, okay? In the meantime, please go to bed, everyone. Emma, grab your stuff, you are sleeping in my room tonight, and Cory…" Sarah shook her head. "Please put a flashlight on your nightstand, and no more exploring tonight."

Cory rolled his eyes and activated the flashlight on his phone, shining it around the room to show his mom that there was nothing to be afraid of. Sarah nodded, knowing her son thought she was making a big deal out of nothing. "Fine," she snapped. "Now please, everybody – back to bed."

Pixie gracefully jumped off the bed and quietly snatched the cookie Cory had dropped. Surprisingly, nobody scolded her this time. Sarah bundled up the shaken-up Emma, her bedding, her favorite stuffed animal, and a few extra pillows and directed all to her bed. They'd be slightly crowded all in one bed, together with Pixie, but the sound of Emma's shriek still echoed in Sarah's ears. She could still see the look of fear on her daughter's face.

I heard a scary woman's voice.

Just a nightmare caused by the thunderstorm – nothing but a nightmare, Sarah assured herself as she closed the door to Emma's room and double-checked it.

Once Pixie and Emma were snuggled in the huge bed in her room she went downstairs again. In front of Emma's room, she paused for just a moment, but nothing stirred behind the closed door. *Jesus, kids have nightmares,* she scolded herself, pouring a generous glass of wine. *Way to go frightening them all. Good job, Sarah. It's probably just an oversize, stuffy closet behind there.*

Did this house have an attic, she wondered and tried to remember the estate listing. She wasn't really an attic person, found them to be creepy, dark, and dusty places.

The thunder rolled again, and, thankfully, it sounded as if it were moving off. Sarah stood on the back porch for a moment, listening to the storm. The rain was slowing down, the clouds were beginning to break up, and she tried to calm her racing thoughts and anxiety. It was just a storm, and the door was probably nothing more sinister than an empty closet.

Old houses creak and groan, and the sooner she got over her fear of everything and everybody and started taking charge, the way she had promised Michael she would, the better it would be for everybody.

Chapter 5

The following morning, Sarah sneaked out of her bedroom before the kids woke and stood on the porch with her morning coffee. In the light of day, watching the steam curl over her cup and smelling the dark, rich coffee, she could almost imagine it had all been just a dream — a nightmare brought on by the storm.

"Just an old closet." she chuckled to herself. Today, she'd let Cory explore the old space. He'd probably be grossed out by dead bugs and spiderwebs, but they'd sweep out that space and perhaps figure out what to do with it. Maybe a walk-in closet with bookshelves — Emma would like that, she mused. The more she thought about it, the more the terror and anxiety of the night before slipped into the background.

A little white butterfly busily flitted between the flowers, and only a few broken branches on the lawn reminded her of the night before. Next door, Mrs. Jenkins collected the paper from the front stoop of their tidy little white ranch house and waved to her. All of this was why they had moved here.

"Can I explore the closet today?" Cory appeared behind her, still in the t-shirt and shorts he had slept in. "I really want to see what's behind that door. Please. Promise I'll be careful."

"All right, you may," Sarah relented. "I can see I won't win, so go ahead. But first, you will get ready and have some breakfast. And absolutely no scaring your sister. Do you understand?"

With a brief "Yes, Mom," he darted off up to his room, though she heard him muttering about what a waste of time it was to get washed up before exploring an old closet. *Good point*, Sarah thought.

Even Emma seemed to have forgotten her night terror, and she and Pixie bounded down the stairs only a little while later, bright-eyed and ready to start their day.

"No more nightmares?" Sarah asked and placed some cocoa in front of her.

"Nope," Emma beamed. "Pixie told me as long as she was around, there was absolutely nothing to worry about."

"Honey, I really—" Before she could explain to Emma that protecting her was perhaps a bit of a big job for a five-pound Papillon dog, her phone chimed with a text message.

"Your father, maybe..." Sarah checked and didn't recognize the number. "Not that Michael would check up on us already."

Hey lady, the text read. *It's Lily from Rosewood Books. I think you forgot your debit card on the counter yesterday. Too much of a hurry to leave?*

Oh my God. Sarah checked her wallet and quickly typed a reply. *Thanks so much, Lily, where was my head? Okay if I come down later?*

No worries – I'm closed Wednesday afternoons – I was going to pop by your house with Matthew later, if that's okay.

Matthew, that old history professor Lily felt Sarah absolutely needed to get to know. Sarah sighed with her finger poised over the screen.

We'll bring some cake, Lily replied when Sarah hesitated. *And a few books for Emma. Gotta build up my future customers.*

All right, you're on. As long as you don't look at my mess.

My eyes never seen a mess I didn't like – C-ya later.

"What's going on?" Suspiciously, Cory had already piled the dishes in the sink and washed his hands again. Somebody couldn't wait.

"I forgot something at the store. Lily is coming over a little while later."

"Yay," Emma chimed in. "Can I show her my room?"

"You most definitely can," Sarah laughed. "I've even been thinking about turning that old closet into a little library for you, if you like."

"Books," Cory made a face. "That's all?"

"And if Emma gets a library, we are going to buy a basketball hoop for you outside, OK? Promise."

Some of the excitement had gone out of the exploration for Cory, even with the promise of a basketball hoop, and Sarah bit off a sigh. "Besides, Cory, Lily is probably bringing someone who knows all about the history of the area. Maybe there are some good old spooky facts about our house. Who knows, it is pretty old."

"Like ghosts, and maybe it's haunted?" he asked, peering sideways at Emma to see if he could scare her.

"No ghosts, Cory. Now if you're ready…"

Sarah paused for a moment at Emma's door, so abruptly the children almost plowed into her from behind. With a hand on the handle, she waited, listening for any sounds from inside. Nothing.

Ready or not, here I come.

❧

A lovely beam of sunlight crept into Emma's room between the curtains, and dust motes danced in the sunbeam. Sarah quickly opened the curtains wide and looked around the room. It was as it had been—a wide, old-fashioned white daybed with pink linens, a matching white desk, a bookshelf with little painted roses and angels, and pink and white wallpaper.

Pixie, with lightning speed, darted through everyone's legs and charged towards the wall adorned with torn wallpaper, revealing the mysterious hidden door. She stood there, ears perked up and on full alert, her tail tightly curled over her back, twitching with excitement. Her head leaned forward, and her nose actively explored the air, as if she were diligently tracking something elusive. After a moment of intense focus, she visibly relaxed, taking a step back, yet her gaze remained fixated on the lower edge of the uncovered door.

"There might be mice in there," Sarah said and made a face. "Be careful if there are droppings, everything will have to be disinfected, aired out, and cleaned before you can come back into this room, Emma. They can be super dangerous."

Cory took hold of the lower edge of the loose wallpaper. "Sorry about the paper, Em. But it is ugly anyway."

"It's not ugly — you're ugly. Mom."

"Cory, we agreed."

"I didn't—" At that moment, Cory almost stumbled and caught himself with an effort. The entire sheet of wallpaper that had been used to cover up the door came away from the wall as one, leaving dust, dried wallpaper glue, and a simple wooden panel door. Cory fought off the giant sheet of wallpaper, bundling it into an untidy heap, and stared at the door. The handle had been removed, and the area patched up with a bit of white filler, but the lock, a big old-fashioned metal affair, was left behind.

"Is it locked?" Emma asked from a safe spot behind Sarah's legs. The burning curiosity over the door overrode even Cory's earlier insults. Cory probed the lock with his fingers and Sarah held out a hand to stop her son. She tried to dig her nails into the gap between the frame and the door, but it wouldn't give.

"I think so," she said, and for some reason, her heart started beating a bit faster again. What was it about this strange door? "Perhaps our handyman can..."

"I'll get some tools," Cory darted out and down the wide double staircase before she could stop him.

༄

"Hello, neighbors, helping hands coming back in!"

Mrs. Jenkins. Sarah rolled her eyes. *Grand Central station*, she wanted to call out. *Walk right in*, but she bit the remark off at the last second. Hadn't Michael always told her sarcasm was not appreciated?

"Up here," she called instead and waited for her neighbor to make her way upstairs. If the house had been empty for a while, perhaps it was forgivable – perhaps – that all of the neighbors wanted to get a glimpse inside.

Emma sat on her bed and cradled Pixie once again. Pixie, Sarah noticed, didn't bark or alert on anything, but her attentive little dark eyes never left the hidden door for more than a second.

"Good morning, I thought you might need some help with— Good lord, what on earth have you done?"

Mrs. Jenkins stopped in the open door of Emma's room and clapped a hand to her mouth.

"Dear God, it's the attic," she said, her normally boisterous voice coming out in a whisper.

"The attic?" Sarah asked and turned around to get an answer, but Mrs. Jenkins reached for the chair by Emma's bedside. She dropped into it as if she wanted to faint and brought her hands to her mouth. All of the color had drained from her face, making her look gray and weak all of a sudden.

"The old attic," she repeated in a hoarse whisper.

"There's an attic in this house — cool," Cory had come back upstairs, swinging the bright red toolbox his father had bought him, now that he was 'the man' in the house. "Let's see."

"No, don't, Cory."

But Cory had already inserted skinny little tools into the old lock and began to twist them gently.

"How exactly do you know how to do this?" Sarah asked, torn between the pale Mrs. Jenkins and her son acting like a talented burglar.

"I dunno – Dad showed me one day. I think you forgot your key or something."

"We'll talk about this later," she said to him, fetched a glass of water from her bedroom, and handed it to her elderly neighbor.

"Here, have some water. Easy now, it's probably the heat. There's really no need for you to exhaust yourself. Look," she pointed at Cory and his toolbox. "I have all the help I need right here."

"It's not that hot, Sarah, and you don't understand. The old attic..."

"Is it spooky?" Cory stopped his work on the door for a moment and looked at Mrs. Jenkins with bright curious eyes. "Zombies? Maybe an old curse?"

"Cory!" Sarah wheeled on her son and raised a finger. "If you're going to insist on acting like this, scaring your sister, you will have to stop right now."

With a little click, unfitting the massive iron lock, it gave way, and Cory slowly swung the door open, swatting at spiderwebs in his way.

"No attic," he finally declared, his voice tinged with a touch of disappointment. "Just an old, boring closet. But hey, don't worry, squirt! We'll turn this place into your very own library. Just give it some cleaning, add a little light in here..."

As he stood there, a hint of a smile played on his lips, giving him the air of a seasoned middle-aged contractor. Thumbs confidently hooked in his belt loops, he nodded as if he were envisioning the library and the work he would have to do.

"Let me see," Sarah took a couple of steps and peeked inside. It was just as he had said, an old dusty closet, the walls unfinished, construction lumber, the corners filled with dust and cobwebs. Even Mrs. Jenkins now got up from her chair and peered inside.

"Well, isn't that..."

"What were you saying about an attic?" Sarah asked, and just then Pixie went berserk. She charged into the middle of the closet and let loose a series of high-pitched shrill barks that would have woken the dead.

"Pixie, for crying out loud – Pixie, quiet."

Sarah reached for her, hoping if she cradled her in her arms the barking would stop, but Pixie was not to be deterred.

Cory finally managed to pick her up and followed her gaze.

"Oh wait, she's looking at something up on the ceiling," he said. "That's weird."

Again, Sarah looked, this time shining the flashlight of her phone at the ceiling of the closet.

"Well, you might get your attic after all, Mrs. J."

"What is it?" Cory asked.

"It's a loop. Likely what you are looking at is a hatch that has fold-down stairs. Long time ago, that's how many attics operated. You had a pole with a hook on it, put it into that loop there, and pulled down the hatch. Along the way, the ladder unfolded, and there you were. Attic stairs."

They all stood looking at it for a moment.

"So, anybody have a pole?" Cory finally said with a smirk, and Sarah grinned in turn.

"Get Pixie outside for a minute, before the barking drives us all batty. I'll get Mrs. Jenkins home, and then we'll go look, okay?"

"All right. Think Mr. Jenkins would give me a hand?"

Pixie had stopped barking for the moment, but cradled in Cory's arm she still growled at the new, strange closet, even though she had been the one to discover it. Her eyes narrowed and she made low rumbling sounds that appeared to be coming from the depth of her soul.

"What is it with you?" Sarah asked, a little annoyed. "There is nothing in there, not even mice."

Pixie's piercing gaze locked onto Sarah, sending a sudden chill down her spine. In that fleeting moment, Sarah empathized with the young kid Damian, sensing an uncanny familiarity in Pixie's dark brown eyes, as if they held a profound understanding of something beyond ordinary comprehension. The intensity in those eyes seemed to convey a secret knowledge, a wisdom beyond her canine years.

As Sarah glanced back at Pixie, her face remained eerily tranquil, and those eyes continued to bore into her own, unblinking and unwavering.

A sense of vulnerability washed over Sarah, making her look away and focus on the closet, attempting to distract herself from the unnerving connection she felt with Pixie.

An inexplicable shiver raced through Sarah's body, sending a jolt of discomfort surging through her. It was as if a mysterious, electric energy had engulfed the very air they breathed, leaving her with an eerie sensation. She couldn't escape the nagging suspicion that Pixie held a secret, something Sarah was yet to unravel.

She closed her eyes, counted to ten, steadied herself, and shone her phone flashlight into the closet once more.

"I'll let you kids explore once. But after that, I'd suggest we do as we planned, turn this into a little library space, and close up that hatch, unless there's a very good reason not to." That was the end of the discussion for her.

⸎

Cory and Emma went to take Pixie outside for a moment while Sarah went to look after Mrs. Jenkins and then grab a vacuum to clean out the worst of the cobwebs.

"You really need to be careful," she said, gently scolding her elderly neighbor. "I appreciate you trying to help, but you looked like you were going to faint there for a second. Let Cory deal with this old closet. I have a handyman who can make all of the repairs. Please."

"You don't understand," the old lady said, clutching the handrail tightly, pausing on the stairs. "This is an old house, it has an enormous amount of history."

"About that. Lily Morrison – the lady who owns the bookstore? She'll drop by this afternoon with a historian to have a look at the house. You're welcome to join us, though I suspect most of it will be boring."

"Oh, Probably Matt Turner," Mrs. Jenkins said with a throwaway hand motion. "Young guy who knows nothing that he hasn't read in books or on that computer of his. The real story – the truth…" She sighed and stopped at the bottom of the stairs. Curiously, Sarah noticed she avoided touching the carved head of the griffin on the newel post.

"Either way," she said, "you're welcome to join us. I believe Lily promised to bring cake – but for now, please go and lie down for a bit."

∞

By the time Lily appeared in the driveway, Sarah had cleaned out the old closet, closed the door again, tidied the torn wallpaper as best as she could, and generally put Emma's room into a semblance of order.

Lily parked her vibrant orange Volkswagen Beetle with a flourish. Today she had woven a scarf of brilliant blue and green batik watercolor through her hair. The little car's retro charm suited her to a tee, the man in the passenger seat, however, had a difficult time extricating himself from the compact vehicle. He was roughly her own age, and tall, Sarah noticed, extremely tall even. Heck, he likely could have reached up inside the old closet without the help of a pole.

When he had squeezed out he stood there for a moment, blinked into the bright sun, and brushed a mop of dark blonde hair out of his face. His dark jeans fit tight in all the right places and his black retro t-shirt bore the inscription, *Do epic sh*t*. Cory would beg her for a shirt like that tomorrow. Lily caught Sarah's stare and winked. This was not your average college professor.

"Had I known I would have to fold up to sit in this – this – vehicle," Matthew said, a little perturbed as he reached back for his leather portfolio.

"Welcome to our home," Sarah said, taking a cake box out of Lily's hands. "You probably shouldn't have, but it is appreciated all the same. Come on in – unless you want to have tea on the porch first."

"Oh, I'd like to look around," the young man said with a gleam in his eyes. "I'm sorry – manners – I'm Matthew Turner."

"Sarah. Lily told me."

"The old Thompson place," he said, letting go of her hand, brushing a shock of dark hair out of his face as his eyes traveled up the wooden façade, over the second-story dormer windows, and the peaked roof. "I have read so much about this house."

"Really? That's surprising. It's just an old home, isn't it? I mean, it is a beautiful Victorian, and the woodwork inside and out," Sarah nodded at the graceful gingerbread carving along the edge of the roof-line and the porch overhang, "is a true work of art, but other than that?"

"Oh, this house has a long history."

"Please don't tell me a serial killer lived here," Sarah laughed and raised her hands.

Matthew stopped, straightened up to his considerable height, and looked down at Sarah with a puzzled expression. "Serial...? No, of course not." Then he caught on to the irony and grinned, and Sarah couldn't help but notice how that smile lit up his entire face and crinkled the corners of his dark eyes.

"No, no, nothing like that, but during the late 1800s—"

"Matt, before we get a history lesson," Lily interrupted, "let's just have a little tour, okay. Then coffee, then history, all right?"

She winked at Lily and led the way up to the porch and the door into the kitchen.

From somewhere Pixie appeared, followed by the laughing children and for a moment the porch became a round of handshakes, introductions, and laughter.

Chapter 6

Matthew appeared to know everything there was to know about the area, especially the little town of Rosewood Hollow and Thompson Hall, their home that had been named around the turn of the century. Thompson was the man who had the house built, though he didn't live there for long.

"Apparently there was some tragedy in his family that remains unclear," Matthew lectured as he steadied Sarah on the stairs. "Thus far, I've only found sketchy details, but his wife did not survive childbirth and his daughter passed away young. Then, two brothers owned the home for a very long time and made extensive renovations, but it's unclear whether they had families living with them. Then completely renovated in 1975."

Matthew looked up and swept his arm around. "This is what you see today."

They stood on the grand landing of the double staircase, with the great hall spread below. Matthew wanted to continue, but Cory tugged at his elbow.

"Look, I want to show you what I found," he said, dragging the historian toward Emma's room. Emma and Pixie followed, and Sarah and Lily brought up the rear.

"I told you he wasn't just an old stuffy historian," Lily said, and Sarah giggled.

"Right. One tall drink of water."

"And single," Lily continued with a wink.

"Thanks, but for the moment—"

"Mom, did you lock the door to that attic room again?" Cory called out and popped his head into the hallway. "I wanted to show Matt."

"No, I cleaned it out and left it to air out." Sarah went into Emma's room and checked the locked panel door. "That's weird, I could have sworn I left it open. Might have shut in a draft?"

"Never mind." Cory took out his burglar tools again, and Sarah shook her head. "We're going to have to talk about those, young man."

This time, it took Cory only seconds to open the door. Pixie, who had been sitting quietly on the sidelines, pushed forward to stand inside the closet once again, her stance equally alert and on edge as it had been earlier.

"This is odd," Matthew said, stepping inside and using his phone to light up the space, just as Cory had done.

"Odd – odd how?" Sarah asked.

"This shouldn't have latched accidentally – that's not how these old locks operate."

Sarah felt a shiver crawl down her back again.

"Can you reach up and let the stairs down?" Cory asked eagerly. "Mom said there should be stairs."

"Usually there are, yes," Matthew replied, still studying the old lock. But just as Sarah had suspected, he could reach up toward the hatch with only a slight stretch.

With a little sigh, the hatch let go, releasing a cloud of dust, spider-webs, and old dead bugs. Cory beat the dust away from his face and coughed.

"But I don't see any—"

Just then, the front door slammed with a bang that appeared to shake the house. Sarah quickly looked around, accounting for her children. "Last person in always closes the door, children. You know better."

"I wasn't the last," Cory defended immediately.

"No, it was me," Lily raised a finger. "But I closed the door – I think."

"Maybe it just doesn't latch right, sorry Cory," Sarah muttered.

"Or it was that neighbor lady again."

"Mrs. Jenkins? She usually calls out when she visits." Sarah wanted to keep an eye on Matthew and her overly eager son and, at the same time, check on the door. One door in the house inexplicably locked, another that should have been closed then slammed shut a few minutes later? What on earth was going on here?

Lily followed Sarah's eyes and put a hand on her arm. "I'll keep an eye on these two here, and Emma and Pixie, you go check on your door," she whispered.

"Thanks, I'll put on some coffee too."

❧

The heavy oak front door was certainly shut, Sarah thought as she checked the entrance hall. Shut so hard one of the little panes in the transom stained-glass skylight above it had popped out of its lead frame and lay on the ground in the hall. Sarah picked it up and turned it over in her hands.

Strange, she thought, the piece of glass had an irregular shape, but was entirely unharmed, even though by all rights it should have shattered on impact with the black and white mosaic tile floor.

She held the glass up to the sunbeam that flooded in through the skylight and squeezed an eye shut. The stained-glass image was a little haphazard and unclear, she thought. Best guess, the scene in the half-round depicted some kind of sunburst surrounded by blood-red triangles of some type.

Very surreal. When did that type of abstraction become popular, she wondered and put the glass aside on a high ledge for safekeeping where Emma wouldn't be able to get at it and hurt herself.

Another item on her list for the handyman. If she ever found someone to take on the job, that list would be endless.

She checked the door again and shrugged. Likely just another mystery in an old house.

⁂

As Sarah turned to the kitchen to prepare some coffee and arrange the cakes on a plate, an intense shiver seized her, forcing her to wrap her arms tightly around herself. It was as though she had suddenly wandered into the heart of an unforgiving arctic winter. A merciless, icy vice constricted around her chest, causing her to gasp silently. Her fingers became stiff, and she felt an icy breeze swirl around her.

And just as abruptly as it had appeared, the bone-chilling sensation vanished, leaving her bewildered and breathless in the sudden stillness.

The cold, heavy feeling drained from her body, and she gasped, drawing air into her oxygen-starved lungs. She reached for a little hall table to steady herself and finally doubled over, her hands on her thighs.

What the heck?

From upstairs, she heard the children, and Lily, and Matthew, chattering animatedly. Nothing at all appeared to be amiss up there. Thank God.

Something white and fluffy shot down the stairs, and almost immediately Pixie put her paws on her knees.

"Hey Pix, give me a minute," Sarah gasped, still fighting for breath. But far from backing up, the little dog became more insistent. She twisted around Sarah's legs, closer than ever, and jumped up now and then, pushing with her paws and her nose into her knees.

"I got you," Sarah said, a little out of breath, and went into the kitchen almost blinded by the overpowering sensation of not being able to breathe. There she found a chair at the long harvest table and simply dropped into it.

Five minutes, she thought, *just five minutes. Deep breaths now – in and out.*

When she had herself under control again, she raised her head and listened. The children and Matthew still chatted upstairs, probably arguing about who should be able to go up the stairs first.

Coffee, she thought, her sense of duty pushing through her confusion and anxiety. She had promised coffee, and juice for the kids. With resolute determination, she compelled herself to action, consciously straightening her back. Yet, just as she was about to take that decisive step forward she froze, hesitation and fear gripping her again like a vice.

There on the scarred wooden counter-top sat the pieces of cake Lily had brought — half chocolate half vanilla – neatly lined up one beside the other while the bakery box they had come in was a mangled, crushed mess on top of the garbage bin.

That familiar shiver assaulted her again.

Lily? Would Lily have done this? But no, Lily was a guest in her house, she wouldn't have, she couldn't. And the way that box was crushed and mangled, that suggested an unbridled anger, fury even.

Or a message?

Gingerly, Sarah picked up the little cakes and examined them. Each of them sat on a pretty little doily, completely unharmed.

Just like the glass outside.

From somewhere far away, she heard Cory laugh out loud, and Emma joining in. Matthew said something, and both of the kids had a fit of giggles.

Pixie had followed her into the kitchen and now stood on her foot. Her two front paws boring into Sarah's bare toes. With a pop, that feeling of being shrouded in a thick piece of cotton wool disappeared, and Sarah could breathe again.

Pixie stepped back, and this time Sarah thought she saw something, a faint yellow glow on the tip of the little dog's tail.

"Pixie?"

The Papillon yipped, spun around in a circle, ran to the kitchen door, and then back to sit with Sarah.

Her tail was pure white once again.

"God, I am losing it."

With an effort, Sarah took dishes and cutlery out and set the table, prepared the coffee and some juice for the children, and checked herself in the hall mirror.

Just because the stress of the past few months was apparently getting to her didn't mean she had to scare the kids. Matthew Turner certainly had nothing at all to do with her sudden preoccupation with her appearance.

"Let's call them down, Pix. They're probably wondering what on earth happened to us."

Pixie spun, clearly advertising for a treat, and Sarah obliged her and instantly put her finger to her lips.

"Ssshhhh, I keep telling the kids not to overfeed you."

Pixie winked.

Wait, what? Sarah did a little double take but already Pixie tore up one side of the staircase to fetch the rest of the family.

Matthew, Lily, and the kids emerged from Emily's bedroom again.

"Well," Sarah called up, yearning for a little bit of normalcy, and Matthew was only too glad to oblige.

⁓

"It's an old attic space," Matthew said, shrugging and beating some dust off his jeans. "Nothing spectacular. In some renovation, they closed it up for one reason or another, I guess. I poked my head through the hatch and there's nothing up there but dust, more dust, and a couple of old trunks pushed into a corner."

"Thank you," Sarah smiled. That warm, matter-of-fact, 'nothing too exciting up there,' was exactly what she needed at that moment.

"I want to explore anyway," Cory said and made a face. "It's an old attic, it's... spooky"

"Cory." Matthew warned. He spread his hands away from his body, and Sarah nodded toward the washroom on the ground floor. "First, we will all wash our hands, then we will sit down like normal people with normal conversation, and then – only then, if your mother says okay, can you go up there and explore."

"Mom, can I – I want to – it's really—"

"Cory," Matthew interrupted. "Did we not agree up there that we were going to take it easy and not scare anyone?"

"Yes," Cory grumbled.

"Wait, wait, I'm getting older, my hearing, you know," Matthew said and put a finger to his ear.

"Yes, I said I would not scare Emma."

"Or Lily or your mom. Thank you."

"He's really good with him," Lily whispered beside Sarah. "Probably because he taught history for a few years at a high school somewhere out west."

"You know for a bookseller, you know an awful lot about this town's historian."

Sarah gently elbowed Lily in the side and grinned. It felt as if she had made a friend in this town. She was off to a good start. Lily rolled her eyes and secretly chuckled.

"And what are you ladies giggling about," Matthew appeared in the hall again, hands clean by now and his hair mostly tidied.

"I was amazed how good you are with Cory, and Lily told me you used to be a teacher."

"Long time ago," Matthew shrugged. "You have to be sharp if you want to get through to these kids. You're competing with phones and messages and games and apps and... well, God knows what else now."

"I appreciate it. I don't know if Lily told you, but Cory could use an adult male to look up to."

"He'll be fine. I hear he's an ace at basketball."

"That's right," Sarah stepped through the wide arched doorway into her old-fashioned kitchen and stopped dead in her tracks. Her hands automatically clapped to her mouth, stifling a scream.

"What's the matter with the cakes, Mom?" Emma stood in the kitchen, her head cocked sideways.

Sarah reached out and grabbed the side of the door frame for support. Lily put an arm around her waist, not quite sure what was going on, and Matthew merely looked around.

"Hey, that's funny," Cory said and wandered into the kitchen, oblivious to anything. "What does it mean?"

He was reaching for one of the cakes when Sarah finally managed to speak again.

"Don't, Cory."

"What? Why are you looking like that?"

All of the cakes Lily had brought, the little delicacies that had inexplicably been lined up like toy soldiers, and then lovingly put on a serving platter by Sarah – they were sitting in the middle of the table now. All of the chocolate cakes had been arranged to form a giant A, and the vanilla ones formed an awkwardly drawn T.

"A T, is that supposed to be funny?" Cory asked, dipped his finger into a bit of chocolate icing on the serving platter, and licked it again. "A T – attic? Really, Mom." He rolled his eyes.

"I put them all on the serving platter," Sarah whispered and sat hard in one of the straight-back cane chairs. "In a little circle…"

Her voice broke, and she hugged her arms to her body in an effort to stop the shivering. Matthew too came to the table now to examine the cakes.

"Well, somebody obviously has a strange sense of humor," Lily said as she took instant charge. She rearranged all of the cakes on the serving platter once more and plopped it down firmly in the middle of the table. "And it is not funny – not at all."

"I was upstairs," Cory immediately defended himself. "With Matthew – holding the ladder."

"Right. And from what I heard, you kind of upset one of those boys who hang around the community center playing basketball all day long."

"Damian? But Damian was just frustrated. He doesn't even know—"

"I don't want to hear it." Lily raised a finger. "It's not funny. You go and tell him..."

"Easy," Matthew said with a gentle clap on Cory's shoulder. "Getting these boys to fight is not going to help anyone. Somebody tried to play a joke on you here. The best thing is to let it go, ignore it. The best kind of revenge is eating those cupcakes. Let's go."

That broke the spell. Emma and Cory sat at one end of the table with some juice and one each of the cupcakes, Matthew in the middle, and Lily and Sarah at the other end. Matthew steered the conversation to basketball and the general history of Rosewood Hollow, and he had the children laughing in a few minutes.

Lily squeezed Sarah's hand under the table in silent communication.

Sarah sighed and forced a smile. Just some kids playing a prank. It was the easiest answer to believe in, even though she knew there had barely been moments between her leaving the kitchen and everyone coming back. She knew Pixie probably would have barked up a storm if someone had snuck in, and those letters – those letters A and T meant something. But what?

Having Lily and Matthew around helped dispel the nervous energy she felt. Matthew really was an inexhaustible font of information about the town and about their house, over and above the few facts he had given her earlier. He had brought a few grainy black-and-white pictures of people in somber black dress in front of the house.

"That is Jedediah Thompson, the original owner, and his daughter Amelia," he explained, handing her a copy of an old photo in a plastic sleeve. "Unfortunately, not much is known about their history – only that he built the house and sold it again after some family tragedy."

Amelia had a bit of a sad look, Sarah thought, although the young woman in the long white dress was a stunning beauty. Sarah imagined her hair to be soft, silky blonde. In the picture, it was braided intricately and piled on her head, secured with long pearl pins. A delicate hand lay on her father's forearm, and she made an effort to smile, except you could see it, Sarah thought. You could see that it cost an effort.

"And this," Matthew said, producing another photocopy in a sleeve, "was taken sometime after that."

The pretty gardens had been trampled, the trees drooped with old leaves and broken branches, and the gate had been torn off its hinges and tossed aside.

Somewhere in the house, a door slammed hard, and Sarah jumped again.

"Probably the door to Emma's room," Lily said with a rueful grin. "Not sure I closed it. Anyway, what say, Emma, until the handyman has fixed the wall in your room, and done something about those stairs, should we move your things into one of the other rooms?"

"Awe..." Emma's bottom lip came out. Sarah knew she had fallen in love with the roses and angels on that wallpaper.

"Just temporarily," she said with a smile. "As soon as everything is put to rights you move back in. You don't want Cory traipsing through your room all the time while he's exploring, do you?"

Emma's lips quivered, and fat tears began forming in her eyes. "Hey," Lily said quickly and swept the child into her arms. "Just let these boys and your mom poke around in the dust up there. Just think of your library when it's finally done. We'll go out in the garden for a bit, maybe pick some flowers."

Emma wasn't convinced quite yet, and only another chocolate cupcake could bring a timid smile back.

"Stay away from that old well," Sarah called after them and shook her head. "I don't know which one of you is the bigger knucklehead," she said to Cory and Matthew, "but go on and explore already."

"Come with us," Matthew urged. "You do want to know what's up there, and worst that happens, you have a story to tell."

"Well…"

"Oh, come on Mom, it'll be fun."

"It really might be an adventure, Sarah. Give yourself a little push." Matthew leaned in a bit, and the good humor blinking in his deep blue eyes made something in Sarah's insides clench with a long-forgotten memory.

"All right," she finally relented. "But let's keep it safe."

"We will."

Matthew and Cory high-fived one another, and Sarah shook her head. "Knuckleheads," she laughed, looking around for her little dog.

"Pixie? Cory, did Lily and Emma take Pixie outside?"

"Maybe, I don't know."

Pixie gave one sharp bark, and Sarah realized the little dog had been sitting out in the hall while they'd been enjoying their coffee and cakes.

"What are you doing out there, little girl? Come here?"

Pixie gave another sharp bark and cocked her head. She lay down just outside the kitchen door and put her head on her paws.

No.

"It's almost like she's saying that, isn't it," Sarah said and turned around, but no one behind her had spoken. Matthew and Cory discussed an old picture of the house from Matthew's collection, and she could see Lily and Emma through the window at the far end of the garden. All at once, that shiver crept down her arms again.

Pixie studied her with unblinking dark eyes.

"Now I know that wasn't you."

"Really?" She heard Cory saying.

"Yes, really. The old well at the back of the property used to be the main source of water for the entire neighborhood here, Cory."

Matthew. Sarah closed her eyes and slowly counted to ten. Just Matthew and Cory talking. Cool it, Sarah.

She felt something at her heel and found Pixie, a paw on her foot, and a tiny pink tongue giving her ankle another swipe.

"It's okay," she said softly and reached down to pat the velvety fur. "It's okay, little girl. Mind yourself while we go explore."

∽

Cory was the first to clamber up the old attic ladder. Limber as a goat, he disappeared through the hatch before Sarah had a chance to say a word.

"You're next," Matthew invited. "And I'll bring up the rear."

"It's been a while since I climbed one of these." Michael, she remembered, had insisted on a one-story bungalow with a flat roof. Somewhere to watch the stars from. She could feel Matthew behind her, steadying her. Not obsessively, but still making sure she felt safe.

With a final push, she hoisted herself through the hatch and scrambled to her feet while Matthew came up behind her.

"Wow, it's a huge space."

"Yep, but too low to do anything with it. Watch your head – the overhead beams."

Sarah reached out and touched the old wood, weathered and warm. Up here in the attic, time had stood still, a few spiders the only living beings who claimed that space. Raw, old wooden planks formed the floor, barely sanded down. An old rope extended between two beams – probably a way to dry laundry in the middle of winter – and the air smelled of dust and long-forgotten summers. At the far end of the house, a round window let in a wide shaft of light, and there stood Cory, between two massive, old wooden trunks.

"Look Mom, look... Aren't these neat? I bet they're a hundred years old. I bet there's something totally valuable inside. Do you think we can get them downstairs? Maybe I could have one in my room and – and..."

"Slow down, Cory," she laughed. "You're tripping over your own words. I'm not sure I want to haul some old trunks down that rickety ladder."

"Yes, but look at how neat they are."

Matthew beat the cobwebs from the angled beams of the roof and went ahead of her. Sarah looked around the massive attic space, but inexplicably, she found her eyes drawn magically to those ancient, weathered trunks, shrouded in a veil of forgotten history. Time had etched its mark on the trunks' exteriors. The wooden surfaces were aged, the once-vibrant color now mellowed to a rich, deep brown, and delicate carvings of long-forgotten symbols adorned its sides, hinting at an ancient origin.

Cory's fingers traced those carved lines, and it was all she could do not to call out to him to stop.

She could feel her heart beating in her throat and knew, without knowing, that she couldn't speak if she tried.

In seeming slow motion, she watched Matthew kneel beside Cory in the dust of the wooden floor and finger the cracked leather latches that held the lids of the trunks shut.

The attic's dusty beams cast flickering shadows upon the trunk, and to a boy like Cory, it promised a treasure trove of untold wonders.

A faint scent of must and history filled the air, hinting at a bygone era. Perhaps this trunk belonged to an adventurer, a scholar, or a wayfarer, and its contents might hold relics and trinkets from times long past.

A crack of thunder filled the air, and Sarah rushed to the window in the south wall to see if she could peer outside, where Lily and Emma had to be. The old round window was dusty and blind, but even through layers of cobwebs, she could see the bright blue sky and sunlight outside. No rain or thunderstorm threatened the beautiful day.

"Oh, it's just a bunch of old papers."

"And they may be more valuable than anything else you might have discovered in there, Cory. Look, there are bundles of old letters and newspapers."

Cory and Matthew's voices brought her back to the present, and Sarah looked back into the far corner. Matthew had pulled the latches out of their metal fittings and propped the lid of the first trunk up with an old brick so it couldn't slam on their fingers.

She watched as he pulled a thick stack of newspaper clippings tied with a black ribbon from the depth of the trunk and felt dizzy in the hot, dusty atmosphere all of a sudden. She reached for an upright beam and took a few deep, cleansing breaths. Down below, past the hatch and the ladder, she could hear little pixie barking up a storm as if she never wanted to stop.

Close it, close it up now.

From somewhere, those urgent words hammered into her brain, and she gasped to take another breath.

Then all was silent. Matthew and Cory had moved on to the next trunk and worked on the latches, and Sarah found herself looking at an old rocking chair in the corner of the attic. Her dizziness and nausea had disappeared completely, and she blinked into the dancing dust motes. The rocking chair was rocking gently back and forth. Back and forth.

Sarah pressed a hand to her mouth and knew she was about to be sick. Without another word to the boys, she ran to the attic hatch, clambered down the stairs, and ran for the washroom attached to Emma's room. She slammed the door hard, locked it, and proceeded to get violently sick, over and over.

When her stomach had released every last bit of food she washed her face and opened the door, only to find Pixie sitting directly behind it.

Are you okay?

Sarah stared at the little dog, her hands clenched by her sides. She had heard those words clearly in her head, *Are you okay?*

"Pixie?" she asked tentatively. God, she was totally losing her mind, but what other explanation was there? She could hear Cory and Matthew upstairs, screeching laughter from outside told her Emma and Lily were having a good time on the old swing. It couldn't be – but what other explanation was there?

It's okay.

"But you can't – you're a…" Sarah struggled with the words.

Dog? In form, yes, but I am so much more.

Pixie came closer and put a dainty white paw on Sarah's foot.

And you are more, Sarah. You are the first person in a long time who can sense me. You don't hear me with your ears, it's your mind that's picking me up.

"The others can't?" Sarah asked and swallowed hard.

Pixie's head went back and forth very gently.

No, Sarah heard, and suddenly the little voice faded. *It's an effort...*

Pixie's eyes closed softly, she struggled to breathe, and Sarah picked her up and cradled her close.

"Pixie, Pixie girl?"

Be careful – upstairs.

With those words, Pixie snuggled tight into Sarah's arms and allowed herself to be supported completely.

"Pixie, my little girl," Sarah brushed her chin over the velvety soft fur on Pixie's forehead and held on. The little dog had gone limp in her arms, but she could feel Pixie's heart beating true and strong.

Be careful upstairs.

With Pixie still cradled in her arms, Sarah went back to the bottom of the attic stairs and called up through the hatch.

"Matthew, Cory – is everything all right up there?"

"Why shouldn't it be, Mom?" Cory's face appeared through the hatch and beamed down at her. The sight of her son beaming from ear to ear made her heart do a little double-take. That was the boy she knew, the excited, smart, happy boy – not the sullen young teenager he had become after his dad left.

"It's just – an old dusty attic up there. Who knows how many years it's been empty? I don't want you to get hurt."

"We won't." Cory laughed brightly this time. "You should see Matthew, he's going gaga over all of this history stuff. I just want to take pictures of that old trunk to see what those symbols mean."

"Still. Wrap it up, would you?"

"Okay," Cory was visibly disappointed and flipped a lock of hair out of his face. "Why are you holding Pixie like that? Is something wrong with her?"

"She's just – exhausted," Sarah fibbed. "She played with Emma and Lily."

Pixie's heart still beat strong and evenly. But her tail, that bushy, feathery tail, usually carried in a proud plume over her back, hung down limply from Sarah's arm. I got you, Sarah thought and held her a bit closer. That tail, was that a little glow right there?

It's tiring, but it will get easier, now that we're connected.

"And the tail?"

That's how you know I am...on.

The voice in her head sounded as if she were giggling. Sarah still felt dizzy, as if she'd stepped through a portal into something entirely foreign. Her new house had a hidden attic, her sullen son suddenly bloomed under the care of an entirely too good-looking stranger, and her dog could communicate telepathically.

Pixie's little paws pushed against her arm with reassuring steady pressure, but she didn't sense another voice.

Gently, almost reverently, she put Pixie into the little pink dog bed she had discovered on their first day in the house and made her comfortable. Pixie sighed softly and snuggled into the curve of the bed.

Chapter 7

Emma and Lily were still out in the yard, so Sarah tucked her phone into her pocket and headed over to the Jenkins' place. Martha Jenkins had adopted Pixie on Sarah's recommendation. She had gone to the pound in search of a dog and then sent an email to Sarah, saying, "I've found the perfect friend for your children." Maybe she knew something.

Mrs. Jenkins opened the door almost immediately, as if she'd been waiting just inside for someone to knock.

"Sarah, what a wonderful pleasure. I hope the house is starting to feel like a home by now?"

"Why Pixie?" Sarah asked without preamble.

"What do you mean, why Pixie?" Mrs. Jenkins asked, stepping onto her porch and closing the door behind her for some privacy. "You asked me—"

"I asked you if there was a local shelter that might have a dog suitable for the children."

Sarah gripped one of the upright beams of the Jenkins' porch, aware of how odd she sounded even to her own ears. "I just wanted to know..." she added meekly.

"Is there something wrong with the little one?" Mrs. Jenkins asked and pointed to a set of chairs. "Is she sick, perhaps, not getting along with the children? You can always ask the shelter..."

"No, there's nothing wrong with her at all." Sarah sat down and ran her hands through her hair, which hung limp and was probably covered in dust and cobwebs. What would Matthew think of her?

"No, it's just odd. A beautiful little dog, purebred, a papillon no less, smart and energetic, at a shelter. I just wondered."

Martha Jenkins fixed her with a long, dark stare for a moment and cocked her head. She might be old, but she was no fool.

"Pixie's owner was a little — different," she finally said. "Didn't have a lot of friends in this town." She looked left and right, though it was a good thirty yards to the front gate, and no one was on the porch with them. "Some say," she whispered, "Well, some say she was a witch."

An alarm bell clanged in Sarah's head, and she licked her suddenly dry lips. *Some say she was a witch.* Pixie had — abilities. Nervously, she laughed and brushed the hair out of her face.

"But that's just talk, right?"

Martha Jenkins wagged her head back and forth. "Who am I to say," she finally said and leaned back in her chair. "You going to tell me what brought you over here, like there's a dozen devils after you? I hope you're not asking me to take that sweet baby girl back to the shelter. She was the most adorable pup in the two days I had her."

"No, no, we've all fallen in love with her." Sarah finally took the other chair, stretched her legs, and looked down at her splayed hands.

"When we found that attic – it was just weird, that's all. Maybe I'm not used to living in a house that's as old as ours."

"That attic is very strange," Mrs. Jenkins said, nodding sagely. "What's inside it anyway? Has anything else happened since you moved in?"

"I sincerely hope that's the only hidden room we'll find, and there's basically nothing in it," Sarah quipped and pushed two fingers into her forehead, where she could feel a headache building. "I'm sorry – I don't know why I stormed over here. Pixie is a perfectly wonderful companion, and we love her. I guess I just wondered about – her history. With the kids, you know."

That was a lame excuse, and she could hear it in her voice and see it in Mrs. Jenkins' disapproving look. Her neighbor had just opened her mouth to speak when the door into the house slapped open, and what Sarah assumed to be Mr. Jenkins stepped out onto the porch. Santa Claus, Sarah thought immediately. He looked like Santa Claus. He was a rotund man with a bushy, snow-white beard, hair, and eyebrows.

"Well, you must be our new neighbor," he said, hooking his thumbs into his suspenders.

"Sarah Anderson," Sarah said and stuck her hand out.

"Mort Jenkins. We had your little dog for a few days until you got here – lovely animal, just lovely. But she is different."

"Different," Sarah asked, her heart pounding in her chest. "Different how? Strange?"

"Lord love us, no." Mr. Jenkins laughed. "Smart as a whip. She'll steal the meat off your sandwich if you give her a chance and you won't notice until you eat it. She's a smart one, you better keep one eye on her at all times. I heard you asking Martha where she came from. She's lucky to have you. That witch who owned her before—"

"Mort, you're just going and spreading gossip now," Mrs. Jenkins complained and pointed at a third chair. "Sit yourself down."

"No, I think I will have my tea now," he said and stood looking at the street for a moment, his thumbs still hooked into his suspenders, not a thread out of place on his well-ironed shirt. "I'll tell you something, though, young lady. There was something not right about that woman who owned her, Selena something or other. Always poking into old history and mysteries and talking about crystals and frequencies and whatnot. Why she even came around here a time or two, looking for some—"

"Mortimer Jenkins, you stop that gossiping now." Mrs. Jenkins got to her feet with surprising agility. "I will not have you frighten our new neighbors with such talk. Sarah, I am so sorry, I'll make his tea now. Don't you mind him."

They went back inside the house, the screen door slapped shut, and Sarah could hear them bickering inside. It actually made her smile. *What a lovely old couple*, she thought, *having been together for so many years*.

From their front porch, Thompson Hall looked exactly as it was described in the estate brochure – a beautiful old Victorian-style house, lovingly restored and cared for, with lush flowering gardens. Nothing sinister, no mysteries, no witches. Everything was as it should be. She sat on the Jenkins' porch for another minute, before Emma and Lily's laughter from her yard brought her back to reality.

❧

"What had you tearing out of here and over to the Jenkins'?" Lily asked a little while later as Matthew, Cory, and even Emma, had commandeered the kitchen table, looking through the pictures and newspaper clippings Cory had dragged down from the attic.

"Just – Pixie – I wanted to know where she came from," Sarah said, playing with a bead on her necklace.

Lily held her gaze for a very long time, searching, and finally shook her head. "Never kid a kidder, Sarah. Something odd is going on. And I might wear hippie clothes and too many earrings, and colors the locals find painful to the eyes, but I also know people. I can see something is bothering you. And I knew Selena."

"Selena?" Sarah asked almost tonelessly, leaning in ever closer, keeping one eye on her children. "Pixie's first owner?"

Lily nodded softly, took Sarah's arm, and led her out onto the porch again, leaving the door just a little ajar, to be able to watch Matthew and the kids.

"Selena made a living reading tarot cards and channeling past loved ones' spirits for the locals. Not a profession that would endear her to a village full of hard-working middle-class Americans."

"Mort Jenkins said she—"

"Mort, and people like him, thought she was a witch," Lily said, swiping the argument away violently with both hands. "Of course, anything they don't understand... Never mind. I was friends with Selena, and I know — I know her bond with Pixie went over and above what happens with other people and their pets. That's all I'm willing to say."

"I can hear Pixie," Sarah said before she could change her mind, and, for a moment, time stopped between the two new girlfriends. Lily's bright green eyes stayed on Sarah's, and she brought a hand to her mouth.

"I knew it," she breathed.

"And if you tell anybody I can hear the voice of a dog, I will call you insane so fast your head will spin," Sarah said, breathing hard. "Don't think I won't. My ex-husband would have those kids back in Baltimore so fast that they wouldn't get to pack a bag if he had the slightest inkling of something spooky happening out here. He's a nice man, but he has hard and fast boundaries, so do not test me, Lily Morrison."

"Relax..." Lily paced to the end of the porch, gave the porch swing a little shove, and came back. "I'm the last person to cause trouble with an ex. I always knew there was something Selena wouldn't tell me."

Sarah said nothing for a moment. I wonder why, she thought, but kept her mouth shut.

"I swear I will not tell anyone," Lily begged. "Unless you specifically ask me to, of course – you have my word."

"Not even Matthew?"

"Not even Matthew," Lily grinned broadly. "I don't want to ruin what's happening there, you know." The joke fell flat. Sarah leaned against the porch support post and took a few steadying breaths.

"It was Pixie who found the hidden door behind the wallpaper," she said, looking out over the yard, the porch swing, and the beautifully normal flowers and birds. "She started acting funny when we opened that door, and then – then I heard her voice in my mind."

"Wow..."

"First she said to be careful upstairs, something about a ghost voice, and that I was one of the few people who could hear her."

Lily said nothing and kneaded her hands together hard. "That's fantastic."

"Lily, I don't really believe in—"

"Sarah, this is pure magic. Selena and I were friends, and I knew she had abilities. Abilities other people might... find strange. She and Pixie had a connection stronger than any I've ever witnessed, and when she passed and nobody wanted that sweet little dog... I just – wondered.

The shelter did their best, I know that, but she just didn't take to anybody. Her attitude turned people off. Until you and the kids came."

"Oh, Pixie has attitude, all right," Sarah laughed. "Papillons usually do, though she is feistier than most. How do you know all of this?"

"Oh, I'm on the board of the shelter," Lily shrugged. "I hear things. I run the bookstore in town, honey – it doubles as a local press office around here."

Suddenly, Pixie wandered through the half-open screen door and sat between the two women. She shook her silky coat, sat regally, and draped her beautiful fluffy tail around her back paws just so.

She's back.

"Wow," Lily said and sat hard on one of the cane chairs.

"Did you hear that?"

"No, I didn't. Although I wish to all hell I had, but I have eyes in my head and I know something just passed between the two of you. She spoke, didn't she?"

"I don't..."

"Tell me what she said — please."

"Lily," Sarah turned away and hid her face in her hands. "Do you know what my ex would do to me and our custody arrangements if he got the slightest whiff of something — like this, going on around here?"

Stop arguing.

Even without the words, Pixie's meaning was made clear with a paw on Sarah's foot. Sarah's eyes met Pixie's, and she held them for a long moment.

Don't worry about that now. There are more important things we have to deal with.

"Holy crap," Lily breathed. "I can see you communicating."

Automatically, Sarah bent down and scooped the little dog into her arms, leaning the silky little head against her neck.

Amelia Thompson is back.

Pixie put her little paws against Sarah's collarbone and pushed back until she could look into her eyes. Clear brown eyes with little gold flecks, Sarah thought irrationally. The next moment Pixie had wriggled free and jumped to the ground.

We need to do something about this. Now. We need to keep your kids safe.

"Pixie, wait" Sarah called out, but with her usual regal attitude, Pixie walked back into the house to sit with Cory and Emma, who were sorting through a mountain of papers with Matthew.

For a moment, neither woman said anything.

"You're going to tell me what just happened," Lily asked, and Sarah sat on an old cane chair, hard.

"Does the name Amelia Thompson mean anything to you?" she finally asked without explanation.

"Amelia Thompson? Jesus – is that what Pixie said? Amelia Thompson?"

Sarah looked up at her new friend, and Lily simply fixed her in a stare of green eyes without saying another thing. Her red curls settled around the colorful headscarf, and she let the silence settle. Sarah swallowed hard.

"Breathe," Lily commanded and nodded inside the screen door one last time before closing it gently. "There's nothing to worry about."

"Says you."

"You might have only been here for a few days, but I consider you a friend, Sarah Anderson. I knew when you came into the bookstore that you were no ordinary person. Now let's go inside and say hello to the kids and Matthew, and for God's sake, let's just act normal."

Pixie came back out onto the porch and sat between the two women, just looking back and forth. Her busy tail curled high over her back, swishing a staccato rhythm back and forth, and Sarah finally felt her insides unclenching.

"Okay, I'm coming," she said with a smile, and all three of them stepped back inside.

∽

"Pixie sure uses that doggie door as if she's never had anything else," Matthew commented, and Sarah looked down to see just that – a brand-new swinging doggie door. Had that been there all along? It reminded her a little of the dog bed she had found earlier, but Cory waved her over with an excitement she had not seen in a while, and she pushed the thought away.

"Come look at this, Mom. We found pictures and articles about this house that go back forever."

"Exactly a hundred and fifty years," Matthew corrected with a smile. "And I thought you were going to draw a timeline."

"I am drawing a timeline. Look," Cory defended himself, pointing to a drawing of shaky lines with names and arrows all along.

"That's great," Sarah put her hand on his shoulder and bent over his work. "You guys ever come across someone by the name of Amelia Thompson?"

"Amelia Thompson? Yes, how did you know, Mom? Did you study all of this stuff before?" Cory pointed to the very beginning of his drawing and looked up at her with an excited grin. "Amelia Thompson was the daughter of the man who built this very house. There was an article about a terrible accident or something while she was abroad, but she – passed away – very young."

Sarah wanted to commend him for not scaring his sister with talk about death and accidents, but her voice caught and stuck in her throat. Her hand froze on Cory's shoulder, squeezing harder than she had intended until he squirmed out of her grip.

"What?" he asked irritated, and Sarah couldn't speak.

There, on her son's timeline, indicating the time period when Amelia Thompson had lived in this house, was an arrow and two large initials drawn in his precise block letters – AT

AT.

Sarah felt herself get weak in the knees and took a few deep breaths so the scream that was forming there wouldn't escape her throat. AT – did none of them notice it? The letters the cupcakes had formed earlier? AT.

And Pixie's warning, she's back.

Amelia Thompson.

At the same time, somewhere upstairs, a door slammed, and then another one, and Sarah began to tremble again.

Chapter 8

"Did you guys not close the windows upstairs when you came down earlier?" Lily asked, chuckling with fake cheer, while at the same time pouring a cup of coffee. "This is an old place, you leave things open you get slamming doors and whatever."

She shoved the coffee at Sarah and held her eyes for a moment.

"Matthew and Lily, if you have the time, why don't you stay for dinner," Sarah managed to say, even though the last thing she felt like doing right now was socializing. "We've taken up your entire day with attic explorations and old documents. The least I could do is offer a meal."

"We'd love to," Lily said quickly, while Matthew was still fumbling for words. Finally, he agreed as well.

"Sure," he said, smiling at Sarah. "If it's not too much effort."

"Not at all," Lily took charge as if she had never done anything else.

The noise of a communal meal was exactly what she needed, Sarah thought a little while later, with the kids arguing about whose turn it was to set the table, and Pixie dancing about, barking excitedly now and then.

"Is everything all right?" Matthew asked, coming uncomfortably close, and Sarah brushed her hair out of her face.

"Of course," she said, making herself smile. "The last few weeks have been hectic, with the move and – everything..."

"It is a very interesting house you have here. I'd love to delve deeper into the history if you don't mind. There are a few articles I found upstairs."

"Oh, Sarah. You should really find out all about it," Lily said with a wink. "It's one of the oldest houses around here."

"Well, I thought..."

"Mom. Cory put everything back."

"Did not."

"Did too."

"Cory, Emma, can we not argue in front of our guests, please? All I asked you was to set the table."

"I did," Emma argued. "Cory picked up all of the plates and put them back on the counter."

"No, I didn't. It was your turn, but if you don't want my help, you can do it by yourself."

Cory dropped a stack of napkins on the dining table and stormed from the room, and Emma wailed. Sarah didn't hear any of it. She couldn't take her eyes off the counter. There, all of her plain white dinner plates sat lined up like soldiers, one beside the other.

Her son would have had to work with lightning speed to do that without being noticed.

A cold draft grabbed hold of her, and she shivered again.

"My apologies," she finally said to Matthew, fighting to get the words out evenly. "I think it would be a lovely idea to find out what you can about this house."

And its ghosts, she added in her head, not daring to say the words. Was that what was going on here, ghosts? Automatically, she looked down at Pixie, but the little papillon sat primly beside her food dish.

"Oh, my poor sweetheart," automatically she refilled Pixie's dish and heated the spaghetti dinner she had decided on for dinner.

Lily persuaded the children to accompany her to a nearby bakery for a fresh loaf of bread, while Matthew neatly organized his papers by the kitchen window in neat piles.

"I'd really like to research your house," he said with a smile that crinkled the corners of his eyes. "But only if you're okay with it. One thing you'll learn about Lily Morrison, she's an amazing friend, but she does have a way of making people do what she thinks is best for them."

"It's all right," Sarah smiled. Matthew's quiet kindness and gentle humor put her at ease in the midst of this chaotic day. "It's fine. I really do want to know. Our house, and indeed our life, is a bit chaotic right now."

"And I'm sure finding a secret attic doesn't help," Matthew chuckled. "I really wonder why they closed it up like that."

"Not wanting to clean the extra space?" she joked while she remembered Pixie's, *She's back*. "Is there much in the stuff you've seen so far about Amelia Thompson?"

"Amelia? Any particular reason why you're asking about her?"

"I don't know. You mentioned her at one point, and the name came up a couple of times, I guess." *And my dog thought it was worth noting.* "So, she was really the daughter of the man who built this house?"

"Jedediah, yes," Matthew said, rubbing his hands. "I would have to go into the old city archives to get a profile on her."

"Would you?"

"I can if you're really interested."

The flapping of the doggie door interrupted them, and with a graceful jump, Pixie came back in and sat close beside Sarah.

"That is the most interesting little animal you have there."

Pixie fixed Matthew with a long stare that made Sarah giggle.

"Oh my, if I didn't know better, I would have to say you insulted her, Matthew. I don't think she likes being called an animal."

"I don't have a lot of experience with... um..."

If Pixie could have rolled her eyes, she surely would have. With a little shake and a toss of her tail, she walked over to Matthew, sat in front of him, and put her paws on his knee.

"I do believe you've been offered friendship."

Matthew reached down, and Pixie took another jump to land squarely on his lap.

"Well, um..."

He looked so uncomfortable, Sarah laughed out loud, and it felt good. So good to laugh with a friend, she was able to push it all aside for now – the attic, the noises, the oddly arranged cupcakes and plates, and the fact that, apparently, she could communicate with her dog.

"She surely doesn't need words to tell you what she wants," Matthew said, and Sarah felt something tense and hard inside her let go.

"No," she said. "No, she doesn't, does she?"

∽

Dinner was a raucous affair, the first such in a very long time. Laughter and stories flew back and forth. Cory regaled Matthew with all of his basketball wins, Emma and Lily bonded over their shared love of books, and Sarah watched and felt... home, she thought. For the first time in years, she felt at home. When she said goodbye to Lily and Matthew at the door, she waved and placed her hands on her children's shoulders. They had agreed that Matthew would come over every afternoon for the next few weeks to research all the papers in the trunk upstairs and decide what to do with them. Cory, who had expressed a keen interest, could help him whenever he felt like it and would earn extra credit for his history courses when the school year started. For the first time in his life, Cory had expressed an interest in something other than sports and basketball talk, and Sarah lit up at seeing him so engaged. When they were done, they would close up the attic, and Emma would finally get her room back, along with her little sitting library. She couldn't wait.

"I want a T-shirt like Matthew's," Cory said with glowing eyes, and she promised he could have one. As she locked the front door, her eyes fell on the little diamond-shaped pane that had fallen out of the stained-glass scene that morning. It still rested on the little ledge where she had placed it earlier.

Chapter 9

Their days settled into a comforting summer rhythm thereafter. Cory struck up friendships on the basketball court and spent abundant time with his new buddies while making time for research with Matthew. Emma, on the other hand, drove their freshly hired handyman to the brink with endless new ideas for her petite library. Meanwhile, Sarah was gradually embracing their new house as her true home. For the first time, she realized she was truly in her own home. She had transitioned from her parent's house to Michael's residence and then to an aging Victorian house that had once seemed like an improbable dream. Now, it had become a genuine home. Consequently, she had to get used to being the boss. Charley, the handyman, adeptly showed her how to fix minor issues and touch up paint. Mr. Jenkins had taken her under his wing and patiently introduced her to the basics of wiring, while Lily – Lily became a constant fixture around the house, always ready with a glass of wine and assorted delicacies from the nearest deli.

"How are things progressing with Matthew?" she inquired about a week after their initial dinner.

"Things aren't exactly 'progressing' with Matthew, Lily Morrison. He's engrossed in researching those dusty papers upstairs most of the time. He's headed to the historical archives for the rest of the day, trying to uncover something about Jed Thompson, his history with his daughter. Something about it is bothering him, and I don't want to ask."

"Well," Lily skewered antipasti with a delicate bamboo pick. "He's bound to return at some point."

"I'm sure."

"He's rather handsome, isn't he?" Lily persisted.

"I guess so."

Sarah continued to stack plates in the dishwasher, a recent acquisition from a local store recommended by Mrs. Jenkins. She was particularly pleased that she managed to install the face-plate that matched her old wooden kitchen without any assistance from the men, not even Cory.

"My dear Sarah..."

"What?"

"You'll get there eventually," Lily grinned. "You can't mourn Michael forever."

"I am not..." Sarah stopped mid-sentence, tilting her head, listening intently.

"Did you hear something?" Lily inquired. She hadn't mentioned the subject since she made Sarah admit to communicating with Pixie, but the question was always on her mind. Sarah could practically see her listening for strange noises, asking about odd occurrences, or if Pixie was 'settling in' all right.

"I'm not sure," Sarah wrinkled her brow. "I thought I heard footsteps upstairs."

"Charley?"

"No, he's not here today. He's shopping for supplies, I think. I should keep an eye on him, he might bankrupt us with all his purchases."

"Wait – I think I heard something too."

The two women sat frozen at the kitchen counter. Lily's hand holding the antipasto spear lowered silently, and she tilted her head.

"Do you suppose...?"

Moments passed without sound, and finally, Sarah giggled. "I guess that's the price of owning a turn-of-the-century home. There's always some kind of noise. Yesterday, Mort Jenkins was trying to tell me that the old sewer pipes might produce wailing noises now and then."

"No, thank you," Lily shuddered. "I've never heard of such a thing."

"Neither have I, but that's hardly surprising. Charley looked at me as if I'd sprouted horns or something when I mentioned it. Maybe Mort just has an off-kilter sense of humor."

Sarah gazed out into the yard where Emma sat on a sizable blanket, engrossed in reading stories to a gathering of her dolls. The sight warmed her heart. "You know she adores her Aunt Lily."

"The feeling's mutual. She is—"

The doggie door swung wildly, and Pixie darted in abruptly, her ears quivering with eagerness, a dainty white paw poised attentively. Sarah noticed it immediately, the distinct golden gleam at the tip of her tail. Her normally composed, dark eyes sparkled with vibrant excitement, and her long, silky coat bristled along her back.

"Pixie?"

Sarah heard her own voice, distorted and muffled as if through a long, echoing tunnel and looked at Lily, searching for help. Lily's lips moved, forming words she couldn't hear. That cold, hard fear she felt when Pixie first spoke to her gripped her heart once more.

Don't worry, I'm here.

As usual, she sensed the words rather than heard them, and instinctively followed Pixie through the kitchen, down the hallway, and into the cozy sitting room at the front of the house, affectionately referred to as the 'parlor' by Mrs. J.

Sarah had asked Charley to revamp the entire room, removing everything, including the old fireplace, transforming it into a games room, with Cory's computer games, Emma's puzzles, and a tidy, secure wood stove. In one corner, she had even arranged a TV screen and several yoga mats for herself, Lily, and their planned exercises – coming soon.

A plush, buttery-soft chocolate brown leather couch dominated the space. Pixie approached it tentatively, taking each step with caution. Sarah followed and paused at the threshold.

"It's... Jesus, you startled me. Um, uh... who are you?"

Seated on the couch was a young woman in a soft, billowing white cotton dress, reminiscent of what now might be called, hippie style. Her blonde hair was piled high atop her head, secured by a lethal-looking hairpin.

"Pleased to meet you. I'm Sarah Anderson. Are you... from the... neighborhood?" Her words slowed, then tapered off, ultimately failing her.

The woman turned to look at her, and Pixie drew close to Sarah. A low, menacing growl emanated from her tiny throat, strangely out of proportion with her size. Sarah had never known Pixie to produce such threatening sounds.

The woman's gaze, however, remained fixed on Sarah, intense and unyielding, her deep, dark eyes so profound that Sarah struggled to discern their color, assuming they had a color at all. Then her mouth opened, and an eerie sound emerged, freezing Sarah's soul and every muscle in her body. Sarah felt her vision fading, her limbs losing sensation. Surely, any moment now, she would...

Pixie let out a sharp bark, and in that instant, the spell was broken, and reality rushed back. Sarah gulped a lungful of air, audible and uneven, feeling it labor to fill every part of her being.

"Sarah, are you okay?"

Lily's voice, but Sarah had no attention to spare for her friend. Her gaze remained locked on the woman in her living room. She felt Pixie's reassuring presence beside her and took another step forward.

"What are you doing in my house?"

What are you doing in my house?

Two thoughts, two women, a single question.

"Sarah, for heaven's sake, answer me," Lily exclaimed, grabbing her arm. "Right now, or I'm calling 911."

Sarah sucked in another deep breath, ragged and loud. She heard it struggle to reach the far reaches of her body.

"I'm fine," she whispered,

She felt anything but fine. The hair on her arms raised as if she had been touching a live electric circuit, and she couldn't look away from the woman on the couch. The woman leaned back ever so casually, one hand touching the back of her hair. Slowly, she turned her head, and her eyes — her eyes were huge black orbs. Sarah wanted to scream but couldn't. Automatically, she reached for Lily's hand, but Lily had taken a step back, looking from Sarah to the stranger, to Pixie, and back to Sarah.

But Pixie... Pixie advanced, step by tiny little step toward the couch. Still, that unnatural guttural growl coming from her tiny throat, and Sarah shivered. The woman stared at Pixie, trying to stare her down. Pixie merely stood her ground, shaking her long ear fringe, holding her tail high, and proudly curled over her back. Her tail, usually pure white, now glowed golden with an ethereal halo and iridescent sparkle.

Not her, Sarah heard in her head and knew instinctively she herself was that *her*.

Lily called out, her voice a panicked screech, and Sarah looked up again.

Her eyes met with those of the stranger and locked on, and just like that, she was gone. Disappeared. She did not rise from the couch or leave, but vanished into thin air as if someone had turned off a light. Something left Sarah, something dark and heavy dropped from her thoughts, heart, and body, leaving her wobbling on unsteady feet.

"Here, sit," Lily took her elbow and wanted to guide her to the couch, the very spot where the woman had been sitting until Sarah pushed back.

"No, I'm fine."

"You're anything but fine. Look at you — and who, what the - what on earth was that?"

"Emma," Sarah cried out and rushed to the window, but her daughter miraculously still sat on her picnic blanket, reading a book to her dolls. Sarah raised a hand to knock on the glass, and Emma waved with a broad smile.

"Hi, Mom."

Everything was fine. Now she did drop heavily into an old wing-back chair and pulled the hair back from her face.

"Do you want to tell me what just went down?" Lily asked, frantically fussing with Sarah's arms and head.

"It was Amelia — Amelia Thompson," she said, repeating the words she heard in her head. Automatically, she reached down only to find

Pixie landing gracefully in her lap, pushing her little body hard against Sarah.

I can protect you—for a while. Her powers have grown immensely since the last time... we met.

But what-why?

"Does anybody want to clue me in on what just happened here, or do I wait to hear it on the crime beat?"

"Lily," Sarah let go of her hair again and took a massive breath, reveling in the sheer joy of being able to breathe. "Did you — see...?"

"Oh, I saw all right. I saw some eerie woman sitting on your couch there, in a staring contest with you, and don't ask me what she wanted. I was too busy making sure you didn't faint on me."

"That was not a woman."

"You're gonna tell me again that was Amelia Thompson, a woman who's been dead for well over a hundred years?"

"I am. And tell me, did you see her leave?"

"No." Lily hesitated for a moment. "I was — not looking, okay? Too busy with you."

Sarah let the silence spread for a moment until Lily raised her hands, left and right of her head, making the golden bangles on her wrists tinkle wildly.

"Fine, so let's say it was — what you say it was. What on God's green earth does she want here?"

Revenge for her death.

Sarah's hand tightened involuntarily on Pixie's collar.

"Revenge," she repeated softly. "That does make sense in a twisted way. Didn't Matthew mention Jed Thompson moved on after some great family tragedy? I bet you it has something to do with Amelia."

Lily sat hard now in the other wing-back chair.

"And Pixie?"

"Pixie," Sarah lovingly ran her fingers through Pixie's long, soft hair. "Apparently she has the power to protect me — us — from whatever negative energy is here."

Lily whistled softly. "Girl, you're going to give me a run for the money when the people around here start talking about that strange woman from now on."

Sarah rose, gently set down Pixie, and looked around the newly furnished games room.

"I'm pretty new to this whole haunting thing, but it seems to me the first thing to do is find out what it she wants, so I can gently suggest to her to move on out of our house. Pixie seems to think it's revenge."

"Pixie…" Lily looked down at the adorable little dog, who just then longingly looked at a plate of cookies on the sideboard. Lily closed her eyes and shook her head. "Never mind."

"Looks like I'll do what you wanted all along. I'll ask Matthew to see what he can dig out about the fate of Amelia Thompson. Meanwhile, I think there's another person who knows way too much about other people's lives."

"Martha Jenkins?"

"The very one," Sarah laughed. "I don't think there's anything in this neighborhood that woman misses. I'll have a little chat with her."

On the way into the kitchen, she found the note she had dropped earlier, read it, and gave a wry little grin. "And you can look through the history books in your shop as well. Oh, by the way, do you know if there's an art glass shop around here somewhere?"

"Hard left," Lily said, blinking a couple of times. "Art glass?"

"That." They passed through the entrance hall, and Sarah pointed up at the stained-glass design above the door. "Not sure what it's supposed to be, but one of the panes popped out. If it can't be repaired, I'm thinking of replacing it. Don't ask me what's artistic about it."

"Weird." Lily stared up at the design for a while and shook her head. "Almost like there's something in the middle, and all of those red little diamonds — a little gaudy for my taste."

"Please."

Lily raised her hands. "Say no more, I won't mention it. And I'll check my business directory."

"Thank you. Speaking of don't mention it…"

"Oh, you don't even have to ask." Lily took a bright orange scarf out of her hair and retied it artfully with a few precise little movements. "I wouldn't even know how to tell anybody what we just saw, mostly because I have absolutely no clue what I saw, or what it all means."

"You're a friend. And I think I hear a bottle of wine calling our names right now."

"Thought you'd never get to that."

જી

As time passed after the incident in the games room, it became easier to think she had imagined the entire scene.

Mrs. Jenkins had taken to dropping in whenever she felt like it, Mr. Jenkins to visiting with his tools, making all sorts of minor repairs, and being a replacement grandpa to Cory. And then there was Matthew. Matthew, who spent most of his afternoons upstairs or on the porch engrossed in ancient texts and boxes of trinkets, documents, and photos.

Whether he had managed to make any progress on his research, she couldn't actually tell, because whenever she looked at him, she would catch him quickly glancing away, as if he'd been caught staring, and he'd actually blush a little.

Lily went on about how charming it all was, and Sarah would deny it, but, every time it happened, she could feel her heart beating a little faster.

Pixie hardly left her side now, and every time she heard an odd noise or felt a cold draft in a room, she'd instantly look for the little papillon. If Pixie was curled up in her small dog bed, calm and relaxed, everything in the world was fine.

Chapter 10

About a week later, an older man arrived at the door, a stained-glass artisan sent by Lily Morrison. Sarah showed him the window above the door, mentally prepared to hear an outrageous price for the repair or receive a lecture on how she should protect the ancient, valuable glass panes in the house a lot better than she had. Instead, the man paled upon seeing the design. He dropped his leather tool bag by his side and took a couple of steps back, as if suddenly terrified.

"I think you should replace the entire pane," he said, rubbing his hands as if chilled on this perfectly hot sunny day.

"But it's just a single piece," Sarah protested. "This is not my favorite, but I'm not keen on tearing the whole thing out just now. Are you sure you couldn't just fit it back into the lead fitting?"

"I won't be touching that," the man said, shaking his head repeatedly. "I'll make you a very good deal on a new transom window, a nice stained-glass floral perhaps, but not that. No ma'am." Again, he shook his head, took another step back, and left his business card on the small entrance table. "Think about it. I have a lot of pretty designs at the shop, but not that, not that."

With that, he left the front door, moving surprisingly fast for an elderly man carrying a heavy tool bag. Sarah looked up at the window and the crystal still resting safely on the ledge by the door. "That was strange," she muttered, as she closed the door behind him. "Well, there have to be others."

She needed to find someone to fix it before fall came and school started. It was tempting to take him up on his offer, the current design had little aesthetic or artistic value, and she certainly didn't care for it. Still, the effort and mess of replacing that transom sounded overwhelming just then.

She decided to ask Lily later, just as a stray breeze from somewhere in the house blew through the entrance, sweeping the glass man's business card to the floor along with an assortment of letters and flyers.

"Cut it out," Sarah said aloud, gathering her papers once again.

Be firm with Amelia, Lily had advised her right after her first appearance. *Don't put up with annoying nuisances, and lay down the law.*

Evidently, Lily had come across this advice in a book about house hauntings. It was easy to offer such suggestions for someone who didn't have to grapple with a ghost regularly, Sarah thought. Somewhere upstairs, a door slammed. Thankfully, until now, the haunting manifestations had been limited to slamming doors, chilly drafts, and sporadic instances of misplaced items, ever since Amelia had unveiled herself to the women. It was as if she were waiting for something.

The thought made Sarah shiver, and summoned by her dark thoughts, Pixie appeared by her side, pressing her body against Sarah's leg.

"Hey, baby," she said, bending down to stroke the soft head.

She needs your help.

No need to specify who she might be.

"Don't we all. When you figure it out, you let me know?"

"This is odd…," Matthew said as he strolled down the wide double staircase while reading from an ancient handwritten notebook. Today he wore black jeans and a black T-shirt. It read in big lettering, I may be wrong, with a smaller font underneath, but it's highly unlikely. He probably had dozens of these, and Cory adored each and every one of them.

"What's odd?" Sarah asked, smiling at the historian. Matthew could find joy in old photos and dusty books like no one else she knew.

"What I'm holding here," Matthew said, looking up to make sure he didn't trip down the narrow stair, and then back into the notebook. "Appears to be an old ledger of Jedediah Thompson's. It mostly concerns the running of this house, which is why I thought it might be useful."

"Probably fun to read about how they kept house in the olden days," Sarah said, pointing toward the kitchen where fresh tea and assorted snacks awaited them.

Matthew had a deep appreciation for tea and could go on at length about various blends and brewing techniques. He often carried a small tin of his favorite loose-leaf blend and enjoyed sharing a cup with Sarah during their research sessions

"So, what's so odd about what's in that ledger?" she asked.

"Actually, it's what's not in it. Several pages have been torn out, quite rudely," he said, pinching a fragment of a page between his fingers. The rest had indeed been roughly torn out. "It's almost as if someone tried to purge every mention of – something – from this."

"I assume that's not a common occurrence with old texts," Sarah asked and poured their tea. "Still…"

"I wouldn't have thought much of it," Matthew said, continuing to read as he sat, pulling his tea closer and reaching for a cupcake. "But this one page didn't tear out entirely. Look at this half-page fragment."

Sarah looked and shrugged. Matthew, she noticed, had gone the extra mile today and wore a faint whiff of an exquisite aftershave. Not enough to be overpowering, just enough to make her want to lean in closer.

"There," Matthew pointed to a faded, old handwritten scrawl in precise cursive script. "For the Lumarian Group."

Sarah jumped back just as she had been leaning in. Upstairs, a door slammed shut, followed by another, then the kitchen door, and finally the screen door leading to the porch. A drumbeat of thunder rolled through the house, even though it was a bright and sunny day, and the papers she had gathered earlier flew off the side table again. Pixie came flying in through the doggie door and pressed herself hard against Sarah's leg, her tiny body quivering with excitement, the hair on her back raised once again.

As quickly as it had come up, the breeze died away, Pixie took a step back and sat on her mat. Matthew removed his glasses.

"My apologies," he mumbled, eyes downcast. "I must have forgotten to close the windows upstairs. I thought I had."

"Don't worry about it," Sarah replied mechanically, exchanging a glance with Pixie.

"Lumarians," Matthew repeated, scrolling with a single finger on a small tablet he usually carried. "Lumarians..."

There was something about the word that caused Sarah's skin to crawl, though she couldn't pinpoint why. A moment later, Matthew had located the information he was searching for.

"The Lumarians believed that the Luminus Crystal was a divine gift, bestowing immense power and enlightenment upon its possessors. It was utilized in sacred rituals and revered as a symbol of balance and harmony between the mortal and spiritual realms. Huh."

"Well, that doesn't really tell us much, now does it?" Sarah said tonelessly. Just then, a cloud passed in front of the sun, briefly casting the kitchen in deep shadows that drew odd, menacing lines over the worn old floors.

"Not really," Matthew continued scrolling on his tablet. "But I remember reading something about them. They were a spiritual group of sorts – not really widespread, and I've never come across them in connection with Rosewood Hollow. Strange indeed."

Thunder rumbled once more, and Pixie lifted her head. Sarah could only hope Amelia wouldn't choose that very moment to make an appearance. She leaned forward cautiously, peering through the doorway into the games room, but all remained quiet.

Emma burst in through the back door, carried on a cloud of enthusiasm and giggles as usual. The screen door slammed shut behind her with a hard bang.

"Why is it thundering, Mom? There isn't a cloud in the sky."

"I don't know, sweetheart. Perhaps it's just an unusual weather pattern," Sarah replied.

Or, more likely, it was Amelia, she thought, reasserting her presence once more. Pixie stood at attention, a faint golden glow shimmering around the tip of her tail.

"Why don't you grab one of your puzzles, Em, and set it up here in the kitchen? Just in case it does start raining. Do you know where Cory is? Did he go to play basketball?"

Emma picked up a reluctant Pixie and hugged her close. "But I wanted to watch Mr. Jenkins work on the old well in the backyard."

"Not now, Em. I don't like the thought of you around that well. Anyway, if the weather's turning bad, Mr. Jenkins won't be working out there either."

Emma pouted, her bottom lip pushed out, wanting to argue. Pixie wriggled out of her arms then, hopped to the floor, and darted into the games room. She returned with a soft plush toy, challenging Emma to chase her and claim it. Forgotten were the tears and complaints as Emma obliged, and the two of them raced through the kitchen and the front hall in lively pursuit.

"Sometimes I think that dog has more intuition and intelligence than many people I know," Matthew remarked, peering over the top of his reading glasses at the pair. "She knew exactly what to do right away."

"Pixie is special all right," Sarah replied with a smile. "Now, what about that strange sect, those Luminaries? Did you find anything?"

"Lumarians," Matthew corrected, patting the chair beside him. "There's some info online. I just hadn't looked into it before, since it never came up."

"I'm home," Cory called as the entrance door slammed and her son strolled into the kitchen, grabbed an apple from a bowl, and headed out in the direction of his room. "Weird weather," he called over his shoulder. "Not a cloud or a rumble while we were playing basketball – then I turned onto our street and there's this cloud right above the house."

"I'm sure it's nothing to worry about," Sarah said, forcing cheer she didn't feel into her voice, but Cory was already dashing up the stairs.

"This is curious," she heard Matthew say and turned back to him. He helped himself to more tea and adjusted his reading glasses with his middle finger. "Not much really about the spiritualist group that called themselves Lumarians," he read from his tablet. "They all but disappeared when the crystal, to which they ascribed magical powers, was either hidden or stolen."

"Hidden or stolen," Sarah repeated, leaning over Matthew's shoulder. "That leaves a lot of room for rumor and speculation." She meant to sound sarcastic, but the website he was reading from appeared to be the official history research page of the nearby university. "Sorry, just saying..."

"No, no, you're not wrong." Matthew winked at her, making her shiver for reasons unrelated to the temperature. "There is indeed even a fair amount of documentation that suggests this group maintained a chapter in Rosewood Hollow. However, many of the records pertaining to that time, the location, or the group itself, appear to have been destroyed or misplaced."

"Or hidden or stolen," Sarah quipped. Just then, her white, sturdy porcelain teapot, which she was sure had been sitting in the center of the table, tipped over, fell to the floor, and shattered into a million pieces.

"Oh my God, I am so sorry," Matthew appeared horrified. "I thought I had put it back on the pad, but I must have..."

"Relax, Matthew."

"I am so sorry, Sarah. Let me at least help you clean up. Can I replace the piece at all?"

"Relax. It's a bargain piece from IKEA. I have kids, okay? Things break." She had purchased it just a few days ago upon finding out that Matthew preferred tea over the coffee she had been brewing all day. But that was another matter.

Thunder rumbled again, though it seemed to be moving away now, and Sarah thought she heard someone laughing somewhere. Cory, perhaps?

She let Matthew help her clean up the broken porcelain and wipe up the spilled tea, and by the time they were done, the Lumarians were the last thing on their minds.

"I will replace that."

"And I told you, don't worry about it." Sarah brushed a strand of hair out of her face and let him help her up from where she'd been wiping the floor. "It's fine."

"At least let me take you to the tea room at the Historical Society. We can do some research at the same time."

"Well..."

"I'm sure your wonderful neighbor will watch the kids, and maybe we can see just how many of these documents have been destroyed or lost.

Chapter 11

An hour later, Sarah found herself ensconced in the cozy tea room at the old Rosewood Hollow Historical Society, sipping lavender tea while Matthew went off in search of the documents he was certain had to be there. The Historical Society itself occupied one of the oldest homes in Rosewood Hollow. According to Matthew, one of the board members had had the brilliant idea to transform the former parlor into an old-fashioned tea room, complete with charming seating arrangements, an abundance of frills, chintz pillows, and delicate China, giving one the impression of having tea at a friend's house. To top it all off, the local bakery delivered a selection of fancy cookies and finger sandwiches every morning, making the tea room an oasis of nostalgia and old-world charm. Sarah breathed deeply and could feel herself slowing down with the ritual of afternoon tea.

"Saw you coming into town," Lily slipped into a chair beside her and gently nudged Sarah's side. "He took you out for tea."

"Because he... Well, my teapot broke," she lowered her voice and looked around to see if anyone was listening to them. "But I'm not entirely sure it was him who knocked it off the table," she whispered.

"But who — Oh!" Lily brought a hand to her mouth. "You haven't told him?"

"No, that's not really a way to start a conversation Lily, 'Thanks for stopping by and doing all of this research. Oh, and by the way, have you met our ghost? She's lovely, just lovely if you keep her away from the dishes.'"

"When you say it like that, it does sound silly."

"I can't believe I'm saying this, but I like the man, and so do Cory and Emma, which is kind of a miracle after what their father..." She let the sentence trail off.

"Ah yes, and how is the esteemed Michael Reynolds?"

"Nosy. He calls me almost every day, and he asked for Mrs. Jenkins' number, in case he couldn't get a hold of me one day." Sarah rolled her eyes and took a cookie from a tray. "He wants to know how the kids are settling in, why they don't call him regularly, and why we have a dog now. And if he ever accidentally heard Matthew in the background..."

"He'll eventually have to get used to it."

"I know, I know." Sarah broke the delicate lemon cookie in half and put one piece into her mouth. "I'd like to delay that moment as long as possible, and I'd prefer the words, 'ghost' and, 'talking dog,' not feature in that conversation either."

Lily shrugged and signaled a waitress for tea. Today, she wore a flowing layered dress of peacock blue and turquoise, with a yellow and orange scarf woven through her hair again.

"The point is, I don't even know myself how to deal with the fact that I have a ghost now. I briefly considered selling the house—"

"No!"

"And decided against it. I can't uproot my kids once again for something they don't stand a chance of understanding. But I have to tell you," Sarah shook her head and wrapped her fingers around the delicate teacup in front of her. "I don't know how I am to deal with a dog I can hear speaking in my mind and a ghost that could pop in at any moment. Not to mention this strange sect that seems to have something to do with it, these Lumarians."

"Lumarians," Lily rested her chin in her hand and grinned at Sarah. "Girl, when you delve into the supernatural, you don't take tiny steps, do you? You just head on in all the way."

"Wasn't by choice, I assure you. I liked the house when that realtor contacted me out of the blue, and I saw Pixie's description on the Animal Rescue website so I adopted her – for the kids. That was it. Now, suddenly I have ghosts and slamming doors, and a glass pane that inexplicably fell out of the window in the entrance. And that repair guy you sent me..."

"Oh, did he show up?" Lily asked and sipped her tea. "What did he say, can he fix it?"

"Where do I even start? He took one look and wouldn't even touch the window. Asked me to come down to his shop to see about replacing the entire thing. Maybe I should, but for just one pane? Also, it gave me the creeps the way he acted around it."

"Hmm," Lily leaned back and said nothing for a moment.

Around them afternoon tea was in full swing. Friends greeted one another with a laugh and a wave, and Sarah could see herself ten years from now, sitting back in a corner with Lily, gossiping. It felt right. Maybe this room was why Matthew favored tea.

Sarah was about to say just that when Matthew came running in with a sheaf of papers in one hand, blonde hair askew.

"Hey Lily, nice to see you. I'm so sorry, Sarah."

He dropped heavily into a chair and set the papers down on the table between them. "One of our historical guides has called in sick, meaning

I have to do guided tours all afternoon. I hate to disappoint you, but I have to cut this short."

"Don't worry about it," Sarah said, trying to hide the disappointment in her voice. Somehow the thought of digging through old papers with Matthew was a nice one.

"I am sorry, truly…"

"No, go on, Sarah and I will just do the research. What have you brought us here?" Lily reached for the stack of papers and quickly scanned the contents. "Lumarians?"

"I just had our archive computer do a brain dump on Lumarians before I was called off. I'll leave this with you if you want to continue on your own?"

Did he sound disappointed as well, Sarah wondered, or was it wishful thinking on her part? She reached for the pages Lily had discarded, and a phrase caught her eye, The magic of the Luminus crystal… *Magic? Wait, magic, what?* She took the page, intending to ask him, but Matthew was already standing and rapping the table with his knuckles.

"I have to run, but I leave you in good hands. Lily knows everybody around here."

And with that, he rushed away, where at the door, one of the exhibit attendants was waiting for him with a clipboard and a lengthy list.

"Well then," Lily put the papers back down. "You don't have to look like you just got stuck with the B team, you know."

"I don't – it's not like that – I…"

"I'm joking, Sarah – just joking. I'm tickled that you like him. He's a nice guy and extremely easy on the eyes."

"Yes, well," Sarah could feel a blush burning on her cheeks. Jeez, it had been ages since she last blushed.

"What were you going to say? I could literally see a question on your face as Matt took off."

"Magic," Sarah said and sifted through the pages again to find the one she'd been holding. "Something about magic."

Some more people wandered into the tea room, an animated group of exercise walkers took the table beside them amidst laughter and jokes, and Sarah suddenly realized how many people were secretly checking her out while trying not to be obvious. She was the new face in town, of course. Or maybe the topic of ghosts and magic and talking dogs did that.

"It's getting packed in here," she said lightly. "Why don't we take a few of those pastries to go and study these papers at the house? I'm sure Cory would be all excited to go through them too."

"I see what you mean." Lily noticed a few people staring, waved at those she knew as customers, and winked at Sarah. "Yes, let's blow this pop stand for something quieter. I have a few books I want to give to Emma anyway."

"You're spoiling her."

"And that's not what somebody else's kids are for?"

Lily signaled one of the waitresses, reached for her wallet when Sarah wanted to, and deftly maneuvered them and their stack of printouts out of the tea room in double time.

Chapter 12

B ack at the house, they found a note from Mrs. Jenkins saying she had taken Emma and Corey for a visit to a nearby farm, and Pixie greeted Lily like a long-lost friend. Sarah looked around the kitchen and in the game room, but, for now, her new house was peaceful and quiet.

"So, what about this magic that had you spooked?" Lily asked and spread Matthew's printouts on the kitchen table.

"Just that, the Lumarians and their connection to magic — and Pixie and Amelia. There's a strange kind of through line here."

"Hmm..." Lily read through the page Sarah handed her. "I'm not seeing it. Other than... all of these things are a little out of the ordinary, nothing jumps out at me."

Sarah poured them two glasses of water from an old-fashioned glass pitcher she had found in the pantry. Mrs. Jenkins, she saw, had dropped some lemon slices into the water.

"I mean, maybe..." Lily looked from one page to the next, put down one, and picked up another. "Why did Matthew think this Lumarian sect was involved?"

"Something he read in a ledger upstairs. A few torn-out pages, and one fragment that referred to them."

"Well then, let's you and I go into the attic and take a look."

"Now?"

"Yes, now. Did you want to wait till tonight, when everybody is back, and the kids will want to climb up there, and you'll start to worry about someone getting hurt or frightened and calling their dad? No, you and I right now. Think of it as an adventure."

Pixie chose that moment to let out a sharp, piercing bark, and Lily laughed. "You see, even she agrees with me. Let's go."

Fortunately, Lily's phone rang just then, and Sarah sifted through the printed material while Lily took the call out on the porch.

"This whole Lumarian thing is quite interesting," she said when Lily returned to the kitchen. "Talk about going all in with magic. Listen to this." She read from one of the documents, "The Lumarians delved into the esoteric realms of magic, harnessing its energies to manipulate matter, shape destinies, and transcend the limitations of the mortal realm."

"Yeah, uh-huh," Lily said and rolled her eyes. "Pretty far-out stuff."

"Their mastery went beyond mere spell casting," Sarah continued. "It encompassed the crafting of astonishing artifacts that channeled and amplified their magical prowess. Specifically, the Luminus Crystal, a gemstone of exquisite beauty and extraordinary power."

"Well, if you happen to find that thing upstairs," Lily chuckled, "you could always try using it to send Amelia back to where she came from. But for now, let's just go and take a look."

"All you want is to sneak up to the attic," Sarah teased. "Away from the kids and Matthew's watchful eyes."

"Coordinated and graceful aren't my strong suits," Lily admitted.

Sarah put her research away. "I took a quick read, but it seems they used the crystal as an amplifier of sorts, a way to focus their magic. Oh, and rumor has it that if you gazed into it for a while, you could glimpse the future. Some even believed you could shape the future into whatever you desired."

"Wow," Lily said, lowering the stairs to the attic. "Same thing happens to me when I stare into a wine bottle for too long. I start thinking I can change the future. Funny, huh? After you, lady of the house."

Lily and Sarah joked and giggled as they ascended the attic stairs, more or less gracefully. Sarah's mom-jeans were definitely better suited for this exercise than Lily's flowing dress. When she had hoisted herself through the hatch, Sarah stood still for a moment, watching dust motes dance in the beam of light from the old window.

"It's kind of eerie up here," she said just to break the oppressive silence. "Don't you feel it?"

Lily didn't respond, but she pulled the cardigan she had borrowed from Sarah a bit closer around her body.

"Don't you have any light up here?"

"Over there, on that far beam." Sarah pointed. She flicked an old black Bakelite switch, and a bare bulb above them came to life, casting a faint, gloomy light.

Sarah shivered, wishing she had brought a cardigan herself. The shadows and unseen corners in the space felt menacing, even evil, as if a thousand eyes were watching her from the dark.

"Here are those trunks the kids and Matthew have been exploring," Lily called out from the far end of the attic, and Sarah turned. A thick net of cobwebs reached for her hair and face, and she beat at it frantically.

"God, I hate spiders."

"You're not the only one," Lily called back, swiping at her own face.

Somewhere down below, Pixie barked, emitting sharp, high-pitched barks that let them know she'd rather be with them.

"Back in a minute," Sarah called out, wishing she hadn't given in to Lily. Walking around in this attic felt all wrong and dangerous. She felt—unprotected up here, and Pixie's barking reminded her of just that.

"Look, Lily, can we—"

At that moment, the light bulb in the center of the attic flashed briefly and burned out, leaving her side of the space in dark gloominess and deeper shadows that reached for her with long, dark fingers. Sarah cried out involuntarily.

"Jesus! I don't think this was a good idea."

"Relax, there's nothing up here but us and a few thousand spiders."

Lily stood in the gloomy square of yellow light from the sole tiny window and waved. "Come over here, look at this."

Grumbling, Sarah carefully picked her way toward the light and her friend, holding onto a vertical beam for balance when her fingers felt something other than dry, rough wood.

"There's something here," she called out and dug in her pocket for her cell phone. "Look."

The hidden side of the beam she had used to steady herself—the one you would never see unless you stood right before it or felt it with your fingers was covered in dozens of carved symbols and letters. Sarah let the beam of her phone flashlight play over the roughly carved symbols and felt something dark and terrifying closing in on her, squeezing hard.

"Lily."

Her friend didn't answer, just a low hissing murmur echoing in her ears, an eerie symphony of dozens of foreign voices entwined in a chilling dance of malevolent secrecy. Sarah couldn't make out any words, but each voice contributed to the haunting chorus that made up a low, menacing whisper, dripping with hidden intent.

The rhythm of the hissing whispers ebbed and flowed, rising and falling like the tide of some forbidden ritual. The tone remained consistently low, a deliberate choice to shroud the words in an aura of secrecy and threat.

"Lily," Sarah called out again, her voice one of sheer panic.

"What?"

As one, the voices were silenced. Lily stood directly behind Sarah and shone the beam of her own cell phone. "What's got you so spooked?"

Sarah could only point at the beam and the carved symbols, then the next one and another one, all in the darkest corner of the attic.

"Wow," Lily said and immediately began photographing the symbols. "Bet you Matthew hasn't seen any of this. This is incredible. We have to get another light bulb right now."

Sarah felt like a strong hand had reached for her throat, gripping it tightly. Pixie, at the bottom of the stairs, barked as if she would never stop, and Sarah stumbled. She couldn't catch her breath and the unseen pressure on her throat squeezed tighter and tighter.

Down. She had to get down those stairs and beside her dog. She pushed Lily aside, almost rudely, and fumbled along the nearest beam toward the bright rectangle of the attic hatch.

No air, she couldn't draw air into her lungs and felt herself become dizzy. Her vision faded and her knees buckled.

Fumbling blindly, she grabbed the support rail and more slipped than climbed down. When she reached the bottom, she sagged to the ground and hugged a whimpering Pixie to herself. The choking sensation abated, and she realized she was almost crushing Pixie.

"Sorry, baby."

I couldn't get to you. She's strongest up there because I can't get to you there.

"She?"

Amelia. Amelia Thompson. She was murdered in this house.

"Murdered?"

"What are you talking about? Sarah — Sarah, talk to me."

Lily had clambered down the attic stairs and gripped Sarah's shoulders. "What was all of that? You couldn't breathe. I thought you were going to... Jesus."

Sarah scrambled to her feet, still hugging Pixie tightly to her chest.

"I don't think we should go up there again – ever. Amelia Thompson — the daughter of the original builder of this house —she was murdered in here."

"But how do you..." Lily looked at Pixie, who sat up in Sarah's arms, turned to face Lily, and stared into her eyes, long and hard. "Oh. But... those symbols. I'm sure they mean something. We have to show them to Matthew. He and Cory will be totally excited when he sees what we found. He might even know what they mean. I don't believe Matt ever went into that corner, and when he does—"

"No."

"Sarah." Lily placed her hand on Sarah's shoulder and turned to face her. "What happened to you up there?"

Sarah took a deep gulp of air, as if to convince herself that she could, and shook her head.

"I – I couldn't breathe. There was something – oppressive and evil up in that attic."

"Evil? Sarah, it's just an old empty space."

"And when I put a light on those old symbols – I heard – voices, whispers, hisses – very eerie sounds."

Her voice broke in a hysterical sob.

"Easy," Lily said and hugged both her and Pixie closely. "I'm sorry. Sounds like you had a bad fright. You probably have a pretty serious dust allergy. That's why you couldn't breathe and frightened yourself right into an anxiety attack. If I had known, I would never have dragged you up there."

Sarah slowly shook her head. "I don't think so."

"Look, sit down, have some water. And I'll just go up there, take a few more photos for Matthew, and close the hatch properly."

"Lily, no." Sarah took both of Lily's hands and shook her head again and again. "Please…"

"Whatever it is, Sarah, it's not affecting me. Look." Lily spread her arms and awkwardly twirled around in the narrow space. "I'm fine, and so were Matthew and the kids. They've been up there all week. Go, sit, and we'll talk about it when I come back down."

"First sign of trouble…"

"First sign of trouble, I'm going to be down those stairs so fast an arrow couldn't catch me. And I would nail that hatch shut personally, okay?"

Sarah laughed involuntarily and nodded. "Fine."

She refused to put Pixie on the ground and carried her all the way out to the large, comfortable porch swing, where she wrapped a fluffy, white blanket around herself and buried her cheek against Pixie's soft fur.

Are you all right?

"I'm OK now, thanks to you."

She knows I cannot protect you up there.

"Amelia? But why is she going after me? Matthew and the kids, and Lily – none of them felt anything."

You are a... sensitive. That's why you can hear me.'

Sarah hugged Pixie again hard. "Precious baby," she whispered into the silky white fur.

A little pink tongue brushed against her cheek, and Sarah sensed a profound sadness emanating from the little Papillon.

"What's wrong?" she asked.

Selena, my owner before you, used to call me her precious baby all the time.

They held onto each other for a moment, but the slam of a car door from next door brought Sarah back to reality. Pixie leaped off her lap and dashed to the front gate, barking up a storm. Mrs. Jenkins had returned with the children, carrying baskets filled with apples and berries. Their laughter and jokes rang through the front yard and Sarah hastily wiped her eyes and ran her fingers through her hair, hoping that Lily had finished upstairs and closed the attic hatch.

～

"Mom, Mom, I saw a donkey with a little baby!" Emma exclaimed, bounding up the porch stairs in a tangle of gingham cloth, flowers, and a basket of fruit. "It was so cool, and there were little ducks, and baby chicks, and—"

"Calm down, sis," Cory said, elbowing her gently and helping Mrs. Jenkins with more fruit. His sharp teenage eyes had already noticed that something wasn't quite right with his mother.

"Are you okay?" he asked softly and Sarah managed a forced smile.

"Of course, Cory, everything's fine. I was just lost in thought for a moment. How was your trip to the farm?"

"Pretty good," Cory replied, setting down the fruit before opening the screen door on his way to his room. "One of their sons is hoping to make it onto the basketball team, so I might teach him a few tricks later this week."

Just then Lily stepped out onto the porch, surveying the abundance of fruit and vegetables.

"It seems like you're planning a feast around here."

"No, I was thinking of showing Sarah how to preserve things," Mrs. Jenkins remarked pointedly. Implying her opinion of Lily's lifestyle, clothing choices, and abilities in the kitchen, "I didn't think you'd be interested."

Lily placed a hand on her chest as if taken aback, then chuckled. "Ouch. That's perfectly fine. I'll manage by going to the grocery store. Sarah, Sarah, I want to go show those pictures to Matthew as soon as I can."

"Pictures?"

Lily bit her lip and Mrs. Jenkins and Cory both stopped what they were doing and stared.

"What kind of pictures did you take?" Cory inquired, trying far too hard to appear casual. "Of the house?"

"Well, you know," Lily said, waving a hand, "that window above your door is broken, oh what's the use? You caught us. Your mom and I were upstairs and discovered some unusual carvings."

"Upstairs? In the attic? We never saw any carvings. Where? Let me see the pictures."

Any thought of canning vegetables or playing computer games upstairs vanished, and both Mrs. Jenkins and Cory crowded in on Lily.

"Show me, I want to see," Cory urged. "Matthew and I have been up there dozens of times and never found anything other than old papers. I was starting to think it was boring. How did we miss them? Where were they?"

Lily glanced back at Sarah once more, her hand nestled firmly in her pocket as if clutching her phone. Eventually, Sarah shrugged and shook her head.

"Go on then. They'll pester us all night, and I wouldn't want anyone sneaking into the attic for a peek."

"Sorry." Lily grimaced, but she retrieved her phone, unlocking it to display the images of the carvings almost instantly.

Lily's camera had captured every crack, crevice, and ridge in the beams and carved wood. Even from a few feet away, the images on the phone sent shivers down her spine, as though something vaguely malevolent had invaded her cherished sanctuary. Sarah shuddered and looked away, only to meet the wide-eyed gaze of Mrs. Jenkins. The elderly woman had turned as pale as the freshly laundered sheets she regularly hung on the line, her right hand covering her mouth in shock. Those symbols had a primal and rudimentary, animalistic aura, yet her neighbor appeared as if she had come face-to-face with pure evil incarnate.

"Wow, do you know what they mean?"

Cory's inquisitive, adolescent voice, still youthful, as he traced the outlines on Lily's phone with his finger.

"I'm not sure. That's why I want to show Matthew."

"Luminus," Mrs. Jenkins breathed, and were she not as close as she was, Sarah wouldn't have caught it. Finally, her elderly neighbor sank into one of the porch chairs, concealing the lower half of her face with both hands.

Emma, who held no interest in Lily's pictures, the attic, or anything beyond a nap following her exciting farm escapade, climbed into Mrs. Jenkins' lap and snuggled close.

"I had an amazing time today," she mumbled, her eyelids growing heavy already.

"Precious baby," Mrs. Jenkins whispered tenderly, and this time the phrase sent a shiver down Sarah's spine.

"All right then. Cory, please let Lily go show those to Matthew, he might know what it is. For all we know someone tried their new carving knife out in the attic for the first time. Please bring the produce inside, and bring a glass of water for Mrs. J., this heat. I'll put Emma down for a little nap. Let's go."

Her children recognized the *no-arguments* tone of voice and obeyed. Emma let her take her upstairs and she heard Cory lugging baskets of fruits and vegetables.

Only Mrs. Jenkins remained on the porch, her hands over her eyes, staring off into the distance.

༄

Pixie followed them up to the room that now served as Emma's and sat while she snuggled the child down for her nap.

You know it has nothing to do with the heat.

"I don't know what it is," Sarah whispered, checking so Emma couldn't hear. "But it scares me."

Pixie parked herself at the foot end of Emma's bed and put her head on her paws.

Be careful.

༄

By the time Sarah came downstairs Mrs. Jenkins had left without another word, ignoring the water Cory had brought for her. Cory eyed the hatch leading to the attic.

"No," Sarah said preemptively, without waiting for any questions.

"But Mom..."

"You're not going up there alone, and I certainly am not going with you."

"But you went with Aunt Lily."

"Once was more than enough."

"Please."

"Don't argue, Cory. It's been a long day, and I just want to sit on the porch and read for a while. Whatever happened to those hundreds' of dollars worth of computer games your father gave you? Go play one of those."

How ironic it was that she would now send her son, who had been holed up behind a computer screen for months, refusing to speak, to his room to play games instead of allowing the exploration he desired.

"They're boring," Cory muttered, but he headed upstairs to his room.

Sarah picked up the printouts Matthew had provided her about the Lumarians and began reading them carefully. If she didn't miss her guess, Mrs. Jenkins had said "Luminus" when she saw those symbols, and that sounded eerily close to "Lumarians" and their magic crystal.

Chapter 13

C hapter Sixteen

Later that evening, after dinner had been prepared and consumed, the kids had gone to bed, and both Lily and Mrs. Jenkins had reassured her via text that everything was fine, Matthew found Sarah on the porch swing, gazing into the distance while clutching a sheaf of printouts.

"Here you are, I tried calling. I wanted to apologize," he raised a bottle of wine but stopped upon seeing Sarah's expression. "Are you upset?"

Sarah lifted the stack of printouts, now neatly separated, and then let them drop onto her lap again.

"This, Matthew. Are you seriously telling me that you've never heard about this story?"

"Well..."

"Well, what?"

"Not exactly never," he said hesitantly, pulling up a chair beside her. "I knew the Lumarians had a presence here in Rosewood Hollow."

"Pretty sure you said, oh, you've never heard of them."

"I didn't want to worry you," Matthew had the good graces to look chastised. He stared down at his shoes briefly and then spread his arms.

"Worry? Oh, gee, I wonder why," Sarah snapped, picking up one of the reports with pointed fingers as if it were filthy. "A religious or spiritual sect of magicians and witches who delighted in building artifacts to amplify their magic."

"But that was a long time ago," Matthew protested. "At a time when some people believed in magic."

Sarah ignored the comment, dropped the report she was holding, and selected another, just as pointedly. "And somehow they unearthed this strange crystal from somewhere, and they firmly believe it could focus their collective power. Get this," Sarah pushed her reading glasses up her nose and read from the report. "They believe that when activated, said crystal could bend time and space, altering the future to the practitioner's will, and allowing travel into any time, backward and forward."

Sarah pushed the reports on her lap away and fixed an intense gaze on Matthew's eyes. "Time travel? Magic powers? That's what you thought would worry me?"

"It sounds pretty far-fetched."

"Oh, of course it sounds extremely far-fetched. I agree with you there," Sarah said, sarcasm dripping from every word. "And I would have dismissed it for a hoax from some extremely misguided people until I came across this..."

Her finger seized another single-page printout that appeared to be an official police report.

"I – I'm sorry, I didn't mean to include that among the papers I gave you," Matthew stuttered. "Listen, can we open this wine, get some glasses, and start over? I want to explain."

"I'm sure you do," Sarah snapped. "Explain how, to this day, in the 21st century – the age of cellphones, AI, and microcomputers –

there are still people hunting for this crystal. People arrested multiple times right here in Rosewood Hollow, hoping to discover it in an old, abandoned house on the outskirts of town."

Matthew's complexion paled a bit. He stood, retrieved a corkscrew and two wine glasses from the kitchen, and offered a glass to Sarah, though she didn't clink it against his before taking a generous sip.

"I think you'll agree that it's a touch concerning," she finally said. "And I might still have a word with the estate agent about this. I specifically asked if this was a safe neighborhood for children."

"It's safe, believe me," Matthew reassured her, reaching for her hand. Sarah felt a shiver of anticipation but quickly pulled her hand away. "Cory and Emma are perfectly safe here," Mathew asserted again. "I care deeply about both of them, and I would have told you if I thought there was anything...dangerous for them."

"I guess I'll have to believe that." Sarah finished her wine and peered into the empty glass. "Still..."

"I should have told you."

"Yes, you should have." Sarah looked up at him, locking eyes with his dark gaze. "So I'm asking you now to be honest with me. Are you one of them?"

"One of them?" Matthew asked, puzzled, and then frowned. "One of... what?"

"One of those treasure hunters who hope to find the Lumarian crystal and either use it or sell it."

"No, no, of course not. That crystal and the Lumarian group have a certain appeal to me from a historical perspective, but, until a few days ago, I didn't even know your house was connected to them or had any kind of spiritual activity attached to it for that matter."

Sarah looked down at her hands. Spiritual activity. Amelia, her very own dog, Pixie. As if on cue, the doggie door gently flapped, and Pixie strolled out to join them.

Everything OK?

Just fine, Sarah thought, unsure if she dared speak to Pixie in front of Matthew at that moment. The way he had mentioned spiritual activity made her hesitate. Pixie settled into her lap, and Sarah sensed amusement from the little dog.

It's fine. You can tell him. He will understand. He needs to know about Amelia. She's getting stronger every day, and she is connected to the crystal.

Pixie turned slightly, allowing Sarah to rub her little white tummy, and finally, she sighed. "Matthew?" She let her head fall back and stared out into the darkening night sky. "When you talk about spiritual activity..."

"Yes?"

"Well, you said it yourself, this is a very, very old house, with a checkered history."

Matthew said nothing, set down his wine glass, and gave her a long, silent look.

"Things have been happening in this house since we moved in," she said carefully, keeping her eyes on his, trying to gauge his reaction.

"What sort of things?"

"At first, it was just slamming doors, items being moved, things being re-arranged in a very specific way."

"Specific how?"

"The day you all came to visit," Sarah said, "after Pixie discovered the attic door. Lily had brought some cupcakes. We put them in the kitchen, and when I came back, they were all lined up to spell the letters, 'A-T'."

"A-T?" Matthew frowned again, and she could almost see him searching his mind for anything connected to those initials.

"Amelia Thompson," Sarah supplied. "The daughter of the original owner of this house. At least, we think so."

"It could have been a silly prank," Matthew shrugged and refilled her wine. "Doesn't have to mean anything."

"I kept telling myself that. Until I saw her."

"Saw...?"

The bottle slipped from Matthew's hand, and only a swift move from Sarah saved it from crashing onto the porch, shattering into a thousand pieces.

"You saw... a person who's been dead for well over a hundred years?"

"A ghost, yes," Sarah said, with the bravery of ripping off a bandage. "It wasn't fun. She wanted to know what I was doing in her house."

Matthew blew out a breath, leaning back in his chair. He reached for the wine bottle again, refilled his glass, and downed most of it in one gulp.

"I'm here on foot," he said, noticing her glance sideways at the road. "But... Your ghost, how do you know?"

"I... just do," Sarah replied, knotting her fingers in Pixie's collar. This particular secret she intended to keep for a while. It was their special connection. Pixie gently licked the top of her left hand.

"So... You think we're all crazy now?"

Matthew laughed. Sarah was startled by the warm, joyous sound wafting through the garden.

"Is that what you're worried about?" he asked, reaching for her hand again. This time, Sarah didn't flinch or pull her arm away. "Of course not. I may be a historian, but if there's one thing I know, it's that there are more things in heaven and earth than we could ever dare to dream about."

"Thank you."

"Oh, don't thank me. This is a gift, an opportunity to conduct some research on a group that's been shrouded in mystery for centuries, right on a property where they used to be active."

"My house?" Sarah asked, struggling to hide the horror in her voice.

"Yes, I was getting to that, until you stole my thunder with a ghost sighting. After the pictures Lily showed me today, I have no doubt about it. The Lumarians used to gather right here in this house, probably up in the attic that was so carefully hidden after they left."

Matthew's hand tightened around hers, and Sarah exhaled.

"The pictures, I'd forgotten about those pictures. But what happened, and more importantly, why? I don't understand."

"I don't either... yet. But we will find all that out once we explore the attic in greater detail, with high-power lamps, cameras, recording equipment, and a whole lot of other tools I haven't even thought of, but will bring anyway."

In his excitement, Matthew stood up from the chair, settled on the porch swing beside her, and drew her close against his shoulder. "Think about it, it could be us who uncover the mystery of the Lumarians' disappearance. Solving an age-old enigma. Cory will love every minute of it."

Most definitely. And so would he. Sarah finally allowed herself to relax and relish the feeling of being held close and secure, smiling into the darkness. Pixie stirred on her lap, and once again, Sarah sensed nothing but happiness and joy from the little animal.

"Tomorrow," Matthew said enthusiastically. "Tomorrow we will get started."

"Whoa, tomorrow already?"

"Yes. I would climb up there tonight, but…"

"Under no circumstances," Sarah sat up a little straighter and shook her head.

"No, I understand," Matthew said, raising his hands, though frustration bled through every one of his movements. "I need to source good lights first, and a fantastic camera, and charcoal to trace these carvings, and…"

"And a good night's sleep," Sarah continued. "And something to keep you all safe up there."

"Safe?" Matthew cocked his head and gave her such an adorable puppy dog look, she felt her insides clench again. "Why would we…? Oh, so nobody can fall through the hatch down the stairs, yes, I can bring safety equipment to make sure that doesn't happen. No worries."

New fear unlocked, Sarah thought. Now she'd worry about her children getting too close to that hatch and the stairs, while still worrying about Amelia up there.

"Everybody will be safe, I promise you," he said taking her hand. "After all, we were already doing this most of last week."

Chapter 14

Despite Matthew's reassurances, Sarah still worried. She lay awake half the night after sending Pixie to spend time with the kids. Emma, in particular, loved the little Papillon dog sleeping on her bed and could usually be found hugging her close.

They had barely finished their breakfast the next morning when a grey pickup truck pulled up, the bed filled with construction lights, a fan, ropes, harnesses, and all manner of things that hinted at mountain climbing rather than a trip to the attic. Matthew bounced up the walkway and onto the porch before she could even open the door.

"Matthew," Emma ran out to hug him while Cory settled for a more manly high-five.

"Are you kids ready to explore?"

"You bet."

In the bright sunshine of a new day, her fears looked kind of silly, Sarah had to admit. It was an old attic, a spiritual group that had disappeared dozens of years ago. What could be up there other than a few historical records and dust? Dust, one could easily be allergic to.

"Somebody bought out the Home Depot," she said smiling, looking at the truck bed.

"All in the name of history and research." Matthew handed her a takeout cup from the local tea shop and a bakery bag that felt warm still and smelled delicious. "Are you coming up there with us?"

"Not me, thank you." Sarah actually took a step back. Dust allergy or not, the memory of those few minutes in the attic still sat in her bones.

"Do you want to take Pixie along," she asked instead.

"Pixie?" Matthew asked, and the look on his face left no doubt what he thought of that idea. "Wouldn't that be rather dangerous?"

"Pixie is more agile than any of you. And she might find something."

"Oh yes, please, please," Emma begged. "Pixie told me last night that as long as she is sleeping beside me, nothing bad could possibly happen."

Her daughter's offhand little comment sent a cold shiver down Sarah's back. Cory rolled his eyes at Matthew, a look that was so much like his father's it hurt.

"Okay then," he said. "But I'll have to carry you up those stairs, girl."

Pixie sat before them, looking rather smug.

You didn't have to do that. The children are safe.

You spoke to Emma last night, Sarah thought.

Yes, Amelia was trying to invade her nightmares. I prevented it.

God, Pixie, are we safe here?

Pixie spun around in front of them and crowded in close to Cory.

"Pixie, you keep an eye on them, okay?" Sarah said out loud and ruffled the soft fur on the Papillon's head. "I'm counting on you."

∽

She had been prepared to wait for the rest of the day, listening at the bottom of the stairs for voices and sounds that let her know everything was okay in that strange attic of hers – but it took a mere hour until Cory excitedly called her from Emma's old room.

"Look, Mom," he called out, "Matthew thought you seemed a bit worried about something happening in the attic, so we decided to bring the trunks of documents down here where we can check them out. He's just taking the last pictures of those symbols and letters on the beams, and he'll join us. Do you think I can write a paper on this stuff? Will I get extra credit?"

Not surprisingly, his last school year had been dismal. It was so bad that if some of Michael's high-powered clients hadn't intervened, he would have had to repeat the year. The fear of being *that* kid still troubled her oldest.

"Good idea," she said, ruffling his hair despite his frown. "Make sure Matthew helps you, okay?"

Then she turned to what they had lugged down those stairs. Two trunks sat in the center of the room, weathered old wooden pieces with cracked leather fittings that looked as if they had seen the world and a land before time. Everything inside her screamed to stay away from them, to have Matthew load them onto that pickup truck out there and drive until he ran out of road.

But they were just old trunks, weren't they? Sarah swallowed hard.

"You see, nobody got hurt," Matthew suddenly whispered behind her. He had climbed down the stairs with a large, expensive-looking camera around his neck.

"Yes, thanks."

Her throat felt tight and scratchy again, and she took a few steps back, partly to clear the small room and partly to put some distance between herself and the trunks.

"There are old books in there," Emma said proudly. "I really want those. And I made sure they wouldn't trip."

"Good for you," Sarah said softly, searching for Pixie. The little dog approached the trunks cautiously, leaning forward as far as her tiny body and neck could stretch. She touched her little nose to it and jumped back. Sarah heard Cory's laughter from a distance as if it came from a long tunnel and her vision blurred. Suddenly, Pixie yelped.

"Pixie." All at once, reality returned, and Sarah scooped up the little dog. "Are you all right?"

There's a powerful energy around those trunks, Sarah.

"Amelia?"

"Why do you say that, Mom," Cory asked. "Do you think those trunks are hers? Did Pixie step into something?"

Sarah pretended to examine the dog's paws and held her even tighter.

Pixie, did they just bring Amelia down here?

There was no response. Pixie felt as tense as a board in her arms, and her tail, that beautiful fluffy white tail, glowed as if lit by a hundred suns.

You will not have them. That wasn't the voice she usually heard in her head when she sensed Pixie. But the little dog quivered with every word.

Not them.

That voice was dark and powerful and broached no argument.

Something laughed somewhere, a sinister echoing laugh and Sarah felt her feet leave the ground as she was suddenly slammed into the wall behind her. Pixie, still cradled in her arms, barked and dug her paws into Sarah's arms.

Whatever you do, don't let go.

Was that a whimper she heard coming from her own throat? Sarah clung to Pixie for dear life as another wave of energy slammed her into the wall behind her. Something emanated from Pixie, something powerful and dense and just as charged as the energy that kept slamming her backward.

A thunderclap echoed through the room and Sarah felt herself sliding down the wall, helpless, still clinging to the little dog who suddenly grew limp in her arms.

Darkness enveloped her and she sat hard on the floor.

"Mom!"

"Sarah!"

Beloved.

Sarah kept her eyes closed and concentrated on feeling her body. Her rear end on the floor, her feet out straight before her and her arms limp by her side. Her head ached with the force of a thousand anvils and on her lap...

Finally, she dared open her eyes. Pixie lay almost lifeless in her arms.

"Pixie!"

Her own voice sounded panicked and frantic to her. Not now, not Pixie, this little loyal friend who had done nothing but protect her family. Their connection was only a few days old, but it felt as if they had known each other for ages, through time and space unknown.

"No, no, no, Pixie."

Sarah knelt and hugged the little dog closer to her chest. The fluffy tail, usually carried proudly curled over her back, now hung lifeless.

The sparkling, golden hue was gone, leaving a dark shadow, much like a mark.

"Please not Pixie," Sarah cried. Frantically, she felt the little chest for a heartbeat and put her ear close to the papillon's nose. Nothing. Was Pixie still breathing? Was that strong little warrior heart even still beating? Sarah could feel Matthew touching her shoulder and shrugged off his hand. Cory and Emma crowded in close, she could hear them speak, their voices concerned, worried. They were okay, no one was harmed; they were here because of Pixie.

I'm here, Sarah.

Dear God, Sarah let out a sigh. The feeling she got was faint, as if it took her the greatest effort to reach Sarah. Pixie's eyes fluttered briefly, and Sarah felt her chest expand with a deep breath.

"What happened to Pixie, Mom, and why are you on the floor? It was like... you flew across the room."

"It's all right, Cory. I'm all right." Sarah scrambled back to her feet, still cradling Pixie, and nodded at Matthew. "I'm fine, really. It's just..."

"Why do you bother with this pointless little creature? I could crush her with a thought."

They all froze. Matthew turned around first, then Sarah. Immediately, she gestured for her children to get behind her.

"What do you want in my house?" she screamed, now beyond furious. There, on Emma's bed, which they had left behind so she could move into her room again soon, sat the same apparition she had seen in the game's room a few days ago.

Her white dress billowed in great folds around her, and her hair was still held by that golden pin that could pierce the heart of a living being. Emma screeched, and the dark, empty eyes of the woman focused in on Pixie.

"She is no match for me."

"Mom," Sarah could feel her children's hands on her back as they crowded in closer. Automatically she took another step back, away from that creature, putting more distance between her and...

"Amelia," she asked tonelessly.

"Who else would I be? And you are in my house."

"Now wait just one goddamned minute," Matthew stepped forward, a thick leather-bound book still in his hand. "Just who are you, and how dare you come into my friend's house and – and threaten her."

"How very chivalrous of you."

Amelia laughed. At least, Sarah thought that was what the echoing sound she heard was meant to be, but it sent more shivers down her back.

"Matthew, don't—"

"Don't what?" He took another step closer to her. "Now listen to me, lady. You are on private property here, and—"

Suddenly Matthew made a gagging sound, clutched his throat, and his mouth opened and closed like a fish dragged onto dry land. At the same time, Cory and Emma screamed, their voices high-pitched and painful as both of them crumbled to the ground in pain, and something inside Sarah stirred and rose to the surface, unfolding as it grew. Just then, she felt Pixie stir in her arms again.

Ready?

"Ready for what? Pixie I don't—"

As if she'd never done anything else, Sarah pushed out her right hand, fingers splayed as if she were a traffic cop trying to signal a stop. She could see it in her mind, a massive red stop sign blocking something that came at them, and at the same time, something shimmering gold and purple emanated from her hands. She locked her right hand behind her left and held it, focusing a massive beam of power through her very being and out into her hands. Her hands felt as if she were grasping a live wire, and still, she held that stop signal as if her very life depended on it, then she heard Matthew cough again.

He stumbled, straightened up again, and turned around to stare at Sarah in wonder.

Enough.

Sarah dropped her hands. Before her very eyes, Amelia appeared to have become smaller, shrunk into herself from the imposing figure she had been, and slid backward on Emma's bed.

"Witch," the word hissed through the room, echoing off the walls.

"Mom, that lady is transparent."

Cory spotted it at once, there, where Amelia had slid back on the bed, they could see the wallpaper behind her and Emma's little book-case through the image of the woman. Sarah blinked and looked again, but the image didn't change. Amelia had become mostly transparent.

Pixie seemed almost magically restored. She squirmed until Sarah set her down, approached Amelia carefully, and sat back after a moment.

She'll be frozen for a while. You hit her with enough power to knock out a demon, Sarah.

"How do I know how to do this?"

"Would somebody like to explain to me what in God's green earth is going on here? I came here for a little historical research, and suddenly – this." Matthew massaged his throat with one hand and gestured at Amelia, Pixie, and back to Amelia again. "This – whatever it is."

"It's an apparition," Sarah said calmly as if she were showing him an exotic type of fruit. "More specifically, Amelia Thompson, the daughter of the original builder, Jedediah."

"And you know this – how? And Pixie," Matthew opened and closed his mouth again, visibly struggling. "How?" he finally asked.

"I don't know that, Matthew. A few weeks ago, I was a divorced mother of two looking for a new start here in Rosewood Hollow. Suddenly, I can talk to my dog, I see apparitions, and apparently, I have powers I'm not aware of – so give me a minute to process, will you." Sarah swept her hair out of her face and turned to her children for the first time. "Are you two all right? Did anything?"

"You can talk to Pixie," was all Cory wanted to know, and looked at his mother with newfound admiration. "Cool."

"Pixie told me everything would be all right." Emma had stuck her thumb into her mouth, something she had not done in a very long time. Sarah knelt on the floor, pulled her into a tight embrace, and held her for a long moment.

"Yes, yes it will be, sweetheart. I promise you that."

She turned to Pixie, still keeping an arm around her daughter, and fixed the little dog in a hard stare.

"I want to know what just happened here, right now."

"Does she answer you?" Cory's voice held even more admiration now.

Simple. You are an empath. You have untold powers that have been dormant until now.

"But how?"

You were drawn here, and I to you. When Amelia threatened Matthew and your children, I could feel your power, raw and unfocused, but I joined it with mine.

The little papillon shook and looked at Amelia as if to say, there's the result.

"Can we get out of this room, please?" Matthew asked, and his face had paled markedly. He still held the leather-bound book he had found in one of the trunks in one hand. "I'm sorry, but this is creeping me out."

Sarah looked at Pixie.

Should we keep an eye on her?

Pixie laughed then, a sweet tinkling sound like a small silver bell ringing.

Don't you know? All you have to do is close the door and sweep your hand across it, and she won't be able to cross the threshold.

That's it?

Oh, she will gain power again, and break the spell, but it will take time. Meanwhile, we have work to do.

Pixie strolled out of the room ahead of everybody, leaving Sarah behind, grappling with what she had heard. She took one last look at Amelia, cowering on the bed, and felt her hatred for the being that had attacked her children. Then she strolled out of the room, head high, slammed the door, and swept her hand across the lock and handle. For the briefest moment, they glowed a bright golden and purple, and all was still again.

Chapter 15

Matthew entered the kitchen ahead of everyone, going straight to the coffee maker. He dialed up the strongest espresso the machine could produce and brewed it. With the delicate cup in hand, he gazed at Sarah, Pixie, and the children, finally downing most of his espresso in a single gulp. He grimaced as the scalding liquid burned his mouth.

"Could someone please explain what just happened?" he asked.

"I don't know," Sarah replied, pouring water for the children and herself.

"That..." Matthew gestured vaguely towards the stairs. "That... Is she — that — out for good?"

"For a while, yes. But it will be good to keep our guard up nonetheless."

Matthew brought his hands up to his face and pressed his fingertips into his temples. "I must be going insane," he groaned. "And you are saying this is..."

"Amelia."

Matthew squeezed his eyes shut, pulled up a chair, and sank heavily into it. "Let's assume you're right for a moment."

"Let's."

"And that's Amelia Thompson."

"It is."

"Cool," Cory exclaimed, his eyes shining with an excitement Sarah hadn't seen in ages. "We have a ghost. Far out."

"Why is she here?" Matthew asked. "In all the time I've lived in Rosewood Hollow, I've never heard of this house being haunted. Believe me, I would have. But more importantly, what are you going to do about her — it?"

Sarah sipped her water, feeling the ice-cold, lemon-tinged liquid glide down her throat. Something within her expanded and grew, a power she'd never felt before, a strength that had been absent for most of her life, while she was busy being an obedient, reticent wife and mother. She straightened up slightly, lifted her head, and felt the tingling extend down her arms and into her hands. She spread her fingers and stared at them in wonder. For once, it was liberating not to be consumed by fear.

"I haven't figured that out yet, Matthew," she replied calmly. "If there's any threat to the children or me, I'll leave this house faster than you can imagine, trust me."

"No," Cory and Emma chorused almost as one. A ghost was the best thing that had happened to them in ages, and they were not ready to let it go. Sarah raised her hand and both of them stopped mid-whine and looked down at their laps. Another new thing in her life.

Pixie strolled into the kitchen then, and Sarah reached down, inviting the little dog onto her lap. Pixie settled on her knees and surveyed the room. For a while, no one spoke. Then, Pixie turned, placed her paws on Sarah's shoulder, and gently nuzzled her cheek, as if wanting to play.

Do you trust me?

Always.

Then listen.

Pixie pressed her head against Sarah's, and suddenly, a torrent of images flooded into her mind — sights, sounds, and stories. The overwhelming onslaught made her want to run outside to escape the tales of destinies, sorrows, and victories that kept coming one after the other. Images of her house, the inhabitants, people, animals, friends and foes. Just as the pressure became unbearable and her breaths grew shallow, Pixie withdrew.

Now you know everything I know.

Give me a heads-up next time. Sarah gripped the table's edge with a trembling hand. *I felt like I was drowning.*

Pixie tilted her head, settled, and curled up on Sarah's lap once more. She seemed weaker than usual, drained and exhausted. Through their connection, Sarah sensed Pixie's battle against weariness.

Rest now.

"Sarah?" Matthew placed his hand on her shoulder. "You seemed, uh, disoriented for a moment."

Sarah nodded, trying to sift through the stories in her mind as fast as she could.

"Amelia Thompson died in this house," she finally said, grasping onto the story she was seeking. "For some reason her father tried to conceal her death by concocting a tale of Amelia visiting family members abroad and some tragic accident occurring."

Matthew took a step back. Questions flickered across his face, and, without a word, Sarah understood what he must be thinking: *How do you know all of this?*

"That's all I know about Amelia," she concluded. "But Jedediah Thompson was the leader of the local Lumarian group, and..." Sarah gasped, pausing as the next memory unfolded in her mind, presenting itself to her as if it were her own. "He was responsible for safeguarding the Luminus crystal from... another group?"

Matthew reached for the large, gleaming white kitchen counter and took the heavy leather-bound book he had been carrying when Amelia appeared upstairs. Slowly, he turned it so Sarah could read the title etched in large gold letters on the old, cracked leather.

A History of the Lumarians.

Cory and Emma looked entranced.

"Is this some kind of real-life role-playing game?" Cory finally asked, glancing around cautiously as if expecting fairies and goblins to appear next.

"No, sweetheart," Sarah smiled. "It's ancient history, but history come to life."

"So, we really have a ghost?"

"A soul that is trying to move on," she said after a moment, realizing as the words left her mouth that it was an accurate and true description of Amelia.

"But why can't she do that?" Emma inquired, always eager to help her fellow human — or ghost in this case.

"Because her father covered up her death," Sarah replied, recognizing again as she spoke that these words were absolute truths. "And it's up to us to uncover what really happened."

Matthew promptly opened the book and scanned through the index; the children whispered excitedly about ghosts and Halloween, while Sarah cradled a slumbering Pixie in her arms, sorting through impressions and emotions in her mind.

☙

That's how Mrs. Jenkins found them not half an hour later when she poked her head in through the screen door.

"Sarah, I heard some awful noises from your house this morning. I just wanted to check..."

Pixie instantly leaped upright in her lap and swished her beautiful tail.

Beware, Sarah heard, just as she was about to respond.

"I'm so sorry," she said instead. "The kids must have had the TV on too loudly."

"But we—" Cory began, silenced by a raised hand once more.

"It won't happen again, Mrs. Jenkins."

The elderly woman held her gaze far longer than necessary, searching for something. What that might be, she had no idea. Yet, her newfound strength allowed her to meet the look without flinching.

"Mort wanted to come over to inspect the old well and make sure the fencing in the back is properly fixed," Mrs. Jenkins mentioned casually, still regarding Sarah with narrowed eyes.

"That would be lovely, thank you. But please don't inconvenience yourself. We're just... engrossed in a game indoors today."

Mrs. Jenkins pointedly looked at the window and the brilliant sunshine outside, then back at Sarah, and Matthew, engrossed in his book. She produced a plate of cookies and set it on the table between them.

"I'll tell him. Let me know if you need any assistance with anything, absolutely anything, you hear?"

"I will, thank you."

Not finding another reason to stay Mrs. Jenkins went home again, and Sarah put a finger under Pixie's chin.

What was that warning all about?

Pixie shook, making her collar tags jingle, and sat up a little straighter on her lap.

There's something that woman wants.

"Mrs. Jenkins?"

"What about Mrs. Jenkins," Matthew asked around a mouth full of cookies. Right, Sarah thought, she always forgot that he was not part of these conversations she had with Pixie. She shrugged lightly.

"I was wondering what she wanted," she clarified.

Matthew peered at her over the rim of his reading glasses before looking back at the half-eaten cookie in his hand. Slowly, he set the cookie down and wiped his hand on his pants.

"Not everybody has an ulterior motive, Sarah," he commented.

"Yeah, I suppose. Now, what about that," She gestured toward the old book he was engrossed in.

"I'm not sure why I chose this one when we were running out of there," he admitted, lifting the book from the table and letting it fall back down. "But back when I was a grad student, I would have done anything for a book like this. Everyone knew the Lumarians were a thing around the turn of the century when there was a lot of interest in the spiritual movement. Yet, hardly anybody knew who or what they actually were. All we had were these fragments of information, and if I could have—"

"Matthew," Sarah interrupted. "Could I have the Cliff's Notes version, please? Much as it's fascinating, I don't think I have time for a dissertation on a sect."

"Mommy," Emma piped up, playing with a discarded crayon on the kitchen table. "Is that lady upstairs who died really a ghost?"

Sarah exchanged a glance with Matthew. Cory might find it exciting, but Emma couldn't quite comprehend what was happening.

"Maybe she can move on if we help her find out what she needs," Emma suggested softly.

Scratch being too young to grasp things.

"Emma, sweetheart, I don't think you need to worry about what you saw upstairs. I'll make sure nothing happens to you. Would you like me to ask Lily to take you to the bookstore?"

Emma looked at her with a serene smile. "I'm not scared, Mommy. I just think we should help Amelia, that's all. But if it makes you feel better, I'll go hang out with Aunt Lily."

An unspoken agreement passed between Cory and Emma, and Sarah pulled her hair away from her face. Despite years of parenting, she still hadn't figured it all out.

"We're just doing research," Matthew explained kindly. "It might be more fun to go to the bookstore."

Cory, however, remained steadfast. He smelled adventure and was determined to join them.

∞

Lily picked up Emma, Sarah prepared some sort of lunch that nobody cared about, and Matthew continued to flip through the book, captivated by every page.

"I wish I could convey how exciting this is," he said now and then.

After another half hour even Cory wandered off to his room, and Sarah finally prodded him.

"Come on, Matthew. Have you found anything? We have a ghost upstairs who won't wait, and if you can't figure out why or how to get rid of it..."

Get rid of it. As soon as she uttered the words, an odd rumbling reverberated through the house.

Pixie? Is she waking up?

She's not asleep, Sarah. Your spell has her immobilized, but she can hear everything we're saying.

Perfect.

"I found a chapter here," Matthew said casually, stroking his chin. "It mentions two rival spiritual groups that believed the Luminous Crystal rightfully belonged to them."

"Gang turf wars, lovely. I thought we had left the city."

"You're not far off. According to this, both the Ascended and the Collective thought the Luminous Crystal was theirs. The Lumarians supposedly stole it during a dispute or raid — details are unclear."

"Got it, gang wars. But if this crystal can bend reality to the holder's wishes, why didn't they just eliminate their enemies? I mean, wouldn't that undermine its supposed powers?"

Matthew regarded her over his glasses. "Ye of little faith," he teased. "Indeed, the Lumarians did just that and concealed the crystal. It hasn't been seen since."

"Fantastic," Sarah exclaimed, jumping to her feet and pacing the kitchen. "We can't see it, and neither can anyone else. Superb. But this isn't helping us. Pixie, how long until Amelia regains her powers?"

The moment she mentioned powers, an odd rumble passed through the house.

The time is coming. She's starting to stir.

What do I do then?

You negotiate.

Pixie sat before her, her mouth slightly ajar and tongue peeking out, a cheery grin on her face.

No pressure at all.

"Any thoughts, Matthew."

"Research isn't just a Google search, you know, Sarah?"

"I'm aware of that, but I need answers, sooner rather than later. I need to know how Amelia's history ties into the Luminus crystal, how and why she died, and why her father covered it up. Maybe then she'll be able to move on. Out of our house."

Sarah's cell phone rang just then, and she fished it from her jeans pocket. She intended to ignore the call until she noticed the caller ID displaying Michael. Changing his label from hubby to Michael had marked a gloomy day. Sarah touched her lip and answered the call.

"Michael, how's everything?" she chimed, forcing an overly cheerful tone that sounded fake even to her own ears. She expected Michael to catch on immediately, but he didn't need her tone of voice to know something was amiss.

"What's this I hear about you chasing ghosts in that ancient house you bought?"

Michael was loud enough that Matthew could hear him all the way across the table. Sarah mentally cursed and forced herself to chuckle. "Ghosts? Seriously, Michael, I don't know who's been whispering in your ear, but chasing ghosts is the last thing we are doing here. Whatever gave you that idea?"

She let that statement hang, allowing him to approach her, to con-front her with what he thought he knew. She no longer felt the need to apologize and explain herself. Another new set of emotions.

"Mrs. Jenkins called me to see if – I don't actually know why she called me, but she had this grand theory."

Naturally, that devious woman. Sarah was surprised by her visceral reaction and clenched her fist. Pixie had been right.

"I should've realized someone her age wouldn't grasp RPGs," she said lightly, making every effort available to hide her irritation. "I'm sorry if she got you worried." *No, I'm not. She pried, you pried, and both of you can just...*

"RPG what?" Michael inquired. "Look, if anything strange is happening around my kids..."

"Role-playing games," Sarah clarified calmly. "Just a typical board game where everyone takes on a role and acts it out. You know, like those murder mystery dinners we used to talk about."

The ones we never attended because you were too cheap and lazy, but anyway, thank you, Cory, for the term.

"Is that all?" Michael sounded skeptical. "If something is going on with my kids..."

"Of course, that's all it is. Do you genuinely believe that I, Sarah Anderson, would actually chase or hunt a ghost? Get real, Michael."

It pained her to say that, but she finally understood how he had seen her all these years. He viewed her as a naive, easily influenced blonde. She clenched her fist in her pocket.

Michael snorted. "You got that right. And by the way, I don't care if you choose to isolate yourself in that small town, but remember this, if I even catch a hint of trouble with my kids, I'll be at the courthouse and on your doorstep so swiftly your head will spin, and Cory and Emma will accompany me. Do we understand each other? Say that you do."

The children you never wanted, and willingly entrusted to my care in the divorce, she thought.

"I understand, Michael," Sarah muttered through gritted teeth, and Michael hung up without another word.

Sarah ended the call, sealed her lips, and only whispered the word she had meant to hurl at him.

"No wonder Mrs. Jenkins was here," she bitterly told Matthew. "She ran off to my ex-husband with the freshest story."

"Problems?"

"Yes, no, I don't know. But the sooner you give me some answers and help me get Amelia out of my house, the better. He's determined to take my children from me if he sees any issues here. Or anything he might consider an issue."

Sarah paced back and forth in the kitchen for a moment until Matthew reached for her arm.

"Alright, Sarah, take it easy. We'll figure it out. Whatever happens, I won't allow this to happen to you and your children."

Like you could, she thought, but took a deep, calming breath and nodded.

Just at that moment, Corey came thundering down the stairs, his slim, silver laptop in his right hand, waving it at them.

"Look at what I found about the Lumarians," he said to Matthew and her. "They passed this famous crystal around between regional group leaders, to prevent it from being stolen. Nobody ever knew where it was at any given time, except the individual leader tasked with keeping it for exactly twelve months. It was a genius system, but the crystal disappeared right here, in Rosewood Hollow."

"What are you talking about," Matthew jumped to his feet and reached for the laptop. "Where did you find this?"

"Google."

"Cory! You can't just google stuff like that."

"Why not? I'm writing a report on Lumarians and their beliefs for extra credit at school, remember?"

"Let me see."

Matthew put down the laptop and quickly scanned the article Cory had found.

"Never heard of this website before," he muttered. "I don't know if they are reputable or not."

"If they come up with a simple Google search, maybe that's doubtful."

"Mom, why do you have to turn everything into something bad? I spent an hour searching to find something about Lumarians and what was going on here."

"I know, I am sorry." Even though she knew he didn't like it, Sarah put her arm around Cory's shoulders and squeezed gently.

"Your dad just called. Maybe you should go speak to him. Mrs. Jenkins called him about our ghost issue, and he was not impressed. I told him it was just a game."

"You fibbed," Cory grinned.

"A little," Sarah smiled back and winked. "But don't take that to mean it's okay."

"And how does Mrs. Jenkins know about Amelia," Cory finally asked, helped himself to a couple of cookies, and opened the fridge, perusing the offerings there.

"Well, she..." Sarah thought for a moment and finally tapped Matthew on the shoulder. "Matthew? Cory is right. How does our neighbor know about what's going on here? Did you by any chance tell her?"

"No," Matthew cross-referenced something on Cory's computer and looked up, frowning. "Why would I? She's a bit of a busybody. Maybe she heard us talking while she was fussing in the yard."

That's not it.

Pixie followed Cory around, picking up the crumbs he dropped along the way.

She has an agenda, there's something very specific she wants.

"What?" Sarah asked, and neither Matthew nor Cory even blinked at her talking to seemingly no one. Pixie did not answer, and satisfied that Cory was done providing crumbs she jumped into the sash window that faced their neighbor's house and sat quietly at attention, not taking her eyes off the Jenkin's place.

"She wouldn't be involved, would she," Sarah said almost to herself.

"This is very good work Cory," Matthew said, running his finger down the laptop screen as he was scanning the contents of the page. "If you were my student, I'd give you an above-average." Cory glowed with pride at that. "This here is an excerpt from an old newspaper, naming some local residents who were picked up in a farmer's field, because some neighbor complained about a strange pagan ritual."

"And," Sarah asked and leaned over his shoulder.

"You're going to laugh at this one," Matthew chuckled. "The leader of the group told the local constable they were merely practicing for a theater play they were planning to perform."

He grinned at her then, a broad, warm grin that made something inside Sarah feel all warm and liquid. "Role-playing games."

"Tale as old as time." Sarah picked up her water again and took a generous sip. "So, what did you find out."

"Like I said, a list of names. This is from the turn of the century, so some of the family names are a little familiar, but nothing jumps out, except for one."

"Oh?"

"The leader of that group? The one who said they were practicing for a theater play? His name is listed as Jed T."

"Jedediah Thompson," Sarah breathed. "That confirms what I – heard. Meaning the man who built this house, who was most assuredly Amelia's father was the leader of this Lumarian group."

"It would tend to confirm that, even though I'm a little unclear where you hear' it." Matthew looked down at Pixie and wagged his head. "It is possible, no, I would say it's extremely likely. He and a woman who was only listed with her first name, no initial – Serena. They must have been—"

A rumble like thunder tore through the house again, making Sarah feel the ground under her feet vibrate.

"Serena," she said. "Where have I—"

Another thunder rumbled and Pixie shot out of the window to sit close by her foot.

"Pixie's first owner was called Selena," Sarah exclaimed. "Selena with an L. Could that be..."

"Selena, the so-called life coach?" Matthew shook his head and held a hand out to Pixie. "I knew her. She came to town a few years ago. Though, it's not that uncommon a first name."

Pixie jumped up on Sarah's leg again and again until Sarah finally picked her up and snuggled her against her shoulder. For once, the little papillon remained entirely silent.

"Don't you think it's an odd coincidence?"

"These people," Matthew pointed a finger at the screen. "These people lived around the turn of the century Sarah. Selena was a bit odd, yes, and her profession even more so, but she had nothing to do with them. Jed Thompson on the other hand means that your house might have been the center of the spiritual life and the common meeting place of Lumarians in this area."

"My house," Sarah said, pursing her lips. "The symbols upstairs in the attic, this book on the history of the group, the destroyed pages from Jed's journal, referring to Lumarians. I think we have ourselves a working theory. Question is, how is Amelia connected to them and how does her death feature into this story?"

"Maybe she was a member," Cory suggested. "If her dad was the boss?"

"Likely, possibly. The spiritualist movement was... was just about the only area where women could hold a position at the turn of the century. Let's find out."

Sarah could feel vibrations rumble through the house again and steadied herself against the kitchen table. Amelia, it seemed was not going to be out much longer.

Sarah straightened her shoulders, not only to convey confidence but also to bolster her own resolve.

"I'm going upstairs to confront our little ghost in the bedroom," she finally declared.

Pixie jingled with a rattle of her collar tags and moved to stand beside Sarah.

I am with you.

Sarah looked down into the little dog's dark eyes and pressed her lips together.

If anything were to happen to you...

I am with you.

"I'm coming with you," Matthew announced, standing beside her. Cory opened his mouth to volunteer, but both Sarah and Matthew raised their hands to stop him.

"Stay here, Cory, please. It's one thing for Matthew and me to confront this — thing," Sarah explained, "but your father is right. If I let something happen to you, I would never forgive myself."

She looked down at Pixie again, who managed an open-mouthed smile with her little pink tongue hanging out.

Sarah, I've handled other things that were scarier than Amelia. I'll be fine.

Other...things, Sarah thought and quickly pushed the thought away as a shiver crawled down her spine.

Pixie went ahead of them out of the kitchen and up the stairs as if her tiny paws barely touched the ground.

"Are you sure about this?" Matthew asked, squeezing her hand reassuringly. She felt the strength in his fingers and took comfort in the knowledge that he had her back.

"Yes," she nodded before turning to Cory once more. "If you hear anything alarming or if we're not back in half an hour, go to Mrs. Jenkins. I have a feeling she will know what to do."

Cory simply nodded. "Mom, you're a badass," he finally said, his face beaming with pride.

When they reached the top of the stairs, Pixie was already sitting by the closed door, her fluffy tail swishing and glowing with a strong, flickering gold light.

Sarah placed her hand on the doorknob, focused on releasing the lock she had placed upon the door, and opened it gently. Amelia still sat on Emma's bed, her arms folded in front of her, a scowl on her face.

"You took your sweet time. Another few moments, and I would have come down to you. This is my—"

"This is my house, Amelia," Sarah interrupted firmly, standing her ground. Amelia still appeared translucent, like a slightly out-of-focus photograph, with the furniture and Emma's books shimmering through her form.

"I can hear her," Matthew whispered in awe, and Amelia rolled her eyes.

"You are powerless."

Amelia's eyes glowed with an unholy fire and she focused on Matthew until he gripped his throat again. Without understanding why, Sarah raised her hands, crossed their palms over each other, and let herself channel the anger she felt toward Amelia. Instantly, the ghost glowed with a brief pink flash and emitted a piercing screech.

"This is just a little taste. I've told you before, Amelia – do not harm me or my loved ones," Sarah warned.

Amelia's ghost hissed, but she didn't retaliate.

"Cory is right," Matthew muttered, massaging his throat. "You're a real badass."

"You ain't seen nothing yet," Sarah responded confidently.

Taking a bold step towards Amelia, Sarah extended her open hands. "I don't seek conflict, Amelia. I only want to understand why you are here, in my house, in this ... form."

Amelia glowered and finally spoke, her desperation palpable and nearly visible at the edge of Sarah's vision.

"This was ... my father's house," she said, her voice tinged with raw and hollow emotion. "He was the revered leader of the Lumarians throughout the entire region, an honorable man whose reputation extended far and wide."

Sarah only nodded. Desperation rolled off Amelia's ghost in giant waves she could almost see at the edge of her vision. If she knew why she was here, she was not getting any closer to the solution to her problem.

"Were you a member as well?" she asked. Amelia shook her head, a subtle gesture that manifested as a flicker of her image.

"Only a few chosen women were permitted to join the order. I had intended to become one of them in due course."

"Like Serena," Matthew interjected softly, "the woman I read about."

Amelia seethed with indignation, her eyes darkly aglow as they bore into Matthew. He instinctively brought a hand to his throat, but this time, Amelia refrained from launching an attack.

"Serena claimed to be a renowned spiritual being when, in truth, she was nothing more than a common hedge-witch pursuing my father and his fortune," Amelia retorted with a touch of disdain.

"Hedge-witch," Sarah repeated, momentarily puzzled.

"Hedge witchery is a form of witchcraft," Matthew explained softly, placing his hand on her arm. "It's often associated with folk traditions and nature-based spirituality."

"Common potion lore," Amelia spat, causing Pixie to shiver in a shower of sparks.

"While it's true that many hedge witches focus on healing, herbalism, and natural remedies, they are no less powerful than other witches," Pixie declared, her voice clear and firm. "They simply value their independence and the freedom to explore the magical realms in their own unique ways."

"Oh, wow," Matthew said, clapping his hands over his mouth. "This time, I heard her clearly, I really heard her."

Sarah interrupted, raising her hand to stop them all.

"This isn't getting us anywhere. I want to know why you're here and if there's anything within our power to help you."

Amelia hissed in frustration, fixing a defiant glare upon Pixie before she dramatically threw her arms up, conjuring a shower of translucent sparks and shimmers.

"I met a young man at art class," she finally began, her shimmering form wavering slightly. Sarah sensed overwhelming sadness emanating from the ghost. "Simon, he was so talented and so dashing and sweet. We took lessons together and dreamt of a shared future. We were to be married, and he aspired to become a professor of art at the Royal College."

"Admirable," Sarah acknowledged, sensing that the story was about to take a tragic turn. "And?"

"And," Amelia snapped, "Simon constantly felt the need to prove himself to my father, so he became involved with a group of treasure hunters seeking a legendary artifact rumored to be hidden within this house."

"The crystal," Matthew and Sarah chimed in unison, and Amelia's figure became even more translucent and ethereal.

"Desperate to secure a prosperous future for both of us, Simon used my trust and knowledge of the house's secrets to aid the treasure hunters."

Thunder rumbled once more, and the house trembled beneath Sarah's feet. She clung to Matthew's shoulder and held Pixie close, but this time, Amelia wasn't attempting an attack. Her ghostly form had nearly become invisible, tattered fragments fluttering at the edges where she merged with reality.

"That's when I died," she said simply, and Sarah blinked in astonishment.

"What?" She took another step toward the ghost, but as if a battery were running out, the translucent image wavered, flickered, and then disappeared. "Amelia, what does that mean?" Sarah called out but received no answer. Somewhere in the distance, she could hear faint thunder and feel a rumble beneath her feet, but then the room lay in total silence.

"I – have – never," Matthew said after a moment, visibly searching for words, grappling with what he had just seen and heard. "I don't — Sarah?"

"The ghost of Amelia Thompson," Sarah said simply. "And before you ask me again what this is all about, remember I know exactly as much as you do."

"But I heard Pixie, clear as day."

"I know."

"And she – speaks? And you hear her like this, all the time?" Matthew had paled a little, trying to process all of this in his scientist's brain. "Sarah?"

"Usually just in my head, Matthew," Sarah sighed and scooped up Pixie.

"What is this all about then?"

I could make him hear me. But it does take a lot of energy.

"Can you explain to me just exactly how you know all about witches — and about Serena who lived a hundred years ago."

Sarah whispered into Pixie's ear, and Pixie planted a little lick on her cheek.

"Are you guys okay?" Just then, Cory gently knocked on the bedroom door and opened it just a crack.

"Fine, Cory, Amelia left."

Matthew chimed in, "Am I the only one who's having an issue with the fact that there is a ghost living in this house? And you know her and talk to her, and apparently," he swept his arm toward Sarah, "Apparently have some special mojo that makes her do your bidding."

"Not as easy as all that, let's go back down into the front room, it's more comfortable there." Sarah stared at the door and the ladder that led into the attic. "We probably have to go up there once more to check if there's anything more about Amelia and what happened to her other than those trunks you brought down."

"I'll go," Cory offered, and Sarah ruffled his hair.

"Later, maybe, and only if you go with Matthew."

Just as they got comfortable in the front room, Emma came back from Lily's, and Cory caught up his little sister on the latest, while Sarah went to fetch some lemonade and glasses. Time for dinner soon, but who in their right mind could set to preparing a meal right then?

"I'm ordering us some pizza," Matthew said, looking up from his phone, just as she came back into the room with a pitcher and glasses.

"Brilliant idea. Kids, can you let Matthew know what you'd like?"

She dropped heavily into one of the deep, thick-stuffed couches Cory liked to use for gaming and tied her hair into a braid down her back. Exhaustion was claiming her, heavy exhaustion and deep, deep overwhelm.

It takes a lot out of you, but I know you are strong. You can do this.

"The magic does?"

By now, no one even looked at her sideways when she had one-sided conversations with Pixie.

Of course. You need to learn to manage your magical energy so you won't burn out.

"I'd rather not, thank you very much."

Pixie snuggled up close beside her and put a tiny paw on her hand.

You didn't ask for this, but you have more strength inside you than you know.

"Are you all right, Mom?" Cory dropped into the deep cushions beside her and handed her a glass of lemonade. "Matthew told me how you fought the ghost upstairs."

"Fighting was not my first choice. It never is. But this time I needed her to stop coming at me, us, and to tell me what was the issue."

Matthew was using Cory's laptop to access some documents back at the historical society.

"Looks like there was indeed an announcement of intending nuptials between Amelia Thompson and a young man by the name of Simon Miller," he said, scrolling quickly. "Simon's occupation is listed as a student here, and he was a little younger than Amelia, so I can see why her father was not too thrilled about it."

Emma snuggled in on her other side, squishing Pixie, and Sarah put her arms around her children.

"Do you know how to help Amelia?" Emma asked softly, and Sarah gave her shoulder a little squeeze.

"Not yet, sweetie. I am not entirely sure what exactly happened to her."

Matthew smiled at the sweet group on the couch and claimed a footstool nearby. "This is a little odd," he said, tilting Cory's laptop so they could all see while he read.

"I have a history chronicle up here, and what is recorded here is that Amelia Thompson left Rosewood Hollow in the spring of 1899 just before her wedding and never returned." He pushed his glasses up on his nose and continued reading. "While visiting family members abroad, Amelia Thompson contracted an illness and tragically never returned to her father's side. Her fiancé, Simon Miller, was not seen in Rosewood Hollow again."

"Well, that's just weird."

A knock on the door announced their pizza, and Matthew rose to get it. "One of the glass panes is out in your transom window," he said coming back with the boxes. "I think we have a guy at the historical society who can get that fixed."

"I spoke to him already," Sarah replied. "Never mind."

Sarah directed Cory to get plates and napkins and settled in with a huge piece of pizza. "What's weird," she said around a big mouthful, "is that Amelia would travel somewhere just before her wedding."

"How so?"

"Matthew, you're a guy, obviously." Sarah giggled. "Just before a wedding — especially a big society wedding as I imagine hers would have been, given the status of Jed – there are a million things to do. If her mother passed away in her childhood ..."

"She did," Matthew confirmed. "Amelia was just a wee thing then."

"Then Amelia had to do all of this planning on her own, maybe with a girlfriend or two. You do not plan a large holiday at that point. Traveling would have been a massive undertaking in 1899 – and abroad? Why not just wait until after you're married, introduce your new husband to family, and make it your honeymoon while you're at it? Makes no sense."

"I don't know." Matthew ate more pizza and scrolled through the document, back and forth. "That's ... women's logic."

Sarah laughed again at his confusion and held out her hand for another slice of pizza.

"And this mysterious illness. Does it say what type of illness we are talking about?"

Matthew checked again and shook his head.

"And Amelia said, 'that's when I died,' not, 'that's when I took a trip, got sick and died.'"

"If there ever was a trip," Cory suggested. "Anybody could just say, 'Oh, that person went on a trip,' and they just never come back."

"You watch too much true crime," Sarah wanted to say but didn't because her son had a point.

"Amelia didn't give us a reason why she is still in this house and either can't or won't move on. Perhaps it has something to do with the circumstances of her death," Sarah mused and stared down at her food.

But Cory and Matthew had already moved on and were studying an old map they had found at the back of the book about Lumarians. Watching them work together, joking about an old-fashioned phrase, Sarah felt a warm glow in her heart. She realized that Cory, the angry young boy, had been craving male companionship. His father's departure had not marked the beginning but the end of their disconnection.

She glanced down at Emma, who was curled up tightly beside her, and noticed that the little girl had fallen asleep. Sarah looked at Matthew and placed a finger gently over her lips, nodding towards Emma.

"Out like a light, huh," Matthew whispered, and Sarah smiled.

"Seems that way. Ghosts have that effect sometimes." She gently touched Pixie's nose with her forefinger.

Do you have a sense of Amelia? Is it okay to let Emma sleep in my room?

Pixie raised her head, perking up her beautiful fringed ears.

All clear, Sarah.

All clear. Sarah set down the remainder of her pizza and scooped little Emma into her arms. "I'll take her upstairs. You two try not to dwell on that stuff too long," she said, nodding at the old book. "I think we've all had enough for the day."

When she returned downstairs, Matthew and Cory were sharing a soda and discussing the mysterious Lumarians in hushed voices.

"Cory, I think it might be a good idea for you to turn in soon too," she suggested. "We've been through a lot today."

"But Mom ..."

"No, your mother is right," Matthew said gently, giving the boy's shoulder a reassuring squeeze. "We'll start early tomorrow. Go upstairs, check the old trunks and all of the documents in there. You'll want to be fresh for that."

Cory made a face. The usual arguments about not going to bed yet were on the tip of his tongue, but a gentle tap on his shoulder from Matthew made him relent. "This isn't going anywhere. Go on up."

Finally, it was just Matthew and Sarah left in the games room. Suddenly, Sarah felt tongue-tied and embarrassed as they cleared the plates and stored the remaining pizza. *What's wrong with you?* she scolded herself silently. *Why can't you find something intelligent and meaningful to say?*

Or even raise your eyes? He's rather good-looking, Sarah.

Get out of my head, Pixie. The little dog shook, making her collar tags tinkle, and gave Sarah an affectionate, tongue-lolling smile.

Suddenly, she felt Matthew's hand on her arm. "Is everything okay, Sarah? You seem tense."

"It's all good, no worries. Are those all the plates?"

"Hey," Matthew set down whatever he was holding and pulled her into a gentle, caring hug. "I can see you're troubled. Are you worried about Amelia? About the kids?"

"Some," she admitted, extricating herself from his embrace. Too much, too intense, too soon, all of her senses screamed. Too much going on in my life. She blew out a deep breath and spread her hands.

"If you're worried, I can stay over tonight. No pressure. I'll camp out in the games room, but if Amelia tries anything, I'll be here."

Sarah clenched her fist in her pocket, torn for a moment. It would be nice to have someone here, but her experiences with Michael were still too recent and raw.

"It's fine," Matthew said, picking up the old book. Disappointment and a hint of sadness showed in his eyes, even though he tried to smile. "I can tell you're uncomfortable. I'll be back tomorrow."

"No, wait, wait." She forced a smile and shook out her arms in an attempt to dispel the tension. "It's fine. I think it would be ... nice to have someone else in the house, just in case."

"Not that you need it, you badass," Matthew said nudging her gently, and the smile returned to his face and his eyes.

Chapter 16

Sarah woke with a start the next morning, uncertain about what was happening. Summer was winding down soon, and before she knew it, she would have to prepare Cory and Emma for school. And she had a ghost in her house. And she had no idea how to deal with it or how to help said ghost to move on.

Sarah sat up in her bed and glanced over at Emma, who was still peacefully asleep on the cot.

Matthew, with Cory's sleeping bag and an extra pillow from her own bed, was camped out down in the games room. Why did that thought suddenly make her heart race?

Quietly, so as not to disturb Emma, she sneaked into her bathroom to get ready and then tiptoed down the stairs into the kitchen.

There, she found a fresh pot of coffee brewing and a mound of pastries on the counter.

"Early riser, I see," she said with a smile. "And, oh look, you've been to the bakery already. That's what my mother would call a keeper." She bit her tongue and made a face, wishing she could take back that last sentence. She had meant it to be flippant and light, but it had come out all wrong. "Err ..."

Matthew looked up at her from beneath impossibly long lashes for a moment and finally smiled.

"And she'd probably be right," he said lightly. "No sightings of Amelia last night?"

"None."

"Listen, if I made you feel uncomfortable offering to stay over, I just ..."

"Not at all, Matthew. Don't worry about it." *Liar.* "I was just surprised." *And cheated on for years and left and discarded, and a man in the house is a little disconcerting.* "I don't deal with ghosts every day," she finished with a weak grin.

"About that ..."

"What about that?" she asked as she poured herself a cup of coffee.

Matthew thought for a long moment, his chin resting in his hand. "I know you did some sort of voodoo thing with Amelia yesterday to push her back. I just ... I worry if it's safe for you and the kids to stay here."

The dog flap clicked softly, and Pixie strolled into the kitchen, smiling and as pleased as if she owned the place.

"Hey, little one," Sarah said, moving to fill Pixie's bowl. "To answer your question, Matthew, I'm not entirely sure. Thus far, Amelia has mostly been angry. I can't explain how I know this, but I believe that if we can find a way to help her, she'll find peace and move on. As long as this remains the case, I'd rather not uproot Cory and Emma again. Besides, we have Pixie."

"That dog ..." Matthew watched the little Papillon enjoy her breakfast. "I've certainly never seen anything like it."

"None of us has."

"I feel like I should—"

"You don't need to protect us, Matthew," Sarah interrupted, feeling at that moment that it was the complete truth, perhaps for the first time in her life. "I've got this – we've got this. But this Lumarian mystery, now that's something I want to solve."

Solve it with you perhaps, she added in her mind and softened the words with a bright smile. That ended the discussion for her, and they moved on to other plans for the day.

Before long, Cory came bouncing down the stairs and into the kitchen with the Maglite and a small explorer tool kit his father had given him a while ago.

"I'm ready," Cory said, beaming at Matthew and counting off his tools. "Flashlight, knives, screwdriver, camera, specimen kit."

"Specimen kit," Sarah interrupted.

"You know, for bugs and sh— stuff."

"I am absolutely sure we will not be finding any bugs in those old trunks we brought down," Matthew hurriedly said and winked at Sarah. "But you've got your hiking boots on, so I say let's go."

"Don't you want to have some breakfast first?"

"Mom, I'm not a kid anymore."

"But you'll always be my kid, Cory."

Matthew put a hand on her arm. "We're just going upstairs to explore some old trunks, and he is positively sparkling with excitement. I'll keep an eye on him."

"Do that," Sarah said, looking after Cory, who was already bounding up the stairs.

"And be careful," she called after them, even as Matthew went after Cory almost as quickly.

She had picked at the pastries Matthew had brought and made another cup of coffee when Emma came down the stairs, sleepy and still wearing her pajamas.

"Where are Cory and Matthew?"

"Upstairs, checking out the old trunks."

"Ahh ..." Emma's lower lip quivered. She had been looking forward to going with the boys. Quickly, Sarah held out a croissant to the little girl.

"We girls will have our own exploration, you, me, and Pixie. We won't bother with old trunks, we'll take the garden and the rest of the house. Who knows, maybe we'll find something way better than they do."

Emma wasn't quite happy yet. She took the croissant and looked out into the garden, where a couple of blue jays fought over a tasty morsel.

"Is Mrs. Jenkins going to come exploring with us too?" Emma asked, and Sarah, washing dishes at the sink, shrugged.

"Maybe. If you want to ask her, you can run over to her house in a little while."

"I don't have to, she's out in the yard, exploring already."

Out there already. At this early hour. Sarah wiped her hands and came to the window to peek out into the yard. Sure enough, out in the far corner of the garden where the old well was, her elderly neighbor walked bent over, moving her hands through the tall flowers and grasses as if she were searching for something.

"That's odd," she muttered and felt more than saw Pixie jumping up on a chair beside her to peek outside.

"She's looking for something. But what?"

"Did Mrs. Jenkins lose something by the well?"

"I don't know, honey. I think I'll go out there and ask her."

"I'll go, I'll go."

Forgotten was the half-eaten croissant as Emma jumped up and raced into the garden, still in her slippers and pink princess pajamas.

Sarah pushed the curtains all the way back and turned around, just in time to catch Pixie with the rest of Emma's croissant.

"You know you'll get fat if you keep doing that."

Is it my fault the kids keep leaving food around?

"No more breakfast for you, then." Sarah waved an empty stainless-steel bowl.

Fine.

"What is Mrs. Jenkins looking for, you think?"

Pixie licked her muzzle clean of crumbs and put her little paws onto the windowsill.

I wish I knew, but she has an agenda. There is something she feels is hidden here, and she wants it.

"That triple darned crystal everybody was looking for way back when?"

It's the one thing I know everyone was looking for.

Pixie's ears stood straight up and turned like little radar dishes in the direction where Emma hugged her old neighbor and adopted grandma.

A moment later, Emma came bounding back into the kitchen, looking around, searching for her pastry.

"Mrs. J said I should go wash my face and get dressed properly, and then I can come and help her search."

"Did she say what she was searching for?" Sarah asked, giving Emma another croissant and gracing Pixie with a stern look.

"Pretty colorful bird's eggs, and there might be some shiny white ones too," Emma called over her shoulder and thundered up the stairs as well. "We need to find them before the fox does."

"Colorful birds' eggs, and a few shiny white ones, I'll be damned," Sarah said to herself and peeked out the window again. Mrs. Jenkins was still searching around the old well, though now she looked over her shoulder every few minutes and tried to keep out of sight of the kitchen window.

"Can you keep an eye on her, Pixie?"

Pixie winked and hopped out through the doggie door. She disappeared into the tall bushes, and only now and then could Sarah see her stalking Mrs. Jenkins through the overgrown flowers.

If she hadn't been threatened and almost choked by a ghost living in her house, it could have been any ordinary, peaceful Saturday morning. The kids were off on exciting exploring adventures, a good-looking, charming history professor enjoyed coming around her house and the kids were truly excited about things for the first time in years. Almost perfect – and then there was her ghost.

Sarah sat down and dialed Lily's number to catch up her friend on all of the latest.

"Emma said Amelia came back," Lily said by way of answering the phone. "And you didn't tell me about any of it? Are you all right?"

"I've had my hands a little full, Lily. And Matthew was here to help me. He even stayed overnight."

For the first time in as long as she had known Lily, the red-headed bookstore owner had no words. Sarah heard a sputtering noise on the line and laughed softly.

"Not like you think, just in the games room, in case something happened."

"I am coming over there right now, and you better tell me everything, you hear? Everything."

"But—"

Sarah wanted to argue, but Lily had already hung up the phone, and she sighed. It was going to be one of those days. Her mother would have advised her to, 'water down the soup, put more chairs around the table, and welcome everyone.'

Pixie slipped back in through the doggie door and circled Sarah's legs.

Emma is with Mrs. J now. We'll see what they find.

"Right. But you – you, my sweet angel dog, were going to tell me how you know so much about witches and what the deal is with Serena, your previous owner Selena, and you. Where is the connection?"

Pixie sat and regarded her with deep brown eyes.

"Well?"

Familiars come in many variations, Sarah.

Sarah sat hard in one of the kitchen chairs, suddenly dizzy. In her ears, she heard a mighty roar, as if she were standing next to a huge waterfall.

"Pixie," she asked softly. "Just how old are you?"

Paperwork from the pound says about five. You do remember that, right?

With that, Pixie strolled off, leaving Sarah sitting in her bright, homey kitchen, her mouth hanging open, a hand half raised as if she were trying to grasp something, and a dark shiver taking hold of her.

Mechanically, she put away the breakfast dishes and stood by the kitchen window, watching Mrs. Jenkins look for bright birds' eggs with Emma, under the watchful eye of Pixie. At some point, Mort Jenkins, carrying a heavy tool bucket, strolled through the yard in the direction of the old well and waved at her as she stood by the window.

"The whole neighborhood is going to come by and pitch tents in my backyard," she muttered, but really she didn't mind. These people cared, and she'd never had more welcoming neighbors.

It took only moments for Lily's orange VW to come to a halt in her driveway, and Lily exited, pushing huge sunglasses into her red hair and toting a large bakery bag.

"Seems like everybody is trying their utmost to feed me sugar," Sarah said, pointing at the bag.

"Desperate times call for high amounts of sugar," Lily said lightly, easy for her to say with her perfect, lithe figure.

"Don't you have a bookstore to run?"

"I left my assistant in charge. Now, spill."

Sarah tore a chocolate croissant in half and, between bites, told the story of Amelia and Simon and Jed Thompson's distrust of the young man.

"Hmm," Lily said, picking at her own pastry. "That's not that un-usual. I assume in those days that was quite common — a father wanti-ng something better for his daughter, especially if he was successful and wealthy."

"You're missing the point, Lily. He was the leader of the Lumarians."

"That is indeed a wild assumption," Lily stepped up to the window and looked outside. "Do you know that Mrs. J is poking around your yard out there?"

"Something about birds' eggs," Sarah said, not really paying atten-tion. "But it keeps Emma occupied for now. Though Pixie thinks Mrs. J has an agenda."

"Pixie thinks?" Lily dropped the edge of the curtain she'd been hold-ing and turned to face Sarah. "Look, if this is all getting a bit much for you, feel free to ask. You all can bunk at my house for a few days, I have the room."

"What do you mean too much?" Sarah suddenly felt anger bubbling up inside her. "Have you been talking to Michael? And Mrs. Jenkins? Does the entire world all of a sudden feel that Sarah Anderson cannot live on her own after twenty years of marriage, and naturally we have to protect her and show her what to do? Poor thing she's helpless. Let me tell you—"

"Sarah, stop, stop." Lily raised her hands. "Nothing like that. I think you are very capable, and the way you faced down that ghost — woof," Lily rolled her eyes. "I couldn't have. I'm just saying, you have a lot on your plate right now. If you need a time out, I'm here, okay."

"Sorry." Mechanically, Sarah began to tidy the kitchen again, putting the pastries into another basket for when Matthew and Cory took a break, opened the fridge to check on things, and closed it again.

"Michael called last night," she finally admitted. "And he did not think I was capable or 'badass' as Cory likes to call it. Matter of fact, he let me know that if he heard anything worrisome at all, he'd be at my front door packing those children into his car so fast I wouldn't have time to say my own name."

Lily muttered something that sounded suspiciously like dumbass and said no more.

"I don't blame him. I just know he's not kidding. Besides, after Amelia dropped that bombshell about dying in this house, she just sort of ... faded. And I have no idea if she'll come back, or if that was it, or if I need to do something about it."

"So, we have a mystery," Lily said. "Amelia died in this house, and her father, who, by the way, was the leader of an oddball cult, covered it up by saying she died abroad. And her fiancé Simon was never seen in town again? That just about cover it?"

"Just about," Sarah said and poured more coffee, maybe her fifth or sixth cup today. Perhaps she should quit, she thought, but if she did, she'd be eyeing the bottle of prosecco in the fridge, and it was decidedly too early for that. "Matthew and Cory are upstairs right now, digging through more of the old materials in those trunks to see if they can find anything else about this mystery. If they don't ..."

"If they don't," Lily asked. "Then what?"

"Tell you the truth, I don't know. Then we wait for Amelia to come back, which I don't relish."

"Do you think Matthew is right," Lily finally asked. "And this Luminus crystal is hidden somewhere in this house?"

"Could be. And that was actually Pixie's theory."

Lily got to her feet and enveloped Sarah in a massive hug, a cloud of colorful Indian fabrics, and some spicy, exotic perfume. She laughed softly, and the golden bangles on her arms tinkled.

"Oh, Sarah, I bet only a few months ago when you were a prim and proper housewife grappling with the idea of having been left for a younger woman, you would never have thought of chasing a ghost and talking to your own dog and solving an almost hundred-year-old mystery."

"Err, no. You got that in one."

Outside, someone honked a few times, quite impatiently. Lily went to the window again and Sarah abandoned her coffee cup to join her.

"Err, that Michael of yours," Lily said softly.

"He's someone else's problem now, what of him?"

"Does he drive an incredibly large Mercedes SUV and have a wife that looks like a black-haired Barbie on steroids?"

"Dear God," Sarah crowded in to look out the window, but there he was.

Michael had pulled up behind Lily's little VW and stepped out of his car, eyeing the little convertible with a large dose of suspicion. He wore his customary uniform of a bespoke Italian suit that exuded sophistication, paired with handmade loafers. His meticulously styled hair appeared as if not a single strand dared to be out of place, and his skin bore the permanent sun-kissed glow of someone who had just disembarked from a jet arriving straight from the heart of Italy. Private, of course.

The young woman in the passenger seat had actually waited for him to come around to her side, open the door, and give her a hand.

"Good God, just get out of the car already," Lily muttered, only to regret it. "Get a load of those heels, no wonder she has to hold on to him."

Mrs. Jenkins had stopped working in the garden and stared open-mouthed. Emma, on the other hand, came bounding up to the man.

"Daddy!"

"Meet Michael Reynolds," Sarah said softly. "And whatever his newest conquest's name is."

"Barbie," Lily said again and angled behind her for another croissant.

"I better welcome them." Sarah turned away from the window and made her way to the front door, knowing that this visit could not mean anything good. As she turned, though, she saw that Emma's little gardening hands had left little mud smudges on Michael's suit, which he desperately tried to brush off now, succeeding only in making a bigger mess. It might be catty, but the sight gave her a reason to smile.

Sarah paused behind the door for a moment, gathered her strength inside, and let out a massive breath as she put her hand on the door handle.

You've got this, lady.

Down by her feet, Pixie had appeared as if out of nowhere and stood close.

Thanks.

She forced a smile and opened the big front door with a mighty swing.

"Michael. How nice to see you. Welcome to Rosewood Hollow. And …?"

"You have my daughter digging in the dirt with an old woman now," Michael asked and swept into the big entrance hall. "Where is Cory? And why is there a hole in this window?"

"Hello to you too." The smile faded from her face, and Sarah pointed toward the kitchen. "Cory is working upstairs with his – history teacher. I'll get him. And …?"

Still, Michael had not introduced his friend.

"History, why on earth is he wasting his time working on history," he snapped instead. "There's no future in it. I told you to steer him towards programming languages or robotics, that's where the jobs are. Jesus, Sarah."

An old reflex made her want to duck away from the conversation, say yes of course, and go do as he had asked, but suddenly there was something else. Pixie stood close, just out of range of Michael's huge loafer-shod feet, and the tip of her tail began to sparkle a little. Michael quite suddenly dropped the keys to the SUV and grabbed his left wrist, where a huge gold watch proclaimed his net worth for all to see.

"Shit."

"Touch of arthritis," Sarah asked ironically and bent down for the keys. "Happens at our age."

"Don't be ridiculous, Sarah."

"Dad!" Now Cory appeared at the top of the stairs, closely followed by Matthew. The hard, angry look that passed between Michael and Matthew was not lost on Sarah.

"Cory, I just wanted to see how you are settling in, son. I am not sure why your mother is making you study history."

"Hey," Unlike Emma, Cory only offered a hand to his father. "You should hear about the history of this house, Dad. It was built by this great leader—"

"Yeah, yeah, yeah, I'm sure. Here," he reached out his hand, and his female companion handed him a plastic bag that bore the logo of a large software manufacturer. "I have some of the latest simulation software for you to play with. If you have any questions, Katelyn here is an ace gamer, she can give you a lot of hints."

"Thanks."

Cory took the bag and looked into it briefly. Sarah's heart went out to her son, but at the same time, Michael had already turned on Matthew.

"And who are you? Not to be rude, but if you're spending time with my son, I think I have a right to know."

The emphasis on, my, could not have been clearer.

"Certainly," Matthew said, smiling and offering a hand. "Dr. Matthew Turner, president of the local historical society."

Sarah blinked for a moment. Matthew had never used his full professional title with her, he'd always been, just Matt, but Michael had to blink once or twice. He massaged his wrist again, and Sarah gently nudged Pixie down by her foot.

"History, huh," Michael said and clamped his hand around his wrist. "Guess while you're busy studying the past, people like Cory and I will be out there shaping the future and making real money."

"Of course," Matthew wanted to say something else when Michael rounded on all of them.

"Now then, what's this I hear about this house having ghosts? Anybody want to clue me in?"

Sarah tensed and held her breath. Behind her, she could hear the soft tinkling of Lily's bangles, as her friend had come out of the kitchen to stand with her. Matthew gave her a questioning look, and Sarah had just opened her mouth when Cory laughed out loud.

"Ghosts? Dad, you don't really believe in ghosts, do you? That's just silly. Everybody knows they don't exist."

"But your neighbor ..." Michael pointed over his shoulder at the front door and again into the round. His face turned scarlet and he looked more confused than ever. "She called me and said—"

"Dad," Cory lifted the bag with the computer games a little and rolled his eyes. "The Elder Scrolls? Skyrim? Ever heard of the game?"

"Oh, that one is super cool," Katelyn piped up and grinned broadly at Cory. "When you're on your quest and you encounter the ghost, and then you have to battle it an—"

Michael raised his hand like a cop stopping traffic coming at him, and Katelyn stopped, pressed her lips together, and looked down at her feet. Had she herself been like that, Sarah wondered.

"Then this is really just a game?"

"Yeah, it's a game, Dad. You ought to try it someday. What did you think it was?"

"But then why did your neighbor ...?"

"Because she's old, Dad, she doesn't get simulations or AI." Again, Cory rolled his eyes, and Sarah could have hugged her wonderful, amazing oldest.

Just then, far-off thunder rolled, and Sarah could feel the vibrations through the floor into her feet.

Not now, she thought desperately and sent a heartfelt plea for help in her mind. If Amelia showed up while Michael was standing in her front hall, she would never have time for another word, and most certainly, her kids would leave with him.

Please not now.

Pixie suddenly shook and tore up the stairs in a flash of white and sparkling gold, and she could see Michael blinking, wondering if he had seen what he thought he had seen.

"Why don't we all sit in the kitchen and have some coffee," Lily suggested. "We sure have enough pastries to feed this entire army, and if you traveled all the way from Baltimore, you must be tired."

"Oh yes," Katelyn took a step toward the kitchen, only to have Michael hold her shoulder.

"I'm sure refined sugars and wheat flour are not what you need right now. Sounds like there's some weather coming in. We're going into town to find a room. We'll stay for a few days." He looked from one to the next and narrowed his eyes. "I don't know what's going on around here, Sarah, but I will find out. And when I do ..." He shook his head. "You will not like it, trust me on that. Cory – call me later, I'd like to spend the evening with you."

"Sure," Cory said without much conviction, but neither Michael nor Katelyn heard him, they were halfway down the driveway toward the SUV already. Not a minute later, Emma came in through the kitchen, with a large bunch of flowers she had picked for her father, and when she saw the departing taillights, her eyes filled with unshed tears.

"Oh, these are beautiful," Lily said quickly and took the bunch out of the child's arms. "You have such a great eye for flowers. Come on, let's go find a vase for them."

Sarah pursed her lips and let out a massive breath she'd been holding ever since she'd discovered Michael on her doorstep.

"You all right?" Matthew took her elbow. "Is he always like that?"

"Thank you, Cory," Sarah said, ashamed that her voice trembled just a little. "I don't usually support lying, but in this case …"

"He wouldn't have listened to me if I had told him about Amelia and Jed Thompson," Cory said bitterly. "All he cares about are profits and balance sheets."

"I'm sure it is not—"

"Yeah, it is, Mom. I'm sixteen, not six. I know that's not the girl he left you for, who was supposed to be the love of his life, and I know he wants me to become some programmer or something."

Matthew put his hand on Cory's arm and shook his head. "It's okay, Cory."

"He barely said hi to Emma, and if he thinks I'm going to go back to Baltimore with him and do what he says, he's got another think coming."

"We won't let it get that far," Sarah finally found the strength inside herself again and wiped her hands over her face. "Not while I'm here. Now come, sit in the kitchen with Lily and me, and take a break."

❦

They sat and poked at their lunch mostly in silence. Lily tried to make a joke now and then, but the joyous explorer atmosphere from that morning was gone. Eventually, Emma went upstairs to take a nap in Sarah's room, Lily went to make a few phone calls, and Matthew and Sarah sat on the porch swing with yet another coffee.

Cory sat with his back against the house wall, staring down at his phone with the concentration of one who needs to solve all of life's mysteries all at once. Sarah and Matthew exchanged a look, and he shook his head just the tiniest bit. He hadn't been able to get through to him either.

"Cory, I want you to know," she started, "that whatever's going on …"

"Yeah, yeah. You support my decisions, and you have my back as long as I'm staying safe, Mom. I know it, I heard it about a dozen times."

"And I am grateful I'm getting through to you and you hear what I'm saying. Here's the thing. I can't force you to go to dinner with your father and … Katelyn, is it? But perhaps it wouldn't be a bad idea if you maintain regular contact with him."

"Hmmm."

Cory's thumbs flew over the glass in a way Sarah had always admired when she was having trouble picking out a single word letter by letter.

"And if it makes you feel better to tell him about Amelia and Jed and the mysteries of this house, go ahead."

"As if," Cory rolled his eyes. "You don't actually believe him when he says he would pack us into the car and take us to Baltimore, do you? To live at his house?"

"Why not?" Sarah cocked her head. "It's what he said."

"Sometimes adults can be so naïve. No, he'd pack Emma and me off to some private school with a great name and a fantastic pedigree, and that would be that for him. He's floated the idea before, and I told him to go and … I told him I was not keen on the idea, okay."

"Thanks for telling me." Sarah abandoned the porch swing and sat on the ground with her back against the house, beside her son. "I didn't know."

"Now you do." Cory still failed to meet her eyes.

"But I'm not convinced that Rosewood Hollow and this house are the safest place for Emma and you until I figure out what is actually happening."

Now his head flew up, and his clear blue eyes bored into hers. That one long strand of hair at the front she always wanted to cut, but he insisted was part of a fashionable cut, fell into his face, and he brushed it back impatiently.

"What, now you're going to send us away too? Great. Make us orphans while we're at it."

Cory turned away from her abruptly and rolled his shoulder just an inch away from her, to create more empty space between them.

"No, Cory, that's not what I mean at all." She tried to touch his arm, but he jerked away from her touch. "I'm trying to keep you safe."

"Then help Amelia first," Cory snapped. "Figure out what happened. She never hurt any of us – not Emma and me, anyway. She just tried to get your attention."

"Well, that worked."

"We're the ones moving into her house and moving her stuff around."

"Amelia has been dead for over a hundred years ago, you know that, right?"

"Yeah, and apparently she died right here in this house, and her deadbeat father was so afraid his precious reputation would suffer he hid the body somewhere and told everybody she'd gone abroad. Sometimes, parents can be real shits, if you really think about it."

Sarah looked down at her hands and said nothing for a long moment while Cory's fingers continued to fly over his phone screen. Giving him a lecture about swearing would accomplish nothing just then.

"So, we keep our guard up and try to figure out what happened," she finally said. "Maybe that will help. I hear you're good at research?"

She tried to smile at her son, but his eyes were hidden behind the curtain of the strand of hair again, and he lifted his phone and let it drop into his lap.

"What do you think I'm doing, checking the basketball scores? That too, but Matthew got me into this site that has newspapers from like hundreds of years ago from everywhere."

"Did he now? Great. But isn't that a paid service?"

"I used Dad's credit card. He said it was fine for education and stuff."

This time he hid a bit of a grin and Sarah shook her head.

"There are about seven things here that I ought to reprimand you for, but I also know you're well aware of what they are, a lecture won't do any good."

"Nope."

"And, way to go, Cory," she elbowed him gently into the side. "Maybe ask me next time, though?"

"Sure."

"Did you find anything?" Matthew joined them now on the ground on Cory's other side. "Didn't I tell you that newspaper site was like a rabbit hole? You can get lost in there for hours."

"Not specifically," Cory brushed the hair out of his face and thumb-scrolled through a few articles. "I found stuff here on when this house was built, and a story that Amelia's mom died when she was born," his face fell a little when he mentioned that. "But you know what I'm not finding? Nobody is mentioning anything about these Lumarians? Don't you think that's strange?"

Cory looked at Matthew with open admiration and curiosity.

"Not necessarily, Cory, when you consider that Lumarians were basically a secret society. Think of Masons, for example. They were a group that valued their privacy and guarded their knowledge. That automatically led to a fair amount of secrecy. So, to answer your question, no, I don't think it's particularly strange."

Sarah got to her feet and went to find Lily. No wonder Matthew and Cory could spend hours together poring over old documents. Cory looked up to him, and Matthew had a way of treating him like a responsible adult that opened Cory's defenses.

She met Lily at the far end of the garden, admiring the profusion of flowers and flowering shrubs in her garden.

"God, this garden is beautiful."

"It's one of the things that drew me to the house."

"I thought you said Michael was pretty good about custody arrangements in the divorce."

"He was," Sarah shrugged. "Originally, all he wanted was to get out of the marriage and move on," Sarah raised her hands, palms up. "That was two girlfriends ago. Maybe he's become bitter and angry because he hasn't found what he was looking for."

"Boo-hoo, sucks to be him." Lily, knuckled the corner of her eye, raised an eyebrow, and smirked toward the porch and Matthew and Cory. "Somebody has, though, wouldn't you say?"

Sarah looked and felt her heart flooding with warmth seeing the two of them side by side, heads bent over Cory's phone, engrossed in serious discussion.

"Yeah," she said and let herself feel the fullness of that moment for a long time before continuing. "I'm worried, though. I don't know how to handle this whole, 'I have a ghost in the house,' thing. If I'm doing the right thing, if I'm endangering the kids."

"Amelia is a ghost, not a demon," Lily said and plucked a long, ornamental grass. "Ghosts usually want something. That's why they can't move on and hang around this plane. Demons only want to mess shit up and hurt people."

"And you know this how," Sarah asked and plucked her own bit of ornamental grass, letting her restless fingers weave it around and around.

"Told you," Lily shrugged. "I was friends with Selena."

"Right, the woman Mort Jenkins called a witch, and who owned Pixie previously. Just what exactly happened to her, and what is the deal with this other woman, Serena, who, apparently, was a Lumarian way back when."

"Whoa there," Lily tossed aside the piece of grass and firmly gripped Sarah's shoulder. "Just because Selena was into Tarot cards, meditation, and manifestations doesn't mean she was up to anything questionable. People like Mort and his ilk can be so damned—"

Lily suddenly clamped her mouth shut, her lips forming a tight line, and clenched her right hand into a fist, shaking it impatiently.

"Yes?" Sarah prompted.

"Nothing. Absolutely nothing," Lily snapped. "I simply can't tolerate close-minded, self-righteous individuals who believe they have all the answers and can easily pigeonhole people at their whims."

Sarah only nodded and let her hands trail over the glorious red blooms of an ornamental shrub.

"Anyway," Lily continued, "Selena had a car about twice as old as mine. Loved the thing. She was driving on the highway one day when a guy in a snazzy new sports car came up behind her too fast, I guess, and must have frightened her. Accident reconstruction said she lost control and shot off the side of the highway, straight into a tree."

"Oh, Lily ..." Sarah hugged her friend.

"Yeah, well, the jerk in the sports car just kept on driving. He might not even have noticed what happened. The only thing that was unharmed was the crate Pixie was traveling in."

"Pixie was there," Sarah said, horrified, and felt a huge pit open up in her stomach when she thought of her tiny, sweet little dog in that situation.

"People say she was probably traumatized. For weeks she wouldn't let anybody come near her. The pound was worrying they might have to ... you know," Lily drew a hand across her throat. "Then one day out of the blue, Mrs. Jenkins walks in and says she's looking for a dog for the new residents of Thompson House, something small and happy for the kids, and you know what? Pixie suddenly was the sweetest, happiest dog you could ever want. Sheer delight. Nobody could explain it."

"Poor thing," Sarah said softly, resolving to ask Pixie about it later.

"And if you need any more reason to dislike bigots, my friend at the pound tells me Mrs. J wanted a guarantee that Pixie would stay like that."

Sarah put a hand on her friend's and shook her head softly.

"Don't worry about that right now."

"I guess I can get a little hot-headed now and then," Lily grinned and shrugged. "For a little town that's supposed to be all safe and homey, we sure do have a lot of drama in Rosewood Hollow, don't we?"

Sarah opened her mouth to answer when the window to her second-floor bedroom opened, and Emma stuck her head out.

"Mom, Aunt Lily, come quick. Hurry, I found something. Come quick."

Now what? "We're on our way, honey."

Sarah took the steps up to the porch two at a time, with Lily not far behind her. Even Matthew and Cory looked up from their intense research and eventually decided to follow.

Sarah's bedroom had been one of the larger rooms in the old house, offering a view of the garden. The walls were adorned with heavy, dark wood paneling and featured intricately carved cornices above each window. Not wanting to part with all of the original decor, Sarah had hired a contractor to repaint it in soothing shades of blue and white, creating her own personal oasis.

In the middle of the room, Emma proudly held a small leather-bound book aloft. The leather had acquired a soft cream hue, softened by frequent, loving handling, and the page edges glistened with gold. A tiny locket and key dangled from a delicate chain.

"Now what's all this?" Sarah asked, frowning up at one of the window cornices where a fair-sized hole had suddenly appeared.

"I didn't break it, Mom, I swear I didn't."

"Didn't say you had. I just want to know what happened and why up there."

Sarah peered closer at the cornice. It was indeed not broken, but the hole was rectangular with regular, smooth edges—just large enough to hide something inside. Something like... She looked back at Emma. A little book, maybe.

"I didn't break it, Mom, I promise. I found it."

Emma now sat on the bed, embracing the small book tightly. Her young brows furrowed, and her jaw set in that stubborn way that Sarah knew all too well.

"No, no, Emma, it's okay. Nobody is mad, what happened?"

Sarah sat beside her and put her arm around the little girl. Like a flash of white, Pixie streaked into the room, through the legs of the boys at the door, and up on the bed. She snuggled close to Emma and nuzzled her cheek.

"See, Pixie is coming to say hi too."

"I woke up, and I wanted to open the curtain to see the garden," Emma said, her voice trembling. "But then I saw the butterfly there," she pointed at the little carved butterflies and flowers at the ends of the cornices. "And I wanted to touch it, to see what it felt like."

Those cornices were at least seven feet off the ground. Sarah closed her eyes and shuddered for a moment. She looked around and realized what must have happened. Emma probably climbed onto the dresser to touch the little carving and lost her balance.

"I slipped," Emma muttered against her mother's chest. "And I wanted to hang on, but I fell. And when I looked, it had just kind of slid aside, and the book fell out."

"It's all right, most important thing is nothing happened to you," Sarah said softly, gently stroking Emma's hair and running her hands over her shoulders and arms, searching for any signs of bruises or scrapes.

Matthew remained in the doorway, clearly wrestling with the idea of entering Sarah's bedroom. Cory, however, had no such reservations. He stretched his lanky frame, reached up on tiptoes, and placed his fingers on the butterfly. With ease, a small access door slid back and forth.

"It's a hidden compartment," he exclaimed, his voice filled with awe. "Matthew, come take a look at this."

Matthew winced and looked at Sarah.

"I, um ..."

"It's okay," she reassured him, a smile on her face as she cradled Emma against her chest. "Go ahead and have a look."

"Come on, Emma," Lily stretched her arms toward Emma, gold bangles tinkling merrily. "Give Aunt Lily a hug and show me what you've got. You definitely found treasure."

"It's a diary," Emma said proudly, showing the little book to Lily. "My friend Katharina had the same one."

"It's not ..." Lily looked questioningly at Sarah, who shook her head.

"Not mine, folks. I'm not the diary kind of girl."

"It's also far too old to be one of yours," Matthew said, eagerly eyeing the little book in Emma's hands. "I'd have to examine it to be sure, but from here it looks to be about, oh, a hundred years old."

"A hun— You mean this could be ... Amelia's?"

As if to answer Sarah's question, somewhere in the house, a deep rumbling sound grew, and the floor beneath their feet shuddered slightly.

"I'd say there's your answer," Matthew said, still standing in the middle of the room, arms tucked close to his sides, looking about as comfortable as the proverbial bull in the China shop. Sarah grinned when she realized he hardly dared look left or right for fear of what he might discover in her bedroom.

Emma held the diary in her open hands as if it were a tray she was presenting. Suddenly, it did not seem so charming or lovely as it had a moment ago.

"Mom?"

"Mind if I take this?" Matthew asked, holding out his hand, and Emma drew back a little.

"Why don't we all go downstairs," Sarah said quickly. "I'll make some hot chocolate, and you can check it out then. It is Emma's treasure, after all."

Emma smiled again, jumped to her feet, and led the way downstairs, followed by a happily wagging Pixie.

"Amelia's diary might hold some answers, Mom," Cory protested, looking back up at the cornice. "I wonder why she hid it, and why up there."

"Your sister found it, so it's hers to share with you. That's just the way it is. I'm sure if you ask nicely, she'll let you and Matthew study it anytime you like."

He rolled his eyes, that big teen boy of hers, but he kept his mouth shut, only whispering with Matthew on the way down into the kitchen.

∽

Hours later, Emma had fallen asleep again in one of the large, comfortable chairs, countless cups of cocoa had been drunk, and even Sarah wiped tired, gritty eyes. Lily had to leave to attend to matters at her bookstore, and if she could have, Sarah would have curled up beside Emma.

"It's ... a girl's diary," Matthew said slowly, twisting his face just enough to give her an idea of what he thought of the concept. "I don't know ..." he leafed through the entries, scanning the dates. "Descriptions of church events, outings, cooking chores, her artwork, and how much she admires her teacher – Mr. Farnsworth."

"I assume that's what Amelia's life revolved around," Sarah said, shrugging, pushing an empty cup back and forth between her fingers. "Chores, art, sewing."

"Not your cup of tea," Matthew asked with a grin, and Cory snorted.

"We had a mother and son art night at school one night—" He closed his mouth and chuckled when Sarah glared at him.

"Trust me, I can't draw a stick figure either," Matthew said and flipped back a few more pages. "Then she meets Simon in the spring of 1899 — now it gets interesting."

"Should we be reading that?"

"No worries," Matthew pushed the diary toward her. "We are in 1899, it's all quite harmless and sweet."

Sarah felt a hot blush rise in her cheeks and quickly pretended to cough into her elbow. When exactly had she started blushing again?

Matthew took the diary back and turned the pages. Was it her imagination, or the light, or was there a little stain of red on his cheeks as well?

"Soo, there are pages and pages on how good-looking she thinks Simon is and how friendly and charming, and ... Maybe those thoughts should remain private."

A rumble somewhere within the house confirmed his suspicion.

"I thought so. Do you think Amelia will ever show herself again?"

"I believe our last encounter weakened her," Sarah said and reached down so Pixie could climb into her lap.

"You must have hit her with a thousand volts, Mom," Cory said and couldn't help the undertone of admiration in his voice.

"I—" Sarah suddenly startled and stared at the window. Even Pixie, who had just got comfortable, perked up again, her pointy ears straight up, turning this way and that to catch the slightest sound.

"You guys hear that?"

Matthew and Cory shook their heads. "What, Mom?"

"I don't know. It sounded like – like somebody was outside, just under this window."

"Mort Jenkins perhaps," Matthew suggested, and Sarah shook her head. "Finished the well cover today."

"Mrs. Jenkins?"

"No, I heard her ask Lily for a ride to the train station. I was sure I saw something."

Gently, she set down Pixie and went to the window, peeking out through the white lace curtains.

"Nothing."

"We are all a little tired here," Matthew said. "Perhaps we should pick this up another day."

"And maybe Dad just sent somebody to check on us," Cory said bitterly. "That would be like him."

"Cory, I don't think ..."

Somebody is outside, prowling around the house.

A deep growl issued from Pixie's throat, making them all stop in their tracks. No one had heard their little dog growl before.

"Pixie?"

A thief, I get the impression of a thief.

"A burglar," Sarah said tonelessly. "Jesus. Cory, take your sister, go upstairs, and stay in your room, please."

He opened his mouth to argue, and Matthew shook his head. "Do it, Cory. If there is a burglar, you don't want to be anywhere near them."

Matthew gripped the heavy Maglite he had used for their explorations earlier – had it just been that morning – and peered into the lengthening shadows outside.

"I'm going to go around the house and check on things. Be ready to call the police if you hear anything out of the ordinary – anything at all."

He looked down at Pixie, who stood stock still facing the back door, growling now and then, her fur ruffled. "Keep your attack dog here close, too."

He is no match for the magic.

The glittering golden glow appeared again around the tip of Pixie's tail, although Matthew was too busy to see it. He opened the back door just a crack and pushed outside into the darkening shadows of the yard. Sarah felt her mouth go dry and a yawning pit open in her stomach. What if he were attacked out there? What if he were injured, all while trying to keep her and the children safe? She cradled her cell phone in her lap, the number of the local police station up and ready to be called.

"Anything, Pixie?"

Stealth, secrecy, deception.

Pixie listened into the gathering dark. Just then, the powerful beam from Matthew's flashlight cut through the shadows, and the big hydrangea bushes at the corner of the house rustled hard and bent, a branch striking the window. Sarah screamed and hit dial.

Chapter 17

The policewoman had draped a blanket around Sarah's shoulders and made a strong pot of tea with what she found in the kitchen.

"There is definitely evidence of a prowler outside your house, Mrs. Anderson," she said in her clipped, efficient tone. "You'll want to be careful about locking windows and doors from now on. Crime is a rarity in Rosewood Hollow, but it does occur."

"Any indication ..." Sarah took a sip of tea and cleared her throat as her voice broke. "Any indication what they wanted?"

The policewoman, Penny Harding, shook her head and picked up a tire iron in a large clear plastic bag.

"None. You're sure this is not yours?"

"Definitely not."

"Then I'd say break and enter, see what valuables might be here and easy to steal."

"I'm a single mother with two kids, we don't really do valuables in this house, Mrs. Harding."

"The kids' dad?"

"He's in town at the Rosewood Inn," Sarah said and wiped gritty eyes. "I spoke to him, he was expecting our son for dinner tonight."

"We'll check that out. Since everybody is all right, and your friend, Dr. Turner, appears to have chased them away, there's not much more we can do here tonight. The men will finish searching the yard, and I'll make sure the patrol car comes down your lane a few times over the night. Be careful."

Sarah only nodded.

"And you really don't have any idea what these intruders might have been after?"

Again, Sarah only shook her head and wrapped her hands tightly around the hot mug of tea. How easy would it have been to say, *Why, yes, there's a rumor that an ancient artifact is hidden in this house?* But she did not. Pixie in her lap remained alert and tense. Even around this police officer, she did not relax.

"No, we haven't been here all that long," Sarah finally said.

"I'm very sorry this has been one of your first experiences. Rosewood Hollow truly is a safe and peaceful neighborhood."

Sarah brought the mug in her hands closer to her body and felt Matthew's arm around her shoulders.

"I'll stay in the house," he said to the officer. "Just to be on the safe side."

"Is that okay with you?" she asked, and Sarah nodded.

"Good, then I'll leave you to it. Expect to see the patrol coming by a few times tonight and give us a call if anything else out of the ordinary happens. Once again, sorry this happened. One of us will bring your statement by tomorrow for signatures, and we'll see if anything else shakes loose in the meantime."

Matthew escorted Penny Harding out to the waiting patrol car. A few lights had come on over at the Jennings' and another house a bit down the road. Great, Sarah thought, they would be the talk of the town tomorrow, but just then, she didn't have the energy to worry about it.

When he came back, Matthew crouched down beside her chair and took the tea out of her hand. "You okay? I can pour you something stronger if you like?"

"I appreciate it, but I want to stay clearheaded tonight, in case - for the kids."

"Got it. I'll be right here."

"What do you think they wanted?"

"Who knows," Matthew shrugged and put the blanket a little tighter around her shoulders. "You're new in town, this is a nice house, maybe they thought there was something worth stealing."

Pixie sneezed right at him, giving her opinion on the subject.

"And you don't believe that yourself for a minute." Sarah let Pixie jump down, took the blanket, and folded it neatly on the kitchen table. "You and I both know all of this is connected to that triple-darned Luminus crystal. I distinctly remember in all of our research that Jed Thompson was responsible for safeguarding the Luminus crystal from another group opposing the Lumarians."

"And you think …?"

"Yes, I think Matthew. I think all of our poking into this and doing online searches and research has drawn the attention of *someone* to Rosewood Hollow and our house." She drew air quotes with her fingers around the word someone. "I don't know who they are, but I do know that they are dangerous, and it's becoming very clear that I should pack up my kids and leave the area for somewhere safer."

"But …"

Matthew looked downcast, and Sarah forced herself to smile. "It has nothing to do with you and me, Matthew, this is all about Cory and

Emma, and their safety. I'm going to work out something with Michael tomorrow. I'll let you know where we are going, but right now I need to keep us all safe, and that means leaving here for now."

"Okay, I understand," he said, but the disappointment was written so clearly on his face that she'd have to be deaf and blind to miss it.

"Cory likes you," she said and took Matthew's hand. "And so does Emma – and so do I. We'll pick this up once we are settled. Without ghosts and mysteries and intruders."

Instead of an answer, Matthew pulled her into a tight hug. A hug that was both a promise and a glimpse of everything that was to come for both of them. Sarah closed her eyes and for just one moment, she let herself fall and be held.

They checked on Emma and Cory in his room, assured them that for the night they need not worry about anything, and finally set up a sleeping bag for Matthew back in the games room. Sarah snuck into her bedroom as quietly as she could, not to wake Emma, and settled Pixie between them. For some reason, Pixie's silent, reassuring presence made her feel safer than any weapon by her bedside might have.

Chapter 18

Sarah had expected to toss and turn all night, but she'd fallen asleep the moment her head hit the pillow and, consequently, was up at first light, making coffee for herself and tea for Matthew. The night had remained totally quiet, whether that was due to the police presence on the block or another reason, she didn't know.

Matthew woke when he heard her up and he stumbled into the kitchen bleary-eyed in jeans and the t-shirt he had obviously slept in. Sarah handed him a tea.

"Couldn't sleep?" she asked, and he shook his head.

"Not really. Every sound …"

"I'm so sorry."

"Hey, no worries," Matthew winked. "Not your fault. I'm assuming you didn't order in for intruders to sneak around the house last night?"

"Not hardly."

Matthew nodded and took a generous sip of his tea.

"That's better," he said with a sigh. "I'm here to help you with anything you need, assuming your decision still stands."

Sarah took her coffee and looked out into the yard, just waking up with the dawn light. Birds sang, a little squirrel climbed through a tree, and the dew glittered on all of the flowers. Her little paradise was doing its best to make it hard for her to leave.

"I'll talk to Michael this morning. I'd really love for you to be there, if …"

If you can handle Michael's attitude, she did not have to say it, Matthew understood with a nod.

"I'm going to run home, shower, and change," he finally said. "Do you want me to call somebody?"

A knock on the door startled them both, and Sarah almost dropped her mug, but it was only Mrs. Jenkins behind the glass door. Sarah unlocked it and ushered her in.

"I saw the police car last night, and Penny Harding told me what happened. You are all right, aren't you?"

"Yes, thank you." Sarah took the offered plate of cookies and put it on the table, while Matthew made his goodbyes. "Thanks for asking, it's just been … a shock."

"This is such a peaceful—"

"Peaceful town, yes," Sarah nodded. "All the same, I think we will take some time away right now to – to figure out what's best for us."

"I can only imagine, it must be quite a shock." Mrs. Jenkins nodded, smiling brightly. Curious, Sarah thought, she hadn't expected this instant agreement. "I can look after the house for you as long as you want."

She has an agenda, Pixie's words suddenly came to her again. Mrs. J has an agenda.

"I can get an estate agent."

"Nonsense, I insist. What are neighbors for."

Upstairs she heard Cory wake and automatically clenched her fists. Explaining it to him would be the hardest.

"The kids don't know yet," she whispered, just as Cory came into the kitchen, looked around, and poured himself some of Matthew's tea.

"What's going on?" he finally asked, and Mrs. Jenkins quietly excused herself. "Mom?"

Nothing could have prepared her for the tantrum she would face next, explaining her decision to Cory. He yelled, he begged, he pleaded, and at one point he even promised to forgo his allowance for an indeterminate time frame, if they would just stay here.

"I need to keep you safe."

"I don't want to be kept safe, I want to stay here and figure this out. This is home now."

Their loud voices brought Emma and Pixie downstairs. Emma started crying when Cory told her, and half an hour of drama later Sarah felt she did not have an ounce of strength left.

"End of discussion," she finally yelled, feeling guilty at that. "We are leaving, and the moment he is up, I will discuss it with your father."

Cory thundered upstairs and slammed the door to his room harder than ever before. Emma, in her nightshirt and hugging a teddy bear, cried bitter tears and Sarah dropped heavily into a chair and pulled the hair back from her face. Just then her phone rang, a number she didn't recognize, but the young day couldn't get any worse anyway.

"Anderson," she snapped.

On the other end of the line, a sobbing cry answered.

"Sarah? It's Katelyn." For a moment Sarah's mind sifted through her list of friends. "Michael's ... friend," the sniffling voice supplied.

"Oh yes, of course." Sarah rolled her eyes. "Listen I wanted to—"

"Sarah, Michael has disappeared."

"What?" Sarah sat up a little straighter and closed her eyes as she listened on the phone. Yeah right, she thought. Trouble in paradise, dude had probably gone out to let off some steam. He did that, Michael did. Just slam the door and make you wonder and worry.

"When he heard about the attempted home invasion last night, he grabbed the car keys and said he was going to check on you guys."

"Probably wasn't too happy," Sarah muttered, only slightly mollified by the fact that he wanted to check and make sure they were okay.

"He – he said he was grabbing those kids right now, and to get an extra room from the hotel. No way he was going to leave them with a ..."

"A?" Sarah asked, knowing this was where the good stuff was.

"Lunatic," Katelyn said softly. "Believe me, I told him—"

"You know what, I don't really care what you told Michael. I have custody of those kids, I decide. I was going to talk to him today about arrangements, but if that's his attitude ..." She pressed her lips together and counted to ten silently. "Then that's just going to have to wait," she finished lamely.

"No, you still don't understand."

"I understand perfectly, Katelyn."

"The car is still here, and the keys are on the ground beside it."

This time Sarah shut up, and the silence hammered across the line for a moment.

"When he didn't come back," Katelyn said, tears choking up her voice, "I thought he'd stayed over."

"As if."

"But then this morning, I got worried and I called him. The message service cuts in immediately without ringing, Sarah. The phone is switched off or ..."

"That's not Michael," Sarah mused. And it wasn't. Michael could not live without his phone in his hand. Not even for an hour at dinner or the movies.

"Have you called the police, reported him missing?"

"They said I need to wait …"

"Twenty-four hours, that's BS by the way. Keep bugging them – I need to think for a minute."

Sarah hung up and held the phone between her palms, close to her chest. Pixie came bounding in and stopped with a paw on her foot.

"Michael has disappeared."

They have Michael.

Sarah stopped in her tracks, "You know?"

Just then, someone hammered wildly at the front door, and Sarah went to let in Lily and Matthew.

"Michael is missing," Lily said and pushed into the kitchen. No pastries and no coffee today, just wild hair, simple jeans, and a sweatshirt.

"How do you know already?"

"Penny Harding came by my store to ask a few questions, the call came in on her radio when she was there, so I grabbed Matthew and came out in case you didn't know."

"Katelyn just called me," Sarah said, omitting that Pixie also knew. She sat heavily at the kitchen table again. "Now what?"

For a moment they all stared at one another without saying a word. Cory had heard the commotion and came strolling into the kitchen, the hood of his sweater pulled over his head, a scowl firmly on his face. Sarah reached out a hand for him and thought she must look awful because he didn't hesitate.

"Change of plans, Cory," she said tonelessly. "I'm sorry, I was wrong. We're staying put right here."

"What happened?" He brushed the hood off his face and took a chair, looking from Lily to Matthew and his mother. "What?"

"Your father disappeared."

"Disappeared? How?"

"We don't know yet."

Sarah rested her chin on her fisted hands and looked at her son long and hard. "Listen, I don't want you and Emma to be afraid. We're going to do everything to find your dad and figure out what happened."

Cory shook his head, drew patterns onto the tablecloth with his fingernail for a moment and finally looked straight at Matthew.

"You think this has something to do with the Lumarians?"

"I don't know, Cory. Speculating won't get us—"

"Of course it does."

Her appearance this time came without thunder or vibrations. She merely swept in from the games room to appear in the kitchen, like a morning mist on a meadow. Sarah automatically rose and squared her shoulders, thinking how silly it was that she could see Emma's books on the shelf right through the transparent Amelia.

"Not today."

Pixie stood beside her, and, where her little body touched her leg, Sarah could feel energy and power going back and forth. To her surprise, Amelia lifted her ghostly hands and drew back a little. The dark pools of her eyes bored straight into Sarah, rife with anger and spite.

Just then, Sarah heard footsteps on the stairs and Emma appeared in the doorway, right behind Amelia. Amelia's eyes shifted and glittered with angry sparks. She looked at Sarah, and back down at Emma, who was gazing at her with open admiration. Sarah had already lifted her arms to gather all of her energy against Amelia when Emma simply stood before her and opened her arms.

"I'm Emma," she said with a smile. "And we're trying to help you get back home. While we're still here, that is."

With a knowing little smile, she strolled into the kitchen and looked around curiously. "Why are you all staring?"

Cory grabbed his sister's arm and pulled her into a chair beside him. "Amelia almost killed you," he hissed and pointed at her.

"No, she didn't. She knows we're only trying to help, don't you?"

Amelia's already gauzy shape blurred for a moment and reassembled again. Sarah still stood at the ready, Pixie by her side. Finally, Amelia made a sound that might have been a sigh or a rush of wind through a long canyon.

"The Obsidian Order," she finally said. "They were the group Simon aligned himself with to find the crystal when I – when I died. I sensed their presence outside last night, and their resolve to do something to make you give up the crystal."

"But why Michael," Sarah asked.

"Because the rest of you are protected." Amelia gave her a pointed look, and Sarah shoved her hands in her pockets.

"They are determined to get the crystal, and nothing and no one will stop them. They will kill him if necessary."

"Is that how you died?" Emma asked, and Sarah cringed, hearing the casual way Emma said died.

"I don't know, child. All I remember is seeing Simon running and my father with a gun."

Could a ghost manage to look sad, Sarah wondered? She cocked her head and wanted to figure it out, but as quickly as she had appeared, Amelia disappeared again, leaving the little group staring at nothing.

Cody produced his tablet out of nowhere and began typing, Obsidian order.

"The fabled Obsidian Order, if indeed it exists, is a secretive and ruthless organization of criminals with a wide variety of interests," he read. "Comprising skilled operatives from various backgrounds, including mercenaries, archaeologists, and mystics, they are driven by a singular goal – to amass wealth and thus power. The Order has existed in the shadows for centuries, with deep pockets and connections to influential figures who seek to exploit this power for their own gain. The order has been the focus of many modern lore and legends, but no concrete proof of their existence has ever been discovered."

Another strange sound rattled from the direction of their games room and Sarah grabbed her upper arms. "I just got chills."

"Let me see that," Matthew reached for the tablet and read the entry. "This is a gaming forum," he finally said and handed it back.

"So? That doesn't mean it's not true."

Matthew frowned, stroked a nonexistent beard, and scanned through the article. "If this is true..."

"Just because it's not some history professor's paper."

"Easy," Matthew raised a hand. "A lot of mythological figures and groups end up in fantasy games in one form or another. But, if this is true, then it would make sense that this group is after the crystal."

"Let me see that." Now Sarah reached for the tablet and quickly scanned the text. "Any way to verify this?"

"Working on it," Matthew awkwardly thumb-typed on his phone until Cory got up to fetch his laptop.

"Here, use this."

"Thanks. Cory?"

"Yeah?"

"You're a pretty good researcher already, you know."

That mollified her son again, and pretty soon the two men were engrossed in online research, comparing notes, while Sarah comforted Emma and tapped her leg so Pixie would hop up.

Now you're going to tell me how you knew this before everybody, Sarah thought.

Amelia knew.

Amelia is a ghost, Pixie. I just want to know. You're part of our family now. How do you have all of this information?

When my owner died …

Sarah brought a hand to her mouth, recalling the terrible accident on the highway.

Just as she was leaving this plane, she reached into my kennel and put her hand on my head. That's all I remember. Now I know things, have abilities.

"She transferred her powers." Sarah didn't know she had spoken aloud until she saw Matthew looking at her curiously, mouthing those words. Sarah shook her head and rubbed Pixie ever so gently.

"I'm so sorry."

For a long moment, there was no answer until finally, she heard Pixie in her head again.

Amelia is right about the Obsidian Order. They believe the crystal will allow them to shape the world around them to their own ideas.

"Criminal ideas, from the sound of it," Sarah muttered, making Matthew look up again.

You must get Michael away from them and find the crystal.

"Well, if there's nothing else," Sarah said and pulled the hair back from her face.

Matthew abandoned his research and flipped the laptop closed.

"Trouble?" he asked, and Sarah allowed Pixie to jump down and go into the yard again.

"Let's just take a shortcut," Sarah said. "And proceed on the assumption that this order has Michael and wants the crystal."

"So far I haven't been able to verify the story."

"That's OK, let's just assume." Sarah got up and went to the window, peeking out into the yard. For the moment all was fine. "Most importantly, we need to find Michael. I'd be willing to hand over that damned crystal if I even knew where it was."

"No, Sarah, you don't know what they'll do with it."

"I'm aware of that," she turned away from the window and began pacing her kitchen. Up and down. "Give me a hand here then. How do I find Michael and keep Emma and Cory safe?"

"And you."

"Yes, well …"

"And what about Amelia?" Emma piped up. "We still need to help her get home, Mom."

"Oh, honey," Sarah stopped beside Emma and pulled her into a hug. "Amelia is a separate mystery for now. We will try to help her, I promise. But first, we need to help your dad."

Emma made a face and fisted her hands in her pockets. "Can I try and help Amelia then, while you are doing … this?"

"Fine," Sarah sighed, rubbing her hands, feeling guilty again. "Fine. As long as you stay on the property away from the well and the attic, and check with one of us before doing anything more than looking around."

"I will."

Emma raced off into the games room. Under her arm, she had Amelia's old diary, her treasure.

Dear lord, help me to avoid traumatizing my children, Sarah thought and sat with Cory and Matthew.

"Ideas?"

Both of them looked at her without speaking.

"Finding your dad? Locating the crystal? Ring a bell?"

Still, no one answered.

"The police," Matthew finally suggested, and Cory rolled his eyes.

"I can just see you explaining to Officer Harding how a ghost told you our dad had been kidnapped and they need to look for him."

"Good point. Amelia?"

"How? Dial a ghost?" Sarah asked, making Cory giggle. "I can't just order her to appear and tell me stuff."

Moments passed. Matthew played with a loose thread on his cuff, Cory searched on his tablet, and finally, Sarah threw her hands up.

"Great, we have nothing."

Her phone rang, and she spent a good ten minutes explaining to Penny Harding that nothing else out of the ordinary had happened, and no, she was aware that her ex-husband was not in his hotel room, but she hadn't seen him either. She had no idea if the officer believed her or not. She certainly wouldn't have believed herself. It was all too complicated and confusing.

Sarah put her arms on the table in front of her and rested her head on it. For a moment, she startled when Matthew gently massaged her shoulders, until she finally relaxed into his touch.

"Michael and this group could be anywhere," he finally said. "Whereas we know or at least assume the crystal is here on the property."

"So, a hunt?"

"Why not? We can start up in that attic. That's where this thing started."

The hidden door, the folding staircase into the attic, the symbols on the old wooden beams. It all felt like ages ago, and they'd barely been at the house for a month. Sarah lifted her head and smiled gratefully at Matthew.

"All right, all right. Another hunt it is."

"Yes." Cory pumped his fist.

"Cory, the same thing goes for you. Stay on the property, preferably within sight of one of us, and check in before doing something – risky."

"Yes, Mom."

"You know what's weird?" Sarah looked around just as the soft flap of the doggie door announced Pixie's return. "Mrs. Jenkins. I haven't seen her since she brought cookies this morning. You'd think with the commotion of an intruder and the police, she'd be over here moth-er-henning everybody."

Pixie put her little paws on Sarah's knee.

I told you she has an agenda. She's dug holes in the yard.

"Holes? Why would Mrs. Jenkins dig holes in our yard?" she repeated for the benefit of everybody.

"Because she's weird," Cory said, rolling his eyes dramatically. "Maybe she's hunting the crystal for herself."

He'd meant it as a joke, but it fell flat entirely.

"Cory is right," Matthew chewed on his lower lip. "We can't assume anybody is *just* a sweet neighbor. This is a small town. Chances are high others know."

"The house has been empty for years, Matthew. For crying out loud, why wait until the children and I moved in to search for the crystal?"

Matthew still worried his chin and lower lip. "That's a good question," he said. "Something about your arrival triggered – all of these events."

"It triggered Amelia, that's for sure" Corey answered and looked toward the games room, where the ghost had disappeared.

"Yes, Corey, but Amelia, by her own admission, doesn't know anything about the crystal, other than her boyfriend-fiancé was ready to make a deal with the devil over this thing to get the money to marry her."

"Wait, you think it was an attack?" Corey got all excited now. "Like those intruders the other day, they came in looking for the crystal and killed her somehow?"

"And why would her father cover up her death then, if it were intruders who killed her? You go to the authorities, tell them there were intruders, and say, my daughter was killed. You start an investigation, you do not hush it all up and come up with a cockamamie story. And what about Simon? Why did Simon leave town in your scenario?"

Corey stared at her for a moment and back down at his tablet.

"This is hard," he finally said and snapped off the screen of his tablet with a jerk.

"Yes, but much of history is hard to figure out, Cory, because you can't just google the answers." Matthew put his hands on the boy's shoulder. "That doesn't mean we're going to give up. Let's go back up and through the attic, and check all of the papers in the trunk again and see if there's anything we overlooked."

"You mean look for the tenth time at stuff we already looked at nine times before? Like that's going to get us anywhere this time?"

Corey sat back in his chair and hunched into his oversized hoodie. The hang of his shoulders and disinterested little circles he drew onto the tablecloth with his finger spoke their own language of frustration. Even Pixie couldn't lift his mood, though she tried jumping onto his lap and covering his face with little kisses.

"Cory, I'm tempted to say take a break and take Pixie for a walk, but with what happened to your dad ..."

"You don't want me alone outside, I get it," he muttered. "Fine, I'll help Matthew – for the tenth time."

Sarah took care of the never-ending stream of cups and plates and mugs and finally stood by the window, staring at her beautiful garden, just in time to see Lily and Katelyn get out of the ancient beetle.

"Lily," she greeted her friend with a hug. "Great to see you."

"I was driving out to check on you. Picked up Katelyn walking down the street trying to find your house."

"The police impounded the car," Katelyn said with trembling lips. "And I had no other way to get around."

"It's fine." Sarah put on more coffee and put her freshly washed mugs back out. "Matthew and Cory are – exploring the attic," she said to Lily, "and Emma the rest of the house." With a frustrated little chuckle, she added, "I'm sorry Katelyn, we are not exactly running a traditional household around here."

"Oh, Lily told me all about the apparitions and spirits in your house," Katelyn said eagerly. "This is so fascinating to me. I've connected with the energies of the spirit world on a profound level. The wisdom and guidance I receive from the spiritual realm are invaluable in navigating the complexities of this earthly existence."

"Are they now," Sarah blinked rapidly. "Well then. Somehow or other this entire thing may be connected to Michael's disappearance although I don't know how, and I wouldn't suggest getting the police involved with talk about ghosts and Lumarians and secret crystals if you get my drift."

"Oh absolutely." Katelyn brushed her raven black hair out of her face and looked straight at Sarah. "It's far better to place your trust in higher powers and follow their guidance, even when it means questioning or challenging the decisions made by earthly authorities."

"Oh, I can't wait for you to meet Amelia," Sarah sighed. "You'll get right along."

"Yes, is she here, can I talk to her?"

"Katelyn..." Sarah sighed. She should have known that sarcasm was lost on this youngster, who was far closer to Cory's age than Michael's. "No," she finally said. "Amelia appears whenever she feels like it."

No need to tell this kid that she had put the fear of – whomever – into this ghost with her own powers. Lily, however, tried her best to hide a chuckle behind Katelyn's back. Sarah shot her a hard glance and raised her eyebrows.

"Why did you want to come and see us then, Katelyn? I assume there was a reason, walking all the way out here from downtown."

"I'm from Baltimore," Katelyn wailed. "I don't know anybody out here, nobody but you. Michael told me we'd just stay here for a day or two, see his kids—"

"Our kids."

"And then go on to visit New York City."

"Nice." Sarah bit her lower lip. She'd always wanted to spend a week in NYC, but Michael wouldn't hear of it. Too expensive, too many bums and pickpockets, he only visited New York on business when he couldn't help it.

"I told Katelyn we'd be happy to have her hang out with us," Lily said and went to get the coffee Sarah had made. "Look, it has to be crazy being all alone, in a strange city." She stared at Sarah. "One more pair of eyes to look."

"Fine then," Sarah threw up her arms. "What's one more person thinking we're completely coo-coo waiting for a ghost to jump out? Grab a coffee and maybe help the boys upstairs to look for – whatever. Matthew will tell you what he needs."

"Great thank you, I promise—"

"And I am warning you. If you annoy Matthew or Cory, that will be the end of it. Matthew is nothing like Michael, do we understand one another."

"Yes, of course."

When Katelyn had gone upstairs to see what Matthew and Cory needed, Lily broke down in a fit of laughter.

"Matthew is nothing like Michael? Really Sarah?"

"You're the one who brought her in here."

"I knew you and Matthew were perfect for one another. I knew it from the moment I met you."

"You did not. You were just matchmaking," Sarah corrected. "And yes, I do like Matthew. And also yes, if she decides to go after him…" Sarah stretched out her arms, forming great claws with her fingers. "She's gonna get a crash course on all of the new powers fighting Amelia has given me, all right?"

"Do you remember what you were like when you got here? Worried about what everybody would think or do?"

"No. and I surely don't want to. They can all go and – you know."

Lily snorted and burst out laughing again, and soon both women were sitting side by side on the porch nursing spiked coffees, laughing at absolutely nothing. It didn't help the situation, it didn't find Michael or the crystal or provide any answers they so desperately needed, but it gave them a tiny bubble of silliness and carefree fun, only a few minutes, which was exactly what they needed on this tense and stressful day.

"I feel awful," Sarah finally said, giggling again. "I should be worrying about Michael, Amelia, and these ... these ..."

"Obsidians," Lily provided.

"Yes, those. I should worry about all of that stuff, but I just – I can't."

"You can't worry about everybody, Sarah. It doesn't work that way. First priority, keep yourself, Cory, and Emma safe."

"I know." Sarah put down her coffee and stared at the riot of colors out in the garden. Reds, pinks, violets, purples, and greens all vied for the attention of her eyes. It could be so beautiful, so peaceful.

"I wanted to leave with the kids today, but now that Michael might have been kidnapped, I can't just take off and abandon him. I think we wait until tonight, then I have to call Penny Harding and see if she can make sense of all of this."

"Tough call," Lily dug her bare toes into the wooden floor of the porch, setting the swing to swaying gently. "Can you? Make sense of it?"

"Mm-hmm," Sarah answered because she honestly did not know. "Where is that dog of mine anyway – Pixie?"

"Ran off into the yard, looking for something," Lily pointed vaguely. "I swear that dog acts like a person sometimes."

Sarah took a breath and debated whether she should tell Lily what she had heard about Selena's accident and the way she had seemingly given her powers to Pixie. She turned her head and looked at her friend in profile, holding her face into the sun with her eyes closed, giving gentle pushes to the swing with her big toes. Accepting a ghost was one thing, but actual magical powers? And where did that leave her, Sarah? She had not had the time to figure out when and how exactly she had acquired the strength, the wherewithal, the sheer *power* to confront Amelia's spirit – and win.

"So, you know … Pixie's owner," she started, just as the screen door opened, and Emma padded out to join them, barefoot, a glass of juice in one hand, Amelia's diary in the other.

Lily peered at her through half-closed eyes and smiled. "Might want to be careful with that beautiful old diary and that glass of juice, Em."

"Oh, I am." Emma carefully set down her juice and joined the two women on the swing. "I read most of it," she said seriously.

"Don't let Amelia hear that," Lily quipped. "When I was a young girl, I would have been furious if somebody read my diary."

"Well, Amelia is dead, and we are trying to help her," Emma said and flipped through the book.

"I know you don't want me to go anywhere on my own …"

"Oh dear."

"Mom, it says here that Amelia and Simon used to leave love letters to one another," she bent down to the diary page again and followed a line with her forefinger. "In the twisty knot of the ancient tree near our property line, it's situated just right. It's so near to the neighbor's place that he can scramble up the fence and stash them away without being noticed."

"A secret letter drop," Lily said and clapped her hands. "How fun. When we were kids, we used to…"

"What's a knot of a tree?" Emma asked, and Sarah put her arms around the girl's shoulders.

"Well," Sarah said, "Imagine a big, strong tree in a forest. And on this tree, there's something really special. It looks like a funny-looking bump, like so maybe," she showed a closed fist to Emma. "Right on the tree's bark. This bump would be special if it's in a good hiding spot because it is usually hollow, it looks different from the rest of the tree, but if you didn't look for it, you would never know. It's kind of like a secret treasure that the tree has been keeping safe. There's probably soft green moss and tiny plants growing around it, making it seem like it has some magic around it."

Emma giggled and leaned against her mother at the mention of magic. "Inside this bump, though," Sarah continued, "something cool happened all on its own over a long, long time. It made a little hidden space, like a secret room inside the tree! It's like a surprise that the tree made for itself. If your hand is small enough and you reach inside, you can leave a secret for somebody."

"Sweet," Emma giggled brightly and hugged Amelia's diary to herself. "I want to go look for the tree and the bump."

"Honey, Amelia wrote that diary a hundred years ago, give or take. That tree is probably no longer even there, never mind anything that may or may not have been inside."

"Can I look anyway?"

"I really don't want you to be out there alone."

"Please, please, I'll take Pixie."

"Emma."

"You are losing this argument," Lily quipped and scanned the garden and far end of the property. "Em, maybe you could take Mrs. Jenkins with you, but I don't see her. That's kind of odd. Usually, she's about somewhere in her yard, or over here."

"Yes, Cory and Matthew said something about it." Now Sarah looked over to the house of her neighbors and realized that all of the shutters and curtains were closed, and the house lay quiet as if its occupants had gone away on vacation. Sarah shivered a little and pulled the orange-patterned scarf Lily had given her tighter around her shoulders.

"Please, Mom."

"Do you think something could be wrong," she asked Lily, and her friend slowly shook her head.

"Why, because they're not around? What makes you ...?"

"Mom, I promise."

"Can you please go inside, Emma, now? We will all go together and look for the tree in just a little while, okay?"

Emma complained and muttered, but she had seen the glint in her mother's narrowed eyes and the firm line on her forehead. From experience, she knew this was not the time to argue with her mother.

Sarah stood up from the porch swing now and tightened the shawl around herself hard. She walked to the end of the porch, facing the Jenkins' house, and stared.

"We've only been here for a month, but I've never known the Jenkins' to have the house closed up like that during the day."

"Maybe they just forgot? Wanted some privacy maybe?" Lily's words sounded hollow and fake. Sarah shook her head.

"No, something's not right. Pixie mentioned that Mrs. Jenkins has been digging holes in our backyard."

"Holes? Is she planting something?"

"Nothing I'm aware of. There's definitely something strange happening here, Lily."

She stepped off the porch and took a few steps closer to the hedge that separated hers from the Jenkins' property. Automatically she looked up and down the property line – no tree. Emma's magic letterbox tree was not on this side of the property. Something drew her to go over there to check it out, and she had taken a few steps when a loud argument from inside her house brought her back.

Lily had already stepped back into the kitchen. Katelyn and Cory were arguing about something, with Matthew trying to make peace. Sarah just caught the end of Cory's sentence, "You were the one who took off with my Dad."

"Enough, Cory," she said sternly. "What's going on here?"

"Katelyn thinks we're just wasting time around here, digging through old papers, 'having fun,' when we should be looking for my dad," Cory defended himself. "And I told her that's a load of bull."

"That's not what I said." Katelyn stomped a black booted foot. "I only meant that our time would be better spent doing something constructive."

"Enough." Sarah raised her hands. "If anybody is doing something constructive to find Michael, it should be the police, not us, all right? We are gathering the clues to a very old mystery." She looked straight at Katelyn and shoved her hands into the pockets of her jeans. "I understand that you might think this is a waste of time, but it helps us cope, so perhaps you'd be better off availing yourself of the door and go ask at the police station if you can help somewhere."

She stepped aside and pointed at the back door with one arm. Not in my house, she thought. You will not come here weeping and distraught, asking for help, and then go accusing my son. It might be petty, but there it was.

Katelyn lowered her head and nodded. Finally, she shuffled off to find a washroom, and Cory washed his hands at the kitchen sink.

"This newfound power suits you," Matthew whispered beside her, making Sarah grin.

"Really?"

"Yup."

Matthew smiled at her, a smile that made her feel all warm and cared for inside, and Sarah felt it like sunshine on her skin before she realized Cory was staring at them curiously.

"So, anything new in those trunks?" she asked, her voice louder than she had intended, feeling the heat of a deep blush creeping over her face.

"Afraid not," Matthew replied, turning away to search through the box of exotic teas he had left in the kitchen. "I hate to let you down, but I don't think we are getting anywhere."

"Well, that's just great."

Sarah sat at the kitchen table and placed a hand on Cory's shoulder. "Thanks for looking bud and for helping Matthew."

"I knew there was nothing new up there."

Lily pulled up a chair and scraped the hair back from her face, braiding it aimlessly. "I feel if we could somehow figure out what happened the day Amelia died ..."

Sarah shook her head. "We can't. We tried, and Amelia does not remember anything about that night. She thinks it was at night, she thinks she remembers the Obsidian Order, Simon, and her dad and a gun – but that's about all."

Matthew raised his head but wisely didn't ask who *we* might be. He had stopped inquiring about Sarah's communications with Pixie, but every now and then, Sarah would catch him sitting quietly, just staring at Pixie as if trying to discover something or attempting to communicate with her in the same way he saw Sarah doing. It just didn't work.

"Amelia and Simon were leaving letters to one another in an old tree somewhere out back," Emma chimed in and carefully put the diary out of Cory's reach. "I know, because she wrote in her diary about it."

"Like a secret letter drop, the way the spies used to do during the war?" Cory asked, suddenly giving his complete attention to his little sister.

"I dunno. She didn't explain. I thought you said the diary was boring." Emma demonstratively turned her back on Cory.

"Not really boring, just ..."

"So, what else did it say?" Matthew asked and gently nudged Cory under the table.

Emma narrowed her eyes at them. The boys had shut her out the last few days, and she was not going to give up her discoveries quite so quickly.

"Maybe it's my secret," she finally said, smirking.

Matthew looked to Sarah for help, who was just passing out the last of Mrs. Jenkins' cookies. Sarah turned away to hide the grin on her face. Finally, when she'd poured tea for them all and settled with a delicious, chewy cookie, she decided to come to his aid.

"Emma wanted to search the property to see if the tree was still there somewhere, but I wouldn't let her go out all by herself," she shrugged and brushed crumbs off her lips. "Maybe if an adult and a big brother wanted to go with her, it might actually be okay."

"I'll go with," Katelyn said, appearing in the doorway again, and Sarah tried hard to stop rolling her eyes.

"I meant—"

"Why don't we all go," Matthew suggested. "Look, there's nothing we can do inside right now, and the weather is nice so why don't we walk the property – as a group."

Sarah had been told there were rather large fruit orchards belonging to the property that were leased to a farmer at the moment. A few years from now, she would be able to choose if she wanted to continue this arrangement or keep the orchards for herself. At the time, she had simply nodded and not worried about it any further. Orchards, best if someone else looked after them, just like the landscapers who kept the gardens trimmed and beautiful when Mrs. Jenkins was not poking around out there.

"All right," she finally said, "we will all go. I need some gardening boots and a sweater, and so will you kids." She looked from Matthew to Lily and Katelyn. "It rained overnight, I imagine it might be quite muddy out there, so ..."

Matthew shrugged and looked down at his jeans and running shoes. "I'm good."

Half an hour later, they had fetched the old property map Sarah had received when she purchased Thompson House and wandered outside, along the fence that separated their property from the Jenkins'.

"Don't you think it is unusual that neither Martha nor Mortimer have been outside or around all day?" Sarah whispered, walking beside Matthew.

"She brought cookies this morning," he shrugged. "That's about all I know. She seems to be usually all up in your business, but maybe she just – I don't know – got worried because of the incident last night."

"Look," Sarah pointed at the house. "It's all closed up. What do you think that means?"

Matthew looked and shrugged again. "It means somebody closed all of the shutters, I think," he said, and Sarah elbowed him in the side.

"Be serious."

"I am serious."

"Look, look, I think I found it." Up ahead, Emma ran up to an ancient maple tree and waved her arms. "Do you think this is it? Can you see anything? Cory, do you know what a knot in a tree looks like? Can you see one in this tree? Do you want to climb it? Can you?"

"Slow down, Emma," Matthew laughed and quickened his pace a little bit. "You're about to boil over."

Lily fell in step beside Sarah, looked at her friend from head to toe, and winked.

"I knew it," she whispered, and again, Sarah elbowed her in the side.

"Shut your face, Lily Morrison."

But she knew what Lily was referring to, and she had to agree with her friend 100%. Matthew was an amazing man, treated her and the kids with respect and love, and had a great sense of humor to boot. He made her feel good, and she hadn't felt that in so long, she'd almost missed it.

"Well," she asked when she and Lily had reached the tree, and Matthew shook his head.

"This is not the one, no knot on this one I can see. Besides, it's too far away from the property line to match up to the description in the diary."

"I could climb into it," Katelyn claimed, making Cory snort.

"I'd like to see that."

"Nobody is climbing any trees unless we are sure it is the right one, okay. That includes you, Katelyn."

Sarah winced. Jesus, it felt like she was talking to an adult daughter around Katelyn. Better to find Michael and get her out of the house as soon as possible.

Her head still swiveled left and right with every step their little group took, checking for dense clumps of brush where an intruder might hide or the path behind them.

"Don't stress out. As long as we are together, we should be fine," Matthew whispered, taking her hand.

"I can't help but worry. Those are my kids up there." She had just opened her mouth to wonder where Pixie had gone in all of the commotion around them when a streak of white blasted past them and around the kids.

Pixie bounced and cavorted, jumping on the kids running ahead and turning back, always in a tight circle around their little group.

"Pixie, where were you?" Sarah called and laughed, only to have Pixie jump and race off to circle the kids again.

I was checking the Jenkins house – there's nobody home.

"Weird, but thanks."

What would you ever do without me?

"I honestly don't know."

"Don't know what?" Matthew asked, looking at her, then at the racing and bouncing Pixie, and back at her. "Oh," he took her hand again and shook his head. "I don't know if I'll ever get used to what you and her have going on here."

"She's – keeping an eye on things," Sarah said a little sheepishly.

"I can see that, but what can she do? Isn't she a bit little to— whoa."

The moment the words were out of his mouth, Pixie jumped at him, planting two little muddy paw prints on the thigh of his jeans, and ran off again. Her mouth was open, tongue lolling out, giving the little papillon the impression of a huge smile. Sarah laughed brightly for the first time in what felt like days.

"She might only be five pounds, but don't ever question her powers, my friend."

The kids checked yet another tree, and another, and especially Cory was getting tired of the hike.

"Man, we've got like way too many trees," he complained. "How are you supposed to find like one specific one?"

"Easy," Matthew laughed and pointed index and middle finger at his eyes. "You look, and then—"

He broke off. Up ahead, Pixie had suddenly stopped. She stood in a rigid, taut stance, tail carried high and curled up over her back, and her ears perked up tall. She looked and listened for a moment, and barked in a loud and piercing voice as only a papillon can.

"Pixie stop, shut up," Cory yelled, and even Emma called her name a few times. Pixie didn't stop. Her nose pointed straight at the far corner of the property, beyond the end of the fruit orchard, where a few old, dilapidated wooden baskets had been piled up, likely in preparation for a large bonfire later on in the fall. A wooden fence separated their property from a dark wood lot beyond, and someone had leaned a shiny, lightweight aluminum ladder against the fence. It looked strangely out of place amongst the ancient fruit trees and the weathered wooden fence.

"What the heck," Sarah was by the ladder in giant strides. "What is this? Matthew?"

"I don't know." Matthew climbed the first few rungs of the ladder and peered over the fence. "If I had to guess, I'd say that's how they got onto the property last night without getting caught in the motion sensor lights out front. It's not that hard. Leave the ladder on the other side, climb up, sit on the fence, take the ladder with you after. You could disappear into that woodlot there, and no one would ever know anyone was here."

"But you caught them."

"You heard them," Matthew corrected. "I just chased them off the property – across the front yard."

"Jesus." Sarah took the ladder and laid it down on the ground, just out of reach of the fence. "We're taking that with us. Maybe the police can look into it."

"Standard outdoor issue, any hiking store will carry these," Matthew began when Emma called them to where she and Lily were looking up at trees. Excitement vibrated in her voice, and she waved her arms.

"Mom, Cory, come quick. Lily and I found the tree. This is the one, there's that knot-thingy, hurry."

∞

Cory and Matthew grabbed hold of the ladder, and they all ran over to where Emma and Lily pointed at an ancient Oak tree, about thirty yards from where they had found the ladder, growing close to the fence.

Pixie stood, her little white paws against the bark of the tree, and she stared up into it. Not a single bark escaped her this time, and she focused a concentrated stare up into the tree.

I am – sensing something, Sarah heard.

What?

Great, great sadness.

Pixie dropped her front paws and sat quietly on her haunches, first looking at Sarah, then back at the tree.

Heartbreak and massive sadness.

"Well, if they left love letters for one another."

No, it's more than that.

"Who are you talking to?" Katelyn, who'd been wandering among the fruit trees, came to face Sarah.

"I am ... Never mind." She pointed up into the tree, far higher than any of them could dare to reach, where a mossy, basketball-sized knot had formed, and just barely visible, turned away from prying eyes toward the center of the tree, the dark shadow of an opening.

"I want to climb up there and check." Emma bounced on her little feet with excitement.

"No, you don't honey, and you don't either, Cory. We're all going to hold the ladder, and Matthew can go up. If you don't mind," she gave Matthew a guilty look. "I just thought ..."

"Tree inspector at your service," he saluted with a grin. "I have to warn you though. After a hundred years, there's likely nothing in there but dust and a few squirrel droppings."

"Eeeuw," said Katelyn, taking a step back. Cory glared at her, and Sarah felt her heart swell with pride seeing her son's protectiveness.

"It's not her fault," she whispered to him, and Cory did his now-famous eye-roll again.

"Here goes," Matthew clambered up the ladder. Halfway up the tree, he pretended to fall, flailed his arms and legs, and laughed uproariously when he heard Sarah cry out.

"That's not funny, Turner," she called up to him, and he winked and grinned at her. "Almost there."

When he had reached the knot in the tree, he fished a tiny little flashlight out of his pocket and tried to shine it inside the little hollow, but it was angled so awkwardly that neither light nor rain nor anything else would penetrate.

"What's he going to do if there is something inside?" Cory asked, brushing the hair out of his face. "Something with teeth?"

"Don't go there, Cory."

For a moment, they heard nothing from Matthew. Then he adjusted his stance on the ladder.

"I don't think there is anything in here. Geez, I hate to poke around in this old— Yikes. Holy crap."

"Matthew," Sarah called, one foot on the bottom rung of the ladder when his face appeared amongst the leaves again.

"Open your hands." Obediently Sarah did, and something dropped from among the branches. Sarah fumbled for a moment and found something dark and cool in her hands. It was covered in dirt, but from under the covering of filth, gold sparkled here and there.

"What is that?"

"A locket," Lily breathed, bending over Sarah's shoulder. "You found a locket in there, bet you it was Amelia's."

Sarah fingered the ribbon that held the locket, faded and worn so much she didn't dare pull on it. Gently she put it into Emma's hands.

"Can you come back down now?"

"In a sec. I think there's something else here."

Just then, Pixie began to bark up a storm.

The ladder wobbled precariously as Matthew angled his arm to reach even deeper into the hollow of the tree.

"Matthew," Sarah called out while trying to shush Pixie with one hand. "If you fall off this ladder groping between bugs and spiders up in there, don't bother coming to me for sympathy."

"There. I've got it."

Matthew's face appeared amongst the leaves again, and he held a small brownish package aloft, wrapped with either string or ribbon, covered in lichen and a grey-brown layer of dirt Sarah didn't even want to guess at.

"Cool," Cory called out and jumped onto the first ladder rung, shaking it precariously. "What is it, do you think it's a treasure map? Maybe to where they left the crystal? Hurry up, Matthew."

Matthew climbed down carefully and shoved the package into the front pouch of his sweater, looking left and right of where they were standing, putting a finger over his lips. He even took a few more steps up the ladder again to peek over the edge of the fence.

Finally, still ignoring Cory's questions and reaching hands, he stood beside them and nodded back the way they had come.

"Come now, back to the house, and close the doors when we are inside. Cory, help me with this ladder."

Matthew picked up one end of the ladder, instructed Cory to do the same, and stalked back toward the house in huge, ground-eating strides.

"Matthew," Sarah called and ran to catch up with the boys. "Matthew, you want to tell me what's going on here?" She gripped his shoulder, but he shook off her hand and continued marching toward the house.

"What?"

Finally, he stopped for a moment and glared at her. "What if Cory is right, Sarah? What if this is some damned treasure map?" He lowered his voice, and his eyes darted around again as if he were a man hunted. "What if this is about the crystal, and every cult follower in the entire county, no, the country, is looking for this?"

He patted the little package in the pouch of his sweater. "I just don't think it's worth the risk to make us targets out here. Let's get inside."

Again, he grabbed the ladder and marched on toward the house, not slowing his pace until they were all inside, and he had bolted the heavy front door behind them.

"Cory, check the back and kitchen doors," he instructed, "and make sure they're locked. Sarah, can you check all of the windows and close them if necessary?"

"What are you talking about, a crystal?" Katelyn asked. "I thought this was some game you were playing."

"Katelyn," Matthew rolled his eyes almost as dramatically as Cory, giving Sarah a little twinge when she realized where her son had picked up the habit. "If I'm right, this right here," he held up the wrapped package he had discovered in the tree. "This right here is why Michael disappeared, and someone tried to break into the house yesterday."

"And the locket?"

Emma put her hand into her pocket and pulled out the little golden locket. The ribbon had become a little more frayed in the girl's pocket, and Sarah gently took it out of her hands.

"I think this is Amelia's. If she and Simon communicated via letters in that tree, it would surely be a token she gave him. Why don't we clean it up and check it out later?"

Thunder rumbled somewhere far off, the door to Emma's room upstairs, which had been standing open, slammed with a resounding bang, and the floor beneath their feet trembled slightly. By now, no one but Katelyn paid any mind to Amelia's little fits and assertions any longer.

"There's your confirmation," Matthew said dryly. "It's hers."

"I don't understand," Katelyn said in a whiny voice, looking from one to the other. "Where's Michael in all of this?"

"Let's find out."

Matthew stalked into the kitchen, the only room that had enough chairs for all of them, and put the package on the table. The outer layer clearly had been some type of calico fabric at some point, tied with a plain brown utility string.

"How is that even still intact if Amelia died in 1904?" Sarah asked, realizing they were all holding their breath.

"That knot was angled inward, toward the center of the tree," Matthew said. "And it was deep. That hollow knot has kept whatever this is safe from the ravages of time, moisture, and light for over a hundred years, and now..."

His long, gentle fingers tried to slip under the string without breaking or damaging it, and his face fell when the string came apart at his touch.

"As a historian, this breaks my heart," he said with a wry smile. "Go get my camera, Cory, before I destroy something of historical significance here."

"It might tell us where the crystal is - and Michael," Sarah urged, and Cory held up his iPhone.

"Still the best camera."

"If we had the time, I would be tempted to argue."

Matthew turned back to the slim package and gently folded back the outer layers of fabric that had wrapped it for so long. Dirt, bits of wood, and what Sarah feared were animal droppings crumbled away from it.

"It's a woven fabric," Matthew said softly. "Rough to the touch, likely hand-spun from natural fibers that have aged gracefully."

When he had peeled back the outer layer of fabric, a new wrapping appeared, this one made of burlap, the fibers coarse and sturdy as if designed to endure. It was secured with twine, wrapped and bound meticulously to ensure its preservation. Beneath the burlap, a final layer of fabric appeared.

Matthew's hands brushed a smooth, silken material, startlingly vibrant compared to the layers above it. The colors had retained their luster and shimmered in deep reds and gold with the faintest touch of opulence.

"Pure Chinese silk," Sarah said reverently and brushed her fingers over it. "Jed Thompson was a wealthy man, perhaps this was a remnant from one of Amelia's dresses."

"Can you hurry?" Cory urged. Emma leaned over and tugged on the scrap of silk that had wrapped the package inside the tree for ages, and Matthew carefully stopped her.

He peeled back the final layer and was left with about five pieces of paper, folded again and again to make a tiny little package. Aged paper, brittle and yellowed, now lay on the kitchen table between them. Matthew, not daring to use his fingers, dug a pair of tweezers out of his pocket and unfolded them ever so slowly and gently.

The contents, though frail, exuded an air of significance. Again, the outer sheet was blank, but beneath, the edges of a letter, now fragile and torn, peeked out. Its ink, once bold, had faded into the sepia tones of time, and the words were written in an elegant script, telling a story of an era long past. Pixie whined a little and crowded close until Sarah picked her up and cradled her in his arms.

Simon.

"Simon," Sarah repeated in wonder and Matthew cocked his head.

"You think?" He noticed the exchange of looks between Sarah and Pixie and shook his head. "Never mind."

"This is fantastic," he finally whispered. "To think this letter is over a hundred years old. I should — no, we should be doing this in a museum, in a climate-controlled document room where nothing—"

"Matthew, can you just please read the letter," Sarah insisted. "Or take a picture and pack it away safely again. Right now, we have more important things to worry about than preserving ancient texts."

He gave her a piqued look but did just that, took a few pictures of the letter then carefully folded it back into its wrappings.

"Cory, could you—" The tablet he'd been meaning to ask for was handed to him automatically.

"What does it say?" Emma asked impatiently. Sarah put her arm around her youngest, and Pixie gave her a little lick on the nose. They all waited for Matthew to start.

He cocked his head to listen for a moment, but other than a sudden gust of wind pushing against the old windows, all was silent.

"This is not a letter," he finally said, adjusting his reading glasses. "Although the last page is signed by a Simon Miller, Amelia's fiancé Simon I would presume, there's a headline here, and it reads, Confession."

"Confession," Sarah asked, and Katelyn and the children didn't even dare to move. "What on earth would Simon have to confess to?"

"Only one way to find out."

Matthew adjusted his glasses again and began.

"I am penning this confession with haste, for I am on the cusp of departing this town. I have, regrettably, lost all that I held dear. The cherished love of my life has departed from this mortal coil, and I must bear the culpability for her untimely demise, though I was not the one who discharged the firearm that claimed the life of my beloved Amelia. Nonetheless, the burden of guilt weighs heavily upon me."

The door upstairs slammed again, and somewhere in the house, a wail rose. Pixie sat up a little straighter, and Katelyn hugged her arms to her body as if she were cold. For a moment, Sarah thought Amelia would appear right there in her kitchen, but all remained quiet.

"We were slated to exchange our marriage vows on the forthcoming Christmas," Matthew continued. "However, I was well aware of her father's disdain for me. At that time, I was but a destitute art student, lauded by my mentors for my talents yet destitute in terms of wealth. It was then, mere weeks ago, that I crossed paths with a man at the Rose

Tavern. He spoke of his quest for the renowned artifact, the Luminus Crystal. Amelia had entrusted me with the secret that her father, Jed Thompson, had been appointed as the Lumarian group's leader and, consequently, the guardian of the precious crystal. I had vowed to protect this knowledge, but alas, I betrayed that promise. The gentleman I encountered at the tavern proffered a substantial sum in exchange for any tidbits regarding the whereabouts of the crystal. I inadvertently disclosed that it could be located within Thompson Hall. Oh, how I rue that momentous lapse in judgment. The weight of the bag of gold now nestled in my pocket is substantial, but it pales in comparison to the burden of guilt that envelops me."

Matthew cleared his throat and lowered the tablet for a moment, looking into the somber faces at the table.

"What happened to Amelia," Emma piped up, and Matthew took a sip of tea.

"Hang on, sweetie, I need to get to the next picture."

Sarah tightened her grip on little Pixie. In her mind, she could see the young couple, Amelia, beautiful and stylish as she was in her portrait at the historical society, and a dashing young artist, talented yet poor. Nowadays, their story would be a 'rags to riches' romance novel with a happy ending. Back then, it barely stood a chance. Even if, on the face of things, Jed would have agreed to let them marry, something would have happened to prevent such a union.

Matthew found the next image and continued. "I came to realize the intentions of the man, as he and his group, called the Obsidian Order, sought to unlawfully breach the sanctity of Thompson Hall to purloin the precious crystal. By chance, I overheard their scheming that very same evening. Swiftly, I sprinted to Thompson Hall, desperate to forewarn my cherished Amelia. Alas, I was on foot, and though I arrived with all haste, not in time to avert calamity. The malefactors had succeeded in their break-in, and Jedediah Thompson, resolute in his determination to safeguard the crystal, stood prepared to defend it with his very life. The image is forever seared into my memory: Jedediah, pistol in hand, aiming with unflinching resolve, just as Amelia emerged from her chambers, drawn by the commotion that echoed below. Regrettably, she was afforded no opportunity for escape or defense. The shot he fired pierced her heart, and she did not draw another breath."

The little tablet dropped from Matthew's hands onto the kitchen table, and he made a fist.

"Jed killed Amelia," he said, almost a whisper.

"Her own father?"

"But what happened to the crystal."

"What happened to Simon?"

Cory, Emma, Katelyn, Sarah — everyone at the table — had a question. They all wanted to know how the story ended. Matthew raised a hand, and they fell silent again.

"It seems Amelia was right," he said. "Simon sold the knowledge about the crystal to the group of the Obsidian Order. When he realized they meant to take it by force, he rushed over here to prevent a tragedy—"

"Only to witness one," Sarah said sadly. "Amelia got caught in the crossfire before she even knew what was going on."

"How is it nobody knows about this story," Cory wanted to know, and only Katelyn looked more confused than ever.

"Hang on, there's one final page to this confession," Matthew said and picked up the tablet again. He scanned over the final words of the document and sighed. "I will spare you the ancient high English. Basically, the Obsidian Order fled when they saw a murder had been committed, Jed immediately realized that Simon was to blame and told him he would testify in court that it had been Simon who had shot his daughter because she'd changed her mind about marriage."

"What a jerk." Finally, Katelyn found her voice. "Really. Why is it always these rich dudes ...?"

"Simon fled to escape prosecution," Matthew interrupted her. "But in a final act of defiance, he returned to Thompson Hall the following night, stole the Luminus crystal, and hid it where it wouldn't be found for a hundred years."

"That's what he says," Sarah asked. "A hundred..."

"Yup," Matthew confirmed with a raised eyebrow. "A hundred years. Then he penned his confession, stashed it where he would hide love letters to Amelia and disappeared. Never to be seen again."

Pixie raised her head then, her nose pointing toward the kitchen door. Sarah followed her gaze and noticed a wisp of white, a mist barely visible, disappear around the corner of the door, and her heart ached for the young woman, a hundred years too late.

"Bloody crystal," Cory muttered, taking back his tablet and scanning the elegant cursive script of Simon. "Now what do we do?"

"One thing's for sure. Whether it is a product of our online searches or some other clue we're not aware of," Matthew said softly. "But this so-called Obsidian Order is aware that this crystal is likely still somewhere here, on this property."

"You think?" Sarah looked around as if she might spot the crystal sitting on her kitchen counter. "What does that thing even look like? How can we search for it if we don't even know what we're looking for?"

"I think I saw a drawing of it somewhere on the internet," Cory said and opened a browser window on his tablet.

"Cory, are you sure that's wise?"

Sarah looked at a drawing of a clear crystal, a little flatter than she had thought it would be.

"This shape looks kind of familiar," she mused.

She stared at the image until Cory snatched the tablet away again.

"We have nothing," he said and snapped the screen off with a forceful click. "Nothing that would help Dad."

"We know how Amelia died," Emma spoke up, and Cory glared at his sister. "Great, Em. Maybe Amelia can help us figure out where Dad is being held, you think?"

"I just called Penny over at the police station," Lily came back in from the entrance hall and flipped her phone case shut. "Nothing new on that end, and to be honest, I get the feeling they're not totally on board with the story that he's even been kidnapped."

"Why would they even doubt that?" Sarah asked. "And how did Officer Harding come to tell you any of this?"

Lily shrugged. "I've known Penny for a long time. The way she inquired about Michael's frustration with how well you're doing in your new life, how you don't need him, I just got the sense she was trying to see if I believed he might stir up some drama here just to feel needed."

"So, you're saying we're on our own."

Sarah slammed her mug down on the table a little harder than strictly necessary. "For once, if they would just do their jobs..."

"Cool it," Matthew put a hand on her arm. "You're not on your own. I'm here, and so is Lily and even Katelyn. We will figure this out."

By then, the sun was beginning to set, and Sarah rose to flip on the kitchen light to chase away the lengthening shadows.

"I know that, I just don't understand why it has to be so hard."

She flipped the switch by the door a few times, but the light wouldn't come on.

"I just changed that light bulb," she swore and went to the counter to try the switch there. Again, the light would not come on. For a second, Sarah froze and swallowed hard. Dread bored itself into her stomach.

"Matthew," she said softly. "Try the light on the porch."

Matthew did, and nothing happened. Sarah tore open the fridge only to find it dark and silent.

"I guess the power's out."

Cory toggled the switch on his tablet again and shook his head. "No net, that means the router is down too, Mom."

"Which means the phone system ..." She pulled out her cell phone and checked, relieved when she found five bars and a strong mobile signal.

"I have a signal here. Is it just our house?"

With shaking fingers, she pulled back the curtains, only to find that the street lights down at the front of the property had come on and were casting a comforting yellow glow.

"General power is on," she said and automatically crowded closer to Matthew. "What's happening here?"

"Could be something harmless," he said, but his voice sounded tinny and not at all convincing. "You know," he cleared his throat, "Like they messed up the transfer of the account to your credit card."

"Why don't I believe that?"

Sarah bent down to pick up Pixie, but for once her loving little Papillon squirmed to be free. She stood taut and quivering, her fluffy white coat almost electric with tension, her nose pointing at the kitchen door, one front paw raised and still.

Something – something is out there.

"Something? Who - what?"

Pixie stayed quiet. Every hair on her body seemed to stand up straight. Her ears quivered and swiveled to all sides.

When Selena had the accident, I had this same feeling. Like something was out there and coming straight at us. But I couldn't do anything to help.

"Pixie."

She had called out loud, and Lily, Katelyn, and Matthew were looking at her. Matthew took her hand and squeezed it hard.

"Cory," he said with deceptive calm. "I know you won't like this, but please take your sister and go upstairs, lock yourselves in your room, and do not open the door unless your mother or I are on the other side. Do you understand?"

"No, I want to—"

"Cory, please do as I say. If something is happening to your father, and here, I only have so many hands to keep everybody safe. I'm asking you as a personal favor."

Cory looked up and saw the seriousness on Matthew's face. All of the arguments, all of the sassy disobedience he had worked so hard to develop in the past few months fell away, and he took Emma's hand.

"Come on, squirt."

"But I want to stay here and talk to Amelia."

"Maybe she'll come upstairs. There'll be lots of time for that later, she's eternal. Come on now."

Chapter 19

"Thank you," Sarah breathed a little easier when the two kids had gone upstairs, but Matthew was not done.

"Katelyn, Lily, you guys aren't really directly involved. If this is the work of the Obsidian Order, they won't have any use for you, but they also probably won't care. This is your chance to leave."

"Fat chance," Lily said and stood on the other side of Sarah, taking her other hand. Katelyn sat at the kitchen table, looking from one to the other.

"I don't understand," she wailed. "I was just looking for Michael. What's this Obsidian Order now?"

Matthew's voice was as steady and as calm as a large chunk of ice.

"This is not your fight, Katelyn. Nobody is judging you if you open that front door and walk out. One of the neighbors will help you hail a cab."

"Michael," she wailed and looked up at the ceiling.

"It might all be something completely innocent, but I wouldn't count on it," Matthew said, looking around, then continued, "I'm not one for weapons, and I absolutely don't know if that would even help, but I think we need a few items to defend ourselves with."

"Are you kidding me?" Even as Sarah tried to grapple with the thought, Lily went to the games room and returned with a baseball bat, the fireplace poker, and the game wand the kids used with their computer games.

"Seriously, you're kidding me, right?"

Matthew nodded and pulled Sarah a bit closer. "She's right, Sarah. Best-case scenario, we're going to be sitting here tomorrow morning feeling foolish. Worst case," he picked up the game controller wand and swung it a few times. "I could club somebody with this pretty good."

Katelyn stared from one to the other, her eyes wide and unbelieving. Finally, with a sheepish grin, she opened her massive purse and pulled out her keychain. With a flick of her wrist, she pulled out a little tube and showed it to them.

"If that's the way it's going to be, I can always mace somebody."

"This is not funny, Katelyn. This is serious. Dead—"

"Not that word," Sarah put her hand on his arm. "It's all right, Katelyn. But remember, we have no idea what we are dealing with, and this could get dangerous."

"Damn straight it's dangerous." Katelyn sat again, stretching her booted feet. "They have Michael. And he might well have only brought me here to get you mad, but he's still a good person and a dad. And that's just wrong."

Matthew nodded and lifted a corner of the curtain to the window that overlooked the driveway and the street.

"I still don't see anything."

They huddled close together then and listened in the gathering dark.

Upstairs, old floorboards creaked as the kids moved around in Cory's room. Sarah's cheerful kitchen clock, featuring bright yellow ducklings, loudly clicked away the minutes, and their own breathing was rasped, strained, and labored.

∾

Matthew had finally got up to fetch a glass of water when someone politely knocked at the back door.

Sarah blinked for a moment. She'd been expecting anything but a polite, mannerly knock at the door. Matthew took the bat, positioned himself just out of view, and nodded to Sarah. She pulled aside the curtains at the door and smiled.

"Mortimer."

Sarah opened the door, and Mortimer Jenkins strode inside, in his careful, deliberate way.

"Looks like you've got a bit of a problem here," he said, overly cheerful, and looked around the darkened kitchen.

"Yes, the power is out, and we thought - we were worried..."

Sarah broke off. All at once, she remembered the Jenkins' odd behavior, the fact that Mrs. J had dropped off cookies this morning, and after that, their house had been as if nailed shut. Sarah stumbled over her words and took a physical step away from Mortimer Jenkins, who came farther into the kitchen, step by cautious step.

"You don't need that bat there, Matthew Turner," he finally said, as if he'd seen Matthew there in the shadows with eyes in the back of his head. "None of you need any weapons."

Sarah stood frozen with her back against her beautiful, pristine butcher block counter, and, at her feet, Pixie stood her ground, facing Mort Jenkins, deep growling noises issuing from her throat.

"Now, you pipe down there, little one," he said, grinning. "You wouldn't want a boot to your little face now, would you?"

Pixie stopped growling, but her eyes never left Mort Jenkins, and the tip of her tail had that peculiar golden glow again.

"You want to tell me what this is all about," she finally asked, putting as much strength into her voice as she could. She remembered facing Amelia, putting her hands in front of her, and channeling strength from – somewhere. But her hands were folded behind her back, and this time she couldn't feel a thing, not even a twinge of power.

"You must have guessed by now," Mort Jenkins said, casually snatching one of his wife's cookies off the plate on the table. "She does make the best cookies in the county, you have to admit that," he said between bites.

"What do you want," Sarah asked again. "And I'm sure it isn't Martha's cookies."

"No, it's not." Mort brushed the crumbs off his hands on his pant leg and smiled at the little group. His mouth smiled, Sarah thought, but there was nothing friendly there. As if someone had taught him how to bend his features to appear harmless.

"To the point then. You see, many, many years ago, there was a trinket connected to this area, and this very house as a matter of fact. It's just a tiny little thing, and since you're not from here, it wouldn't hold any meaning to you. But to us, who have lived here our whole lives, it has great ... sentimental value. We'd like to have it again, and all will be well. Even that banker from out east who is enjoying the hospitality of our group can carry on his filthy business again."

Sarah wanted to answer, but Matthew stepped out of the shadows and stopped her with a raised hand.

"Shame on you, Mortimer Jenkins," he said. "I'm the director of the local historical society and a professor, and if you for one moment thought I would not know that you're talking about the Luminus crystal, not a droll little worthless trinket, then you are sadly misinformed."

"As you wish," Mort Jenkins nodded. "The Luminus crystal then. Makes no difference. If you will hand it over then, the young ones upstairs can have their dad back, and life can go on all peaceful-like."

"Why do you want it that badly," Lily asked, and Mort Jenkins gave her a short, dismissive look.

"What does it matter to you? If I were you, I'd sit good and quiet. Things happen so easily at a bookstore. All that paper. Be a shame to have a fire or something."

"Are you threatening me?" Lily jumped to her feet, only barely restrained by Sarah.

"And you think I'm just going to sit here and take it? You are sadly mistaken. I am going to—"

"Going to what?" Mort rounded on Lily and suddenly gave her just the tiniest push. Lily stumbled for a second and would have fallen if Sarah had not caught her. The temperature in the room changed all at once. Sarah couldn't see Pixie any longer but hoped she was safe. Her eyes were focused now on Mort Jenkins, who squared off against the little group, all joviality and smiles gone from his face.

"All we want is the crystal, and nobody will get hurt. Put your bat away, Turner. What are you going to do, hit an old man over the head?"

She saw Matthew opening his mouth to answer, and time slowed down to a crawl. Mort Jenkins, the nice old neighbor who came around to fix things, reached into his pocket to pull out an ancient, small but lethal-looking pistol.

"Why do you make me do this," he roared just as the back door opened again, and Mrs. Jenkins walked in, just like always as if she owned the place and, behind her, one other person.

She knew this man. Sarah blinked once and again just to be sure. Mrs. Jenkins carried an old-fashioned lantern to spread some light, and finally, as the light hit his face, Sarah and Lily both gasped.

"You."

The man spread his arms and sighed.

"I don't know why you didn't just let me change out that old transom window, Sarah. Everything would have been fine, and you and your kids would live a lovely life. Now," again, he spread his arms. "Who knows."

"What does my window have to do with anything?"

"Haven't you guessed yet?" The man actually laughed, a harsh and ugly sound. Sarah tried to remember his name, but after his odd behavior, she had put his business card away, to be forgotten somewhere.

"This all seems to have solved a riddle that is over a hundred years old."

"What has," Sarah asked, and then it came to her. "The piece that fell out of the stained-glass window, the shape Cory showed me in the drawing. That — that was the ...?"

"That was the Luminus crystal," Mort Jenkins confirmed with a nod. "Lumarian historians always suspected Simon hid it inside the house somewhere, but no matter how hard we looked, we could not find a trace of it."

"Hidden in plain sight. Until it fell out of its frame," Sarah said tonelessly. "And you came."

"And I recognized the shape," he confirmed. "Now if you will just cut this short and hand over the missing piece, we will be on our way, and your kids won't have to grow up – alone." He nodded at Mort's pistol. "He may be old, but he's an excellent marksman."

Sarah put a hand to her throat, and for a moment, the room lay in silence.

"Well," Mrs. Jenkins said. "I'd hurry – the kids' dad, he doesn't have much time."

"What are you implying?"

"Don't do it, Sarah," Matthew warned. "You don't know what they're going to do with that crystal."

"Turner, why don't you do as you're told and shut up."

Mortimer wheeled on Matthew with surprising agility, and an ear-splitting bang filled the room. Sarah saw the muzzle flash and the splinters of wood from the floor in front of Matthew's feet, at the same time as she smelled the stench of gunpowder.

"Now, unless you want that wretched dog to be the first of many to meet their fate," Mortimer's voice was ice, his resolve unshakable.

"Pixie," Sarah screamed, and almost instantly she felt her in her heart. *I'm fine, he missed me.*

"My dog," Sarah screamed again, turning on the Jenkins. Fury coursed through her veins; her fist clenched in righteous anger. "You worthless, inhuman thug, you are—"

"Armed." Jenkins aimed the pistol straight at her midsection now.

"Now, either you give me the crystal, or I'm going to keep shooting, and one by one, everybody in this room will fall."

"There are four of us," Matthew said bravely.

Jenkins smirked, unyielding. "And I hold the power here. Put down that futile bat and surrender the crystal. Remember, Michael doesn't have much air where he is right now. You wouldn't want any accidents, now would you?"

"You are..." Lily hugged her arms around herself. "I will ruin you when we get out of this, you hear me?"

"No, I don't," Jenkins retorted, his grip on the pistol unwavering. "The crystal. Now."

Matthew's eyes darted around crazily, searching for a weapon, Sarah thought. She couldn't put his life at stake, she wouldn't feel like she had moments ago when he had fired at Pixie. Not again, not with Matthew. Guilt weighed her down, but she could feel Pixie's reassurance in her heart.

It's fine. You are doing the right thing.

Why don't I feel like it then?

Because you are a decent person.

"OK," Sarah raised her hands. "Put away that gun. I'm giving you the crystal."

"I knew you'd have sense."

"No..." Matthew yelled and threw himself at her, but the glassmaker roughly grabbed Matthew, pushing him hard against the wall, and raised a fist.

"You stay right there, mister, and you won't have to watch what I can do to these little ladies right here, do you understand?"

Matthew's eyes glittered with pure hatred, but he didn't answer.

That earned him a hard cuff against the side of the head. A cut opened below his eye and blood trickled down his cheek. Sarah's heart ached for him.

"I said, do you understand, Mister Professor? I don't like having to ask twice."

"I understand," Matthew said from between clenched teeth.

A knife appeared in the man's hand. A sharp, lethal-looking knife with the kind of blade that could pop in and out of the handle, ending a life at will. Katelyn paled visibly.

"Sarah," she whimpered softly, and Sarah glowered at her once-friendly neighbor and his menacing associate.

"Put that away. There's no need for this violence. I'm going to get your damned crystal, and then I don't ever want to see you again."

But therein lay the rub, didn't it? If her lovely neighbors and this surely respected local tradesman took off with the crystal, they wouldn't want to leave an entire house full of witnesses behind. People who could tell others in the area what they had seen, that they were Lumarians indeed and now in possession of the crystal. This would have to end here, so no matter what Mort Jenkins told her about having a lovely life once she handed the gem over – he was lying. Lying through his teeth, meaning she had to act.

If it's nothing else, she thought and kneaded her hands behind her back. Nothing happened, no burst of power, no sparkle.

Pixie, if I ever needed your help...

Something is interfering. It's drawing all the power.

She spotted Pixie in the far corner under the table, well out of range of boots. The tip of her tail sparkled, but only the tiniest little bit.

"Get on with it then," Jenkins waved his gun in her face. "Where are we going? Upstairs, downstairs, the attic? Where did you hide the Luminus?"

Sarah turned slowly, ready to head for the front hall, where she had put what she thought was a piece of glass safely on a ledge, so none of the kids would pick it up and get hurt. It felt as if it had been years ago.

Mortimer stayed close behind her, so close she could smell him, a mixture of tobacco, sweat, and old linens, as she walked out into the hall, step by painful step, and ran her fingers along the ledge, feeling for the crystal and closing her hand over it.

"Give me that." He motioned with the gun, and Sarah was about to hand it over when Martha called out.

"Bring it out here into the light, so we know she's not cheating."

Again, Mortimer waved his gun, and together, they walked back into the kitchen. All the color had drained from Matthew's face, and Katelyn cried softly. Lily sat glaring at the man she had sent to this house to fix a transom window.

Sarah's friends, her family now. If she was going to do anything, this would be the time. And still, her hands felt like – hands. No burst of power, no defense. Sarah approached Martha and the light as slowly as she could, buying for time, when she heard it in her head, *Watch out, something is happening.*

Sarah automatically ducked out of range, but whatever was happening, it didn't originate with Mortimer Jenkins.

First, it was a sighing breeze, growing stronger and stronger, pulling at her hair, her clothes.

"What the ..." the glassmaker muttered, whose hair hung down in a tidy little braid. A braid now being pulled in the direction of the entrance hall.

The draft became stronger yet, and with a resounding bang, the door to the hall flew open. Amelia, Sarah thought, but it wasn't Amelia she saw standing there in the hall.

Amelia had been a young girl, dressed in a pretty white dress, blonde hair piled high on her head, smiling a sad little smile. This – entity – was nothing but darkness. A black shimmering cloud that seemed to pulse from within. A dark space where nothing existed and nothing ever had. Dark, deep emptiness. It moved closer then, narrowing as it glided through the doorway and widening again.

Katelyn screamed and covered her face, and somewhere far away Mrs. Jenkins began reciting the rosary in a loud, angry voice. Sarah took a few steps back. She was directly in the entity's path.

For a moment, she felt her skin tingle and her hair stand on end as the entity passed over her.

"Mort," the glassmaker screamed. "Hell, you never said anything about – that."

Mort said nothing and stood his ground. Calmly, almost casually, he raised his pistol and fired at the entity, once, twice. The bullets passed straight through, spraying splinters as they stuck in the door frame.

Still, the entity never made a sound.

Don't touch it. Pixie, in her head, and respectfully, Sarah took another few steps back and stood staring.

She put her hand on Katelyn's shoulder and gave her a little squeeze. The girl was crying helplessly as if she would never stop.

"What do you want," Sarah asked softly, and the answer stunned her for a moment.

Help you as you have helped me.

The voice was in her head, but it sounded like – Amelia?

Then the entity laughed, and if she never had to hear the sound of a gravelly, deep, frightening laugh like that again, she would live well to the end of her day, Sarah thought.

"Oh, hell, it's just a cloud of fairy dust," Mortimer cursed, advancing on it and firing again, three shots, this time, that lodged in the cupboard behind her.

"It's a piece of wind," Mortimer screamed. "Like the devil farted, nothing else. Now give me the Luminus."

Mortimer Jenkins reached for her, grabbed her by the wrist, and shook. Automatically, her hand opened, and the crystal clattered to the ground in a spark of rainbow showers. Triumphantly, Mort dove for it, and Sarah acted.

She kicked out a knee and pushed her neighbor, hard, straight into the middle of the cloud of darkness. She thought his scream would never end.

Martha and the glassmaker now dove for the crystal, and Sarah tried to kick it out of the way when one tiny wail stopped everything – Pixie.

Time slowed down to an eternity for Sarah. She wheeled around to see Mortimer by the back door, suddenly holding Pixie by the scruff of her neck. He shook her hard, and the little dog wailed pitifully.

Sarah wanted to run to him, to wrestle Pixie from his grasp forcefully if needed, but her legs wouldn't move. Mortimer Jenkins hauled out with one arm and flung the tiny little Papillon against the wall where she collapsed in a heap of white fur and golden sparks and didn't move again.

The fury that had been building within her from the moment she had recognized Mort Jenkins for all he was, suddenly unleashed its full force. She shot her arms up and let out an ear-piercing scream. An unholy sound surged toward Mort Jenkins, while an endless torrent of energy and power erupted, enveloping him and illuminating him like a fireworks display until he crumpled and ultimately dissolved into nothingness.

Martha and the glassmaker screamed and ran from the kitchen, out into the yard and into the street, and Sarah sagged to the ground.

She had nothing left, no strength, no power. Matthew, Lily, Katelyn, and the kids were alive and unharmed. They might never see this house and her the same way they had, but they were alive.

But Pixie. Her lovely little companion, that sweet spirit with the sparkly tail, insatiable sweet tooth, and sarcastic wit was gone. The voice in her head that had reassured her and calmed her down, given her courage and showed her how to use her power – silenced forever.

Sarah crawled on her hands and knees to the wall where Pixie had collapsed when Mort Jenkins threw her. She remembered their first morning in the new home, and Emma telling her, 'Pixie said to stay away from the old well, it's dangerous.'

Emma cradling her in her arms, whispering her secrets to the magical little Papillon. Cory playing basketball and sinking every shot, while his opponent withered under Pixie's stare.

The memories assaulted her hard and fast, and the tears spilled down her cheek.

Familiars come in all shapes.

Her knees scraped roughly over the crystal shards on the ground, and she finally reached Pixie, pulled her into her arms, and cowered down, protecting the tiny little body with her own.

"I would never leave you, never."

A hand on her shoulder. Matthew, it had to be Matthew.

"Sarah?"

Sarah shook her head. She wouldn't look up, she wouldn't return to a world that surely would be empty.

Lily came and sat beside her, putting an arm around her shoulder and leaned her head against Sarah's. Katelyn did the same on the other side, and the women sat together, Sarah's sobs the only sound in the room.

Why didn't you take me?

Sarah felt the softest touch on her face, a mere breeze, and she lifted her head just enough to see the white flutter of Amelia.

"You came to help us," she said tonelessly.

"You solved the mystery around my death and Simon's disappearance, I owed you that much."

"The Luminus?"

You broke it when you lashed out at Mortimer.

"Good," Sarah said savagely and hugged Pixie closer to herself. "At least it won't cause any more harm."

"There's a piece left under your foot."

Amelia's voice faded quickly now, her apparition dissolved and re-assembled slowly. Sarah raised her head another inch.

"What do you mean?"

You have the power.

Amelia faded before her very eyes, and Sarah desperately contorted to fish with one hand under her foot until her hand closed around a sharp piece of crystal.

"The Lumarians believed that the Luminus Crystal was a divine gift," Sarah said out loud. "Bestowing immense power and enlightenment upon its possessors. It was utilized in sacred rituals and revered as a symbol of balance and harmony between the mortal and spiritual realms."

Sarah tightened her hands even harder around the sharp object, until the razor edges cut into her palm, and blood dripped down on her lap, on the tiny little shape there.

"How do I do this, how do I use it? You were always the one to show me how to do things."

You have the power.

"Sarah, let it go. Come on, get up, I don't want Cory and Emma to see you like this when they come down. And Pixie. We should – do something — about," he looked down at Pixie in her lap, and Sarah shook him off like a pesky fly.

"Come on, come on, come on."

Lily and Katelyn had gotten to their feet again and stood, staring down at her, without speaking. Sarah wanted to scream. Fury had focused her energy against Mort Jenkins.

Fury. Love.

Love.

"Turn on the light, quick."

"But Sarah, the power is—"

"Turn it on," she screamed and held up the crystal in one hand, hugging Pixie to herself with the other.

Matthew flicked the switch, and triumphantly, Sarah watched the light flicker, steady, and shine again. She held the crystal even higher until a beam of light passed through it, and a hundred rainbow facets poured over little Pixie in her arms.

"By the light of my love I command you ..."

"Sarah, what are you doing?"

The rainbow flames became stronger and more powerful, dancing now from the crystal in Sarah's hand, showering down at Pixie.

"By crystal's gleam,

and radiant stream,

I call upon the ancient dream.

Life's spark concealed,

in shadows rest,

Awaken now, at my behest."

The crystal in her hand burned with unholy cold fire, and still she held it fast in the light. She let all of the love she felt for Pixie flow out of her, into the crystal and into the little dog in her arms.

I would never leave you, I will always be here for you.

A moment later, as suddenly as it had come on, the light died away again. Sarah sagged back against the wall and cowered down, her forehead touching little Pixie.

Why did I think I could do this? she thought desperately. What made me believe that I had any power? I failed, and now she's gone. My little magic puppy, gone.

The shard in her hand, black, soulless, and lifeless now, clattered to the ground like so much worthless rock, and Sarah rocked back and forth.

"Sarah, please get up now. We have to ..."

"I can't, Matthew, I can't. Don't you understand - I failed."

"Failed at what?"

"Because I did. Because I— Pixie—Pixie??"

Sarah stopped for a moment because she had felt something, the tiniest little flutter, a spark, somewhere in her arms.

Easy, I can't breathe.

Sarah relaxed her tight grip on the little dog just a bit. All at once, Pixie's little front paws pushed into her chest. She did not dare speak or breathe. Pixie still lay in her arms as if lifeless, but her paws were twitching, her eyes fluttering.

"Girl," Sarah asked. "Come on girl, talk to me, please. Please. You can do it."

With one free hand, she tried to feel a pulse or a heartbeat on the tiny body, and finally, Pixie gasped and took a huge breath.

It's okay, Sarah, it's okay. What happened?

Sarah closed her eyes and lowered her head to Pixies. Unashamed, she cried hard tears into the soft white fur.

"Jenkins threw you against the wall," she said.

Pixie shook and stretched each of her dainty legs in turn as if testing them. Finally, she shook and bent her back.

Must be why I feel like I got run over.

"And I—lost it on him. Amelia and I hit him with everything we had."

Amelia, huh?

"I don't know where Jenkins is right now."

Pixie gave her a little kiss on the cheek, and Sarah could have sworn her little dog winked at her.

If you and Amelia hit him together, that bit of sand there by the door would be my guess.

"My girl. And you?"

Pixie shook again and stretched through her entire body, testing that everything still worked.

I'm good, really. I'm sorry I couldn't help you. When Amelia realized Jenkins meant to kill you all for the crystal, she drained all of the power in the house to focus it on that – dark entity.

"Is there any way for you to tell us what is happening here?"

Matthew. Sarah looked up and into the stunned faces of Matthew, Lily, and Katelyn. They'd been watching her carry on one side of a conversation without understanding what was happening. She tried for a weak smile and Matthew put a hand on her shoulder.

"Sarah, it looked like Pixie was—well—gone, you know. I—I don't understand."

No, you wouldn't, Sarah thought. *The light, the power, the crystal, and my love for this little one — we brought her back.*

She rose and cradled Pixie in her arms once again, unwilling to let go of her quite yet.

"She was stunned, that's all," she said instead and smiled. "Go get the kids. I need to have everybody here, make sure everyone is okay. Then call Penny. I — we need to report what happened here tonight."

"Really," Lily said and chuckled. "You're really going to explain to someone what happened here. How they broke into the house looking for a magical crystal, you know the kind, and you were going to give it up, then a ghost came to your rescue, and together you defeated one goon, who, by the way, is your neighbor and he kind of evaporated, and the other two ran to God knows where. That is what you are going to tell Penny Harding? I really want to see that. Especially when you get to the part of Pixie and that — that resurrection. That should be fun."

Sarah wanted to answer when she heard Cory and Emma thundering down the stairs.

"Mom—what happened to Pixie? Where is she? What happened down here? All we could hear—"

"Easy," Sarah raised a hand and opened her arm so her children could get close to her. "Pixie is right here, everything is fine, at least I think it is. I'll have the vet check her out tomorrow."

Oh no, you won't.

"What happened to her?" Cory, her tough, scowling kid, put a hand under Pixie's little chin and leaned his head close to hers, nuzzling her face.

"Mr. — someone tried to hurt her, but we didn't let it happen. Everything is fine."

"But Emma and I - upstairs we heard ..."

"Amelia was here," Emma said with a knowing little smile. "I knew she'd be back."

"No, she wasn't. How would you even know?" Cory snapped, not wanting to be the one who had missed something.

"I just know."

Pixie struggled to get down on the floor, and Sarah let her. She looked around at her little family in the kitchen, needing to make sure that everybody was okay, just as someone knocked at the back door again.

"I'll get it," Cory turned and wanted to go, but she clamped a hand on his wrist.

"No, you won't. Matthew is going to take this one. And everybody, stand by me until we know who's there."

"But I—"

"Cory, I said no."

Matthew cautiously answered the door and pulled it open all the way.

"Officer Harding, come on in."

Sarah bit her lip, and Lily and Katelyn rose to stand with her.

"We received a notice of a disturbance here tonight," Penny Harding said. "But they failed to mention that your power had been interrupted as well."

"Yes," Sarah didn't know anything more intelligent to say. Finally, she gathered her thoughts and forced herself to smile. "And, an attempted home invasion, you might say?"

"Attempted? Attempted how?" Penny Harding's eyes zeroed in on Lily and stayed there. "What happened here tonight? Exactly."

Lily looked around from one to the next, but no one would meet her eyes. Matthew busied himself with a tea kettle, Katelyn and the kids looked around uncomprehendingly, and Sarah had her hands together, resting on her face.

"Some people tried to get in - again," Lily finally said with a shrug. "Couldn't see much because, well, no power and all. Something really spooked them, though, and they ran, that's all I remember. You?"

She looked around for confirmation and received only shrugs. "Nah — couldn't see anything — we were upstairs — it was dark."

"Why am I having a hard time with this?" Penny Harding pulled up a chair and sat, looking at the uncomfortable group around her. "One of the neighbors said they heard screams coming from here."

"Which neighbor," Sarah wanted to know.

"Does it matter?"

Sarah put a hand to her forehead and shook her head.

"Look—"

"We were pretty frightened when the power went out all of a sudden," Matthew supplied. "I mean, it is an old house, suddenly it was dark, we couldn't find any flashlights. Then somebody tried to get in. So, yes, I think someone might have screamed. I might have screamed. It is a rather normal reaction."

"Possibly."

Penny Harding looked at her notes and up at the little group in front of her again.

"I'm not sure what's going on with your power supply. Considering you had the second attempted break-in in just a few days, your ex-husband is still missing, and it's far too late tonight to do anything about the power outage, perhaps all of you would be more comfortable at one of the small hotels downtown. I know I would be if you went there."

"We'll be fine," Sarah said just a tad too quickly, and just as the officer wanted to argue with her again, someone else knocked at the back door.

"Grand Central Station, welcome," Sarah groused, "Who is it this time?"

Matthew went to the door again and looked through the curtain.

"Oh, my God."

He tore open the door once again to admit Michael. Disheveled, dirty, and confused but definitely Michael.

"Sarah, I have my reservations about you living in this godforsaken... Oh hello, officer. Katelyn, what are you doing here? Didn't I ...?"

He, too, glanced from one to the other with a definite, *what the heck happened here*, look on his face.

"Welcome," Penny said to him. "Grab a chair. Maybe you can tell me what happened to you. And, if you have any idea at all, what happened here a few hours ago?"

"What happened here, I wouldn't know," Michael said, piqued, looking down at his stained trousers. "All I know is my wife apparently engages in some odd computer games with my children. An unsavory pursuit to be sure, but that's her business. I'm entirely not sure why my — friend — is here."

At the mention of the word friend, Katelyn huffed and rolled her eyes.

"I was about to come over here to pick up my son," Michael continued. "When Sarah's brainless old neighbor approached me with some nonsense about something I needed to know. Next thing I knew, somebody was hitting me over the head, and I woke up in the bloody garden shed next door just a while ago. They stole my watch too, look," he shook his wrist to show it was empty. "You can be sure I will be laying charges against these — these —criminals. That was an original Patek Philippe, and I will not—"

"Mr. Anderson, that was last night."

"What?"

Michael stopped in his tirade and looked around. "Will somebody turn on the light, for God's sake, and tell me why I was out for an entire day?"

"We don't know. But maybe you should all head to the hotel right now."

"My kids and I are staying," Sarah argued. "It's far too late tonight. Michael, you and Katelyn can try to get comfortable in one of the guest rooms."

"As if."

"But we are staying."

Penny Harding did not like it. She still suspected something was going on here that nobody was telling her about.

In the end, Katelyn refused to go with Michael as well and found a guest room. Pixie, Emma, and Cory settled in Cory's room, Lily went home, and only Matthew and Sarah remained in the dark kitchen.

"I can go," he said cautiously, and she shook her head.

"I think I would feel better if you stayed. I'm pretty sure they won't be back, but — you never know."

"You think or you know?"

For once Sarah was happy that the darkness in her kitchen hid her blush and her silly smile.

"I know," she said softly, and together they went up the old curved staircase.

The next morning brought the power workers bright and early and another set of policemen who still could not quite understand what had happened in the old Thompson house. There was a rumor going around that it may be haunted, but, of course, that was just silly. They gathered the vague descriptions Matthew, Lily, and Sarah could provide about the home invasion, and left to file their report.

No one answered at the Jenkins' place, which was not entirely out of the ordinary, as Martha Jenkins had let it slip at the grocery store that they were coming into some money and wanted to look at places in Florida. Eventually, a locksmith was called to check, but the place was clean and tidy – and as empty as if it were waiting for new tenants. Everything was gone, leaving another mystery.

Several people left town in a hurry in the early morning hours, leaving Matthew to speculate later on that the news of the crystal's destruction had spread among the remaining Lumarians and Obsidians, leaving them to scramble for the remainders of their organizations.

Michael laid charges against Mortimer Jenkins for assault and the theft of a luxury watch. Another report was dutifully filed, and, when Michael's back was turned, shuffled to the bottom of the pile. Until Mort Jenkins was spotted again, there was nothing they could do.

Sarah carefully swept the sand around the kitchen door into an old receptacle and left it at the Jenkins' place in an unguarded moment.

Noon had come and gone, lunch had been made and consumed when Michael finally showed up at the house again.

"I don't know why you felt like you had to stay here last night," he groused at Katelyn. "I'm sure you wouldn't have been much help in an emergency, and after everything that happened to me—"

"You're fine, Michael, and you have a dozen other watches just like that one."

"Yes, but ..."

Sarah offered him a plate of sandwiches and chips, which he eyed with a certain amount of suspicion.

"I, for one, am glad we had Katelyn around last night. Are you hungry?"

"Not for that, thank you. I hope you're packed, Katelyn, because we are leaving just as soon as you can make it out to the car."

"Well, actually ..."

"As for you, Sarah," he raised a hand stopping every argument. "As for you, the last word in our custody settlement has not been spoken. This place — these people — this is not a place where I want my children to be growing up. I'm going to petition the court to—"

"Michael, for once will you just shut up," Katelyn suddenly snapped and jumped to her feet to stand in front of him. "The world does not always accommodate you to reshape itself and be the way you want it."

"Katelyn, I'm amazed."

"You see, it's always about you, Michael. Did you ever ask me whether I wanted to come out here with you? No, 'we are going,' end of story. Now, 'we are going home,' end of story. Meanwhile, you miss the fact that Sarah is doing an amazing job with these two kids. On her own. They are outstanding human beings."

"I send money, and lots of it."

"Yes, you send money. But let me tell you one thing, Sarah is the strongest woman I have known in maybe forever. She has more power in her little finger than you will ever have."

"My Sarah?" Michael stared and said nothing. His eyes went from Katelyn to Sarah and back. "You've got the wrong person. My Sarah says 'yes' to everybody who asks a favor of her. Doesn't have a bone in her spine."

"Shut up, Michael. Just listen to me. You are blind to everybody but yourself. Now go back to Baltimore. I'm staying here in Rosewood Hollow."

Sarah, who hadn't known any of this blinked a few times and said nothing, but Cory, who had come running down to fetch the tablet he'd forgotten, shook his head at his father.

"I don't want to move, Dad. If you want that, you're going to have to force us. It's great here. We have this fantastic spooky old house, and new friends, and a garden, and a dog."

He picked up Pixie, who'd been yapping around his feet, jumping at the boy.

"You'd go nuts with a dog like her in your condo, but we love her. She's special. You never let us have a dog no matter how often we asked. Basketball and sports at your expensive gym that was it, that was all we were allowed to do. Two kids in the house? Too much mess, too much bother, not for you. Listen to your girlfriend."

Michael got to his feet and rose to his full height in front of the boy. "How dare you talk to me like that? You will go wherever the hell I tell you to go, do you understand."

For a moment, the outburst stood in the room. No one would look at Michael until he sat again and looked at his hands and his bare wrist. Cory took his tablet, and knowing better than to argue, turned on his heel and stormed upstairs. The bang when he slammed the door shook the house.

"That's right," Katelyn said softly. "It's all about you. It's been fun. Have a good trip back." She picked up her little duffel bag and looked at Sarah. "Okay if I use your landline to call a cab? I'll take a room in that B&B down the road, and I think Lily said she needs help at the store."

Sarah waved her hand and nodded, and in the end, it was only her and Michael sitting in the kitchen, staring at empty cups of coffee.

"So," Sarah finally said. "I have to go look at what these hydro guys are doing, then I have plans with Matthew and Lily. You?"

"Matthew appears decent," Michael admitted, though it visibly cost him. "But what's this about you having all of this strength and all now, what happened here?" He spread his arms and hands as if he could make himself grasp the concept, and Sarah smiled.

"I don't know, just life, I guess." She caught sight of Pixie, who came in through the doggie door quietly and picked her up in her arms. "And she ... she gave us all a new center, and taught us about unconditional love and acceptance."

"Am I supposed to understand that?"

"Nah," Sarah said and kissed Pixie's little forehead. "You wouldn't. It's magic."

Free Bonus Book

Thanks for reading! Please leave a review and watch for the next Magical Papillon Mystery novel featuring Pixie.

For more fun and updates follow Pixie on TikTok, @papillon_pixie

Want to know how this magical adventure began? Uncover the secrets of the past.

As a special thank you for reading (and, I hope, enjoying) **Whispers in the Attic,** I'd like to offer a free copy of the prequel to the Magical Papillon Mystery series, **The Mirror and the Matrix.** This short story reveals the heartwarming moments and spooky encounters that led to the enchanting mystery of **Whispers in the Attic.**

To receive your free epub copy of **The Mirror and the Matrix**, please follow this link, https://forms.gle/wf6s7GGf8TSbrVv8A or scan the QR code with your phone.

The Mir-ror and the Matrix

Also by Sabine

Cozy Mysteries: The Magical Papillon Mystery Series
Whispers in the Attic
The Mirror and the Matrix

∾

Financial Thrillers: The Cannabis Preacher Series
Sermon One
Sermon Two
Sermon Three
Sermon Four
Box Set

∾

Romance Novels (Pen Name, Sabine Keevil):
SoundMaster Romance Series:
Guitars & Cadillacs
Foolish Pride

Coming Soon

Sapphires & Secrets (Magical Papillon Mysteries)

Joyce Ai (Financial Thrillers. *She knows everything about you!*)

Ghost Mountain Gold (An Indonesian Financial Thrillers)

This Time (SoundMaster Romance)

Spotify Playlists

Enjoy the following Spotify playlists with music mentioned or inspired by my novels.

Guitars & Cadillacs:

https://open.spotify.com/playlist/71ymCTx5YJPzroWBg4g WHF?si=fcf531d7a84b46cc

Foolish Pride:

https://open.spotify.com/playlist/1lR5rhB840RyeecFLvb1pG

The Cannabis Preacher:

https://open.spotify.com/playlist/4P90ZeynKOI7gyGUcVF HJE?si=484f28ffa7fb4b2a

Whispers in the Attic:

https://open.spotify.com/playlist/46FQGJn3T7qnAnoau63 BxU?si=379b6a6be4874ef3

www.ingramcontent.com/pod-product-compliance
Lightning Source LLC
Chambersburg PA
CBHW061148210726
48294CB00006B/1626